I0598272

A Shadow on the Ground

by

Rebecca Lee Smith

This is a work of fiction. Names, characters, places, and incidents are either the product of the author's imagination or are used fictitiously, and any resemblance to actual persons living or dead, business establishments, events, or locales, is entirely coincidental.

A Shadow on the Ground

COPYRIGHT © 2013 by Rebecca Lee Smith

All rights reserved. No part of this book may be used or reproduced in any manner whatsoever without written permission of the author or The Wild Rose Press, Inc. except in the case of brief quotations embodied in critical articles or reviews.
Contact Information: info@thewildrosepress.com

Cover Art by *Kim Mendoza*

The Wild Rose Press, Inc.
PO Box 708
Adams Basin, NY 14410-0708
Visit us at www.thewildrosepress.com

Publishing History
First Crimson Rose Edition, 2013
Print ISBN 978-1-61217-981-0
Digital ISBN 978-1-61217-982-7

Published in the United States of America

Gage leaned forward with his elbows on his knees. The words weren't exactly pouring out. He took a deep breath and clasped his hands in front of him, like a preacher signaling for the congregation to bow their heads. Then he took another breath. "Jeremy lost his mother two months ago, and he's a mess right now. He keeps lashing out at me, hoping to make me hurt as much as he does. I'm sure you've figured that out. But I want you to know I did not kill his mother."

"I didn't think you did."

"It was an accident. She pulled out of the driveway into the path of an oncoming car. There were extenuating circumstances which Jeremy blames me for. Actually, he blames me for all of it. But I did not— I could never—" He lifted his eyes and looked at her. "I don't want you to think badly of me."

"That's why you came back here tonight? So I won't think badly of you?"

"Yes. I mean, *no*. I just—"

"Well, I do think badly of you. I'll always think badly of you."

"You don't mean that."

"Why not? I can think badly of you if I want to. Most girls have a guy in their past they wish they'd never met. You're mine. Of course, most girls don't get to experience the thrill of having the guy show up out of the blue twelve years later. With his kid. On the worst day of their lives."

"If I'd known you were going to find a dead body today, I would have waited until tomorrow to show up."

She leveled her gaze at him. "I can't tell you how much better that makes me feel."

Dedication

For John Lee, the best of brothers,
destined to be born the year I turned five.
Thanks for knowing how to put life in perspective
in twenty-five words or less,
for always seeing the big picture when I'm lost
in the details,
and for still making me laugh until I cry.

Other Titles by Rebecca Lee Smith

A Dance to Die For
available from The Wild Rose Press, Inc.

Chapter 1

Morgan Maguire slid the phone in her back pocket and tried to kick the fertilizer clumps off her work boots without gagging. She hated manure. It was right up there with blue mold rot and apple maggots. Her brother was an incurable optimist, but the sooner he realized she would never be cut out for farm work, and could serve the cause more efficiently by living in the city—any city—and sending him a monthly check, the better off their lives would be.

Her life, anyway.

She fastened the fencepost latch out of habit even though the five dogs belonging to her step-grandmother Opal had long since run away or died. Opal had flown the coop too. All the way to a one-bedroom suite in the town's new assisted living wing, where she had all the gossip she could handle, a ten minute walk to the Dairy Queen for her daily Blizzard fix, and never had to look at an apple tree again.

Tonight. I'll tell Sean tonight.

She couldn't keep putting it off. She had to tell him she was moving back to Nashville. He was her twin, for God's sake. He was supposed to want the best for her. Why couldn't he understand that the bucolic life he cherished ate away at her soul like rust on an iron pipe?

"Crystal!" Morgan called. The little girl's head

bobbed up from her comic book. "Get in the truck, honey. Ethan Spannagel just called. His dad didn't show up for his doctor's appointment, and we need to find him. Come on, this is serious. Move your little butt. *Quick, quick!*"

"Can I bring the cookie bag?" Crystal asked.

"Yeah, just don't tell your mother."

"My mom says this old farm is on its last legs."

Morgan laughed. "Well, that's actually kind of...true. But don't worry. Mr. Spannagel has a plan to make it *all* better." She didn't even try to filter the sarcasm out of her voice. "He and Sean are meeting with some hotshot business consultant tomorrow who's going to tell us all the things we're doing wrong."

Crystal carefully bit a chocolate chip out of her cookie and blinked her huge blue eyes. "What's a hotshot?"

"Someone who thinks they know everything. And gets paid for it."

"Will you and Sean still make apple butter? I like to eat it on my toast."

"Me, too. But if it were up to me, I'd level this dump. Then set fire to it."

Morgan's grandfather was probably turning over in his grave at that blasphemy, but she didn't care. Sean was the one who loved the farm, not her. *Well, he can have it. Every scrappy, backbreaking, weed-infested acre of it.*

She adjusted her straw hat in the rearview mirror and guided the old pickup around potholes left by the recent rain. Tall weeds whipped against the running board and side mirrors, filling the truck with the pungent smell of damp hay. Mr. Jenkins' cows nudged their huge brown faces through the fence openings and eyed her suspiciously. Cows were one of the few things Morgan liked about living in the country. They weren't the smartest beasts in the barn, but they had a way of rolling their eyes and looking at a person sideways that caused many a man to glance down and make sure his fly was zipped.

She pulled into the Spannagel's yard and parked behind Harlan's mud splattered Chevy.

"Stay here, kid. I just need to make sure he's okay." She swung out of the truck and waved to Mrs. Cowden across the road without looking. Morgan didn't have to look. The old bat spent her days spying from the upstairs window, wispy gray hair flying around her fat face, binoculars resting on her nose like a giant pair of fly eyes.

"Harlan!" Morgan rapped on the door. She cupped her hands over her eyes and peered through the slanted window. "Harlan, it's Morgan! You in there?"

If he was asleep, he'd never hear her. He rarely wore his hearing aid, and turned the volume down out of spite whenever his son Ethan made him put it on. The thought of Harlan napping troubled her. At the orchard, he rarely took a break, preferring to hang around the barn, whistling a tune and taking bets from the hired hands that his seventy-four-year-old muscles could still heft two bushels of Stayman Winesaps. Of course, that was back when they employed hired hands for him to impress.

"*Harlan!*" She jiggled the metal knob. The door clicked and swung open. A moldy smell, clammy and thick, rushed past her as if it were trying to escape the airless room.

Morgan hadn't been inside the Spannagel's house in over twenty years. Not since the Christmas Eve Mrs. Spannagel invited some of the Riverbirch children over for hot chocolate and reindeer cookies, bid them a cheerful goodbye, then went upstairs and blew her brains across the room with Harlan's old Winchester. Ethan had stayed with Morgan's family that night, bedded down on the parlor sofa, wrapped in one of her mother's handmade quilts, his muffled sobs lulling Morgan to sleep as they echoed through the silent house.

"Harlan! Where are you?"

She walked through the dining room, past the old desktop computer nestled in a messy sheaf of papers, and climbed the stairs to the second floor. She pushed open the first door. The sour odor of unwashed socks pricked her nose. Her gaze flicked around the room, from the unmade four-poster bed to the vitamin and prescription bottles lined up neatly across the dresser. In the corner, a pair of Harlan's overalls draped across the back of a tattered wingback chair.

She closed the door and went across the hall to Ethan's old room. Remnants from his youth were everywhere—plastic model airplanes, a Red Sox pennant, his collection of vintage record albums, painstakingly alphabetized from Aerosmith to ZZ Top. A stack of freshly laundered shirts lay on the bed beside a canvas toiletry bag, and she wondered if Ethan had moved back home, at least temporarily. Everyone in Riverbirch knew how worried he'd been about his father's deteriorating health.

Why hadn't she watched Harlan more closely? She'd known he hadn't been himself lately, but she'd been too busy daydreaming about leaving the farm and resurrecting her old life—or any life—to notice he had left for the day.

On impulse, she crossed to the table beside Ethan's bed, looped a finger around the wooden knob, and pulled. The last thing she expected to see was her own face staring back at her. She lifted the yellowed newspaper clipping from the drawer. Large wary eyes, dark curls bunched beneath a bridal wreath of wilting daisies, drug store makeup not quite covering the fading bruise on her left cheek. She threw the clipping back in the drawer and slammed it shut.

Poor pathetic sap.

In those days, she'd clung to hope as if it were the safety bar on a rollercoaster. As if it could save her. But that was all in the past. She'd spent years making sure the girl in the picture had ceased to exist. She'd taught herself not to dwell on the things her heart wanted that would never be in the cards, and she wasn't about to start dwelling on them now.

She went downstairs to the kitchen. On the counter sat Opal's best ceramic cake carrier. She lifted the lid. Jam cake with caramel icing, Harlan's favorite. Opal had had her eye on Harlan since the day she'd become a widow, taking him all the foods he loved, flirting with him shamelessly at church potluck dinners, making him dance with her at the bluegrass concert. Some of the church women sniggered at her, but Opal didn't care. Among the over-seventy single females in town, Harlan was considered quite a catch. He'd had a few health problems in recent months, but he was still a vigorous, handsome man, with a full head of silver hair and an easy, infectious laugh. He also owned a prime piece of riverfront property, rumored to be worth a small fortune.

Morgan let herself out the back door. She followed the path down to the Spannagel's old slaughterhouse. Patches of goldenrod filled the abandoned holding pens, pushing up and through the rusty wire fence to sway in the September sun. She'd never had the nerve to look inside the slaughterhouse, but sneaking in after dark had been a rite of passage among the teenage boys living on Milltown Road.

She gazed up and down the valley. *"Mr. Spannagel!"*

He was probably hiding. He detested doctors and lab technicians. Ten bucks said he was sitting on the bank of Deer Creek, leaning against a river birch tree, sneaking a cigarette and swigging applejack moonshine out of a Mason jar.

The sudden tinkle of music stopped her cold.

A perky rendition of "Dixie" trilled deep inside the slaughterhouse.

The second ring sent Morgan racing across the soggy ground to the ramped entrance. She grabbed the wrought iron handle and pushed the heavy door open.

She stopped, her heart pounding.

Jagged shards of light spilled into the cavernous room. Huge meat hooks hung from ropes. Twisting black hoses and pairs of corroded chains looped down the wall from the high beamed ceiling. The sharp smell of moldering wood, mingled with a sweet metal odor she couldn't place, coated her throat until she wanted to heave.

"Oh, God," she whispered. "Harlan?" Her gaze trailed along the far wall, then to the left.

Harlan lay on his side against one of the pig chutes, a hulking, motionless heap. Dust motes swirled around his head like glittering insects, disappearing then reappearing inside a cone-shaped shaft of light. Blood had seeped from both nostrils, flooded his gaping mouth. It smeared along the metal railing beneath Harlan's hand, fanned out from his shock of silver white hair, burbled into the grid-covered drain.

Morgan knew he was dead before she touched him. His cloudy gray eyes were fixed on the stall doors, his shiny lower dental plate balanced on bloody, purple gums.

Saliva gushed to the back of her throat. Her stomach lurched and roiled. She forced herself to kneel and place her fingers against his neck. She mashed the spongy flesh again and again, gulping in air, willing some insignificant little beat to throb against her fingertips.

Oh, I wish I wa-as in the land of cotton.

Morgan cried out, which miraculously squelched her need to vomit. She spotted Harlan's cell phone lying on the ground beside the stall door. She picked it up and snapped it open.

"Dad!" Ethan shouted. "Dad, where are you? Are you okay?"

"It's me, Ethan."

"Morgan? What's wrong? Why hasn't Dad called me back?"

"He's in the slaughterhouse." She swallowed hard. "I just found him. He's unconscious. I need to call an ambulance."

"*Morgan!* What are you—"

"It's okay, Ethan. I'm not sure what happened, but

7

I'm here with him. You need to come home."

The Maguire coping mechanism had kicked in, but she'd said all the wrong things. She should have warned Ethan to be careful driving over Blackstone Mountain. She should have had the courage to tell him his father was dead so he wouldn't break his neck getting there.

"Morgan? Whatcha doin'?"

Crystal.

"Don't come in here!" Morgan jumped up and blocked Crystal's view. She couldn't let an eight-year-old see a dead body. The image of Harlan's blood smeared corpse had already seared into her own brain, promising cold sweat nightmares for decades to come.

"But I *want* to *see* the *barn.*" The little girl leaned against the doorway. Her huge blue eyes stared at Morgan from beneath a cloud of white-blond curls. Her inverted index finger hooked deep into the recesses of her right nostril.

"Get in the truck, Crystal, *now!* Or I'll tell your mother!"

"What's that stuff on your pants?"

Morgan didn't have to look. She could feel Harlan's blood seeping through the worn knees of her jeans. "Dammit, Crystal! *Get your butt back in the truck!*"

Crystal scampered up the hill.

Morgan dialed 911. Halfway through the call, the muscles in her legs turned to rubber. She stumbled outside and lowered herself onto a bed of chickweed.

How was she going to tell Sean? How could she tell her brother that the one man who thought he could keep their family's orchard from plunging into bankruptcy was dead? Tears welled up in her eyes. Hot selfish tears. The kind Morgan's mother always said would scald her soul. She should be crying for the poor man lying dead in the slaughterhouse, drenched in his own blood. Or for her brother, who had lost a trusted mentor and friend. But all she could think of was herself.

And how she was stuck.

Again.

She slid Harlan's phone into her pocket and looked up. A low cloud clung to the side of Blackstone Mountain, like a climber frozen in his tracks, unable to move up, down, or sideways.

A quiet, hysterical laugh tried to work its way past the dry, thin pockets of air she kept swallowing. The realization of what had happened, and what it could mean for all of them, tightened in her chest. She gulped in more air.

Harlan was dead. How could she desert Sean now? Her brother was the only real family she had left, and she could never leave him in the lurch no matter how desperate she was to cut and run. She knew Sean better than anyone. He would fight the good fight until there was nothing left to fight for. He would never give up. She had no choice but to stay. At least until things settled down.

But the instant it became clear whether Maguire Orchard and Apple Butter Barn was destined to survive or go belly up, she was going to pack her bags, get the hell out of Riverbirch, and return to civilization.

And this time, there'd be no looking back.

The distant wail of a siren reverberated across the valley. Morgan took a deep breath and blew it out. Then she stared at the blood on her hands and waited.

Chapter 2

Gage Kirkland forced himself to calm down. The raw anticipation that had burned through his gut for the last forty minutes was beginning to give him the kind of heartburn no amount of antacid could touch.

The woman he'd found pacing the Maguire's front porch in a low-cut ruffled blouse, chain smoking menthol cigarettes as fast as she could light one off the other, was worried Morgan hadn't shown up with her kid. What was the woman's name—Peach? Peach was sure something bad had happened to them. And who was Gage to say she was wrong? If he'd learned anything skulking around the most dangerous streets in Atlanta, it was to respect another person's fears. Sometimes they were unfounded. Most of the time they weren't.

"I'm not a rich woman," Peach wailed. "I live in a trailer park and work two jobs. I can't afford daycare, so I pay Morgan to keep Crystal every day after school. If she takes my baby somewhere, she's supposed to leave a note." She gazed up and down the road, panic growing in her dark kohl lined eyes. "Being a single parent can sure be the pits sometimes."

"Yes, it can."

"I'm just glad I don't have to worry about my two boys. They live with their father in Cherokee Bluff, so I only have to fool with them every other weekend." She batted her thick black lashes. "Dammit! Where are they? I've gotta be at work at five." She turned back to Gage. "You're not gonna leave me here alone, are you? Please say you're not gonna leave."

"I'm not gonna leave."

"We're *staying*?" Jeremy glanced up from a dog-eared copy of *The Time Machine* and scowled. He managed to avoid looking directly into Gage's eyes, a feat he'd perfected during the last two months. "*Jeez!* How long are we staying here? Until it's time to eat?"

"Maybe."

Jeremy threw the book on the wicker loveseat. "Then can I go inside and take a—" He glanced at Peach, thought better of it. "Can I use the bathroom?"

"Go ahead," Peach said. "Morgan won't mind. Top of the stairs to your left."

Jeremy shuffled into the house. The screen door banged behind him.

"Is your boy here to take piano lessons?"

"Uh...no." Gage ducked under a string of wind chimes. "I'm here to meet Sean Maguire." He leaned against a wooden porch post and followed Peach's anxious gaze to the road winding in front of the house. It had taken him half an hour to find the place. He lived on the other side of the mountain in Cherokee Bluff, and had forgotten how tricky the back roads near Riverbirch could be.

He glanced over his shoulder. The view from the big wraparound porch looked like the picture postcards he'd seen at the Tennessee Welcome Center. A large painted wooden square decorated the front of the gray weathered barn—some kind of quilt pattern that looked like apples. He'd seen painted wooden quilt blocks with different colors and patterns hanging on barns all over Tennessee, and they always made him smile. Such a sweet, homey way to decorate the countryside. As if the idyllic scenery wasn't beautiful enough.

Below the Maguire's rambling three-story Victorian, neat rows of apple trees, heavy with fruit, spread across a lush, rolling valley. According to the tax records, theirs was a high-density orchard, 175 trees per acre, on about thirty-seven acres, flanked on one side by Deer Creek and the other by the south end of Blackstone Mountain. He sighed contentedly. A little slice of heaven plopped down in the middle of nowhere. "Nice place," he said. "I'm from Georgia. Is Blackstone part of the Appalachian Mountains or the Smokies?"

"Appalachians. And I'm glad you pronounced it the right way. It's downright insulting when some of those big know-it-all announcers on *The Weather Channel* pronounce it 'App-a-*lay*-chuns.' The only people who say it like that are the people who don't live here."

Gage glanced behind him. "This house is huge."

"This house is a monster," Peach said, laughing. "In winter, they close off half the rooms just to heat it." She sighed. "But I love it here. Morgan doesn't know how lucky she is. She's never been much of a country girl."

"Has she always lived here?"

"She lived in Atlanta while she was married, then moved back here, then moved to Nashville for a few months until last spring. She keeps trying to get off this farm, but somebody always needs her for something. Then she has to come home again."

"What did she do in Nashville?"

"Played the organ for some big church.'Course, she had to quit to help take care of her grandpa." Peach shook her head. "Robert Maguire was a hard man, but I wouldn't wish a death like his on anyone. Cancer. The poor man was eat up with it. That's where Morgan and I met. I work at the nursing home part-time, and I stayed with him at night."

"You're a nurse?" He tried to keep the surprise out of his voice.

"Well, not yet. But I'd like to be." She took a breath and went on. "After Mr. Maguire died, his second wife, Opal, said she never wanted to see another apple tree as long as she lived. She threatened to contest the will, and forced Sean and Morgan to give her part of their inheritance. It left them in a pretty bad place financially, which is why Sean begged Morgan to stay until he gets the farm back on its feet. She won't hang around, though. Once they get the harvest apples in, she'll leave again."

Gage wondered what Morgan Maguire would look like now.

He hadn't allowed himself to trust the memory he carried in his head, buried so deep no amount of effort or whisky could destroy it. Its luster should have faded, or at least morphed into the kind of hazy fantasy that had been trotted out and brooded over so many times, it had nothing to do with the real thing. Her eyes, her hair, the smile that had made his twenty-two-year-old heart ache with desire, couldn't be the same as he remembered. People never stayed the same. Life changed them. Other people changed them. Chances were he wouldn't even recognize her.

He'd know her voice, though. Low and throaty, with the barest hint of a rasp. A voice no man in his right mind could ever forget. When he'd called to confirm the appointment with her brother, the sound of her voice on the answering machine startled him into tripping over a crate of empty wine bottles. Then sent him sprawling headfirst into the tasting room wall.

"Your son looks like you," Peach said. "Cute kid. He isn't real thrilled to be here, is he?"

"At the moment, Jeremy isn't real thrilled to be anywhere."

"They sure go through phases, don't they?"

"Oh, lady," he said softly. "This is way more than a phase."

Gage glanced at the screen door. He wished Jeremy would come bounding out and flash him the laid-back grin Gage had always taken for granted. But those days were gone. The last few months had turned Jeremy into a boy whose pinched face couldn't hide his anger. Whose volatile temper remained cocked and ready to explode at the slightest provocation. Refusing to look his father in the eye was something Jeremy withheld out of spite. It was the knife he could plunge into Gage's heart, the revenge he could exact without breaking a sweat.

He's just a kid. He deserves to feel happy.

Gage didn't believe in happiness. Not for himself, anyway. Not anymore. It was something reserved for the elderly with brains so ravaged by dementia, they couldn't remember their own names, much less the person who had ruined their lives fifty years ago. And for the children, young, innocent souls still untouched by the meanness in the world. He'd always considered a person's innocence a sacred thing. Which is why he would never forgive himself for destroying it for his own son.

"They're here!" Peach jumped up and down. Polka dot ruffles flapped against her ample, bouncing bosom.

A pale blue truck, so beat up it looked like it should be balanced on cinderblocks in somebody's front yard, turned into the driveway and rumbled toward the house. It ground to a halt beside the white fence. A little girl, the spitting image of Peach, sans about a hundred pounds, scrambled out of the cab and ran toward them. Her thin arms flailed in the wind.

"*Mama, Mama! Morgan found a—*"

"Crystal Darlene! Where have you been?" Peach flipped her cigarette behind a clump of azaleas and scooped her daughter into her arms. "I've been worried sick about you."

"Listen, *listen*, Mama! Morgan found a dead—"

"Not now, sugar. Mama's talking."

Gage stared at the truck cab, waiting.

If he thought for one second she'd even remember him, he'd...no. He laughed softly. He couldn't imagine she would. It had been too long. The time they'd spent together had only been a spit in a bucket. They'd danced around each other for a day and a night like opposite ends of a magnet, shared a makeshift bed, made a few empty promises. By the next morning, she'd probably forgotten all about him, shaken off their time together like a dream barely worth remembering. He'd thought their lovemaking had been pretty spectacular, even by twenty-year-old standards, but what had he known? A kid who had hidden his inexperience and vulnerability beneath a veil of bravado, then let his better judgment and raging hormones get the best of him?

Nothing much had changed there.

The shallow part of him hoped she'd let herself go, turned into one of those hefty women he saw at the grocery store, who smelled like bacon grease, and enjoyed speeding down the aisles, terrorizing the other shoppers in their motorized carts. Or maybe that was the cowardly part.

He blinked at the truck. Why didn't she get out? Had she seen him? Did he look familiar to her? He took another deep, ragged breath. Something sharp stabbed at the shell surrounding his heart, leaving it scratched and sore.

What would she think of him now? Irresponsible? Inadequate? Disappointing? If she did remember him, how surprised would she be he had changed so little? That beneath the grown-up, slightly weathered exterior, he was still the same immature kid afraid to trust his own judgment? That he was still making the wrong choices and blaming himself because the life he'd screwed up hadn't turned out like he wanted? He used to think that at least his heart was in the right place, but he wasn't even sure of that anymore. He wasn't sure of anything.

He crossed his arms and shifted his weight from one foot to the other. His heart thumped against his ribs. Double-time. Like Bugs Bunny staring down the barrel of Elmer Fudd's shotgun. It occurred to him that when they finally came face to face, he might actually be required to speak. He tried to swallow, but all available spit had left the building.

Two scuffed brown leather boots slowly emerged

from the truck, followed by a pair of jean clad legs that seemed to go on forever. The woman attached to them slid from the cab, stepped back, and slammed the door. She took off her dilapidated straw hat, shook out a cascade of dark brown hair, then stood for a moment, looking at him.

Had she always been that tall? As tall as him? Maybe. They'd only spent one day in each other's company, and they hadn't wasted much time standing. They'd sat on a bench at the Harvest Festival beside a huge copper kettle while she stirred figure eights into boiling apple butter with a long wooden paddle. Then later, they'd lain on a cot in his uncle's Lake Shanleigh boathouse with the moonlight streaming through the wooden slats, caressing her pale, smooth skin until it shimmered. She still had the kind of porcelain skin that looked as if she spent her days indoors, protected by steel and UV coated glass, instead of trailing through a sunny apple orchard in the foothills of the Appalachian Mountains.

As she rounded the fence, he took in her soft curves, her slim, square shoulders, the mud streaked, beige and blue plaid flannel shirt. Her glossy dark waves tumbled across one full breast as she bent to open the gate. Then, the moment he had been waiting twelve years for, and dreading more than any single moment of his life, came and went. She lifted her head, blinked her clear gray-blue eyes, and gazed directly at him. Without one single hint of recognition.

Something twisted in his chest. He tried to swallow the knot lodged in his throat. He glanced at the toes of his carefully shined boots and willed his pride to stop scorching a path through his insides.

Okay.

Morgan Maguire didn't know him from a can of paint.

That was one giant blow to his ego. But in the end, it would make things easier. The street smarts he'd always relied on had pretty much flown out the window the second he'd discovered she was involved in this case. If she knew the real reason he was there, it would complicate things beyond belief. He had enough on his plate without adding humiliation and heartbreak to the mix.

He'd only agreed to take this job because he needed the money for his son, and he would do anything—*anything*—to help Jeremy. No matter what moron was paying for it.

He'd been curious to see how Morgan had turned out. Who wouldn't be? But now that his curiosity had been satisfied, it was time to jump back on the reality train and act like the professional he was. Or used to be. He'd give Morgan's brother the two hour consultation he'd promised, do what Tyson had hired him to do, take his boy, and get the ever-lovin' hell out of Dodge. Then maybe, just maybe he could start to forget her.

"Morgan," Peach said, "I don't think you've met—"

"Gage Kirkland," he said. He started to hold out his hand, but as soon as it was airborne, he lost his nerve and pulled back. Not exactly the smoothest of moves, but he didn't trust himself to touch her. "I'm...I'm from In the Black. We're a small business salvage company, relatively new to this area. I don't know if your brother told you, but he's won a free consultation for me to look at your operation. See if I can help get it back on track."

"Sean isn't here." Morgan looked at him impassively. "He thought you were coming tomorrow."

"I was," Gage said. "I am. But I was in the neighborhood, and I thought I might drop by and see the orchard. You know, get a head start." Why couldn't he stop smiling at her like an idiot? Why did he sound like he was selling used cars?

She laid her straw hat on a chair and looked right through him. As if he wasn't there.

Had he changed that much? Sure, he'd filled out, grown a muscle or two, started shaving semi-regularly. But he was basically the same guy. On the outside, anyway.

"In the neighborhood?" she said. "Way out here?"

"I had some free time," he said, scrounging up a more plausible excuse. He blew out a short, silent breath, then settled his gaze on her face. God, he'd missed that face. He hadn't known just how much until that moment. A tiny dimple still creased the skin beside her full, perfectly shaped mouth, the same mouth that had never stopped haunting his dreams. "I had to pick up my son from school, and I thought if you didn't mind, I could—"

"You have a son?" Morgan's head jerked toward the barn. "Is he here with you?"

"We just moved from Atlanta," Gage said. "Right now he's—"

"He's in the can," Peach said. She pointed to the stains on Morgan's jeans. "What happened to you?"

Crystal tugged at Peach's blouse. "Morgan found a body, Mama. A real live dead one."

Peach clutched Crystal to her hip. "Are you serious? Oh, my God, Morgan, who?"

19

"Harlan Spannagel. He's taking a blood thinner, and had some kind of hemorrhage."

"Crystal didn't—"

"No, no," Morgan said quickly. "I kept her away from it. That's why we're late. I tried to call on the way back, but couldn't get a signal. You know how iffy cell service is once you start around the mountain. I haven't been able to get hold of Sean either."

"You mean, he doesn't know?"

Jeremy pushed his way out the screen door.

The sight of his gawky legs and arms clutched Gage's heart. Oversized jeans hung on his slight frame. The curved bill of a navy baseball cap covered the back of his neck. A black T-shirt with the message 'Earth's Full—Go Home!' hugged his thin collarbones. Gage had worried Jeremy's Atlanta clothes might set him apart from the other kids in Cherokee Bluff, but, except for the expensive athletic shoes supplied by his indulgent grandparents, Jeremy was a perfect clone of every other boy who stood slouching in front of the county school.

Jeremy's light brown eyes studied the people on the porch with cool indifference. His sharp chin, identical to the one Gage scraped shaving cream off every other morning, jutted out in a sullen declaration of disgust.

"I like your shirt, kid," Morgan said softly. "I've got one that says, 'Why are you still here? The stupid people left hours ago'. Maybe we could trade sometime."

Jeremy's gaze flickered to life for a moment. Then it was gone.

Morgan smiled. "So, Jeremy, how do you like small town life? Must be like getting hit in the chest with a stun gun after living in Atlanta."

Jeremy stared at the porch.

"The lady asked you a question," Gage said.

Jeremy lifted his head and looked at Morgan. "Okay, lady. You wanna know how I like living in East Bumfuck? I don't. I don't like it at all. In fact, everything about it sucks a big one."

"That's hard to believe," Morgan said, nonplussed. "I mean, there's so much to do here—4-H Club, Friday night Bingo, Saturday night fish fries, square dancing. Now, you know you want to learn to square dance. Swing your partner? Allemande left and do-si-do?"

"I'd rather poke my eye out with a rusty nail," Jeremy said.

"Yeah, me too, kid," Morgan said. "It was a joke."

Gage cleared his throat. "Peach said you give piano lessons. Jeremy took lessons while we were in Atlanta. Didn't you, Jeremy? He was pretty good."

"How would you know?" Jeremy said. "You never showed up at any of the recitals."

"How long have you been playing?" Morgan asked.

"Let's see," Gage said. "He's eleven now. Since he was eight. Right, Jeremy?"

"Gosh, *I'm* eight," Crystal said. "You're supposed to be eleven? You're not as big as me."

Jeremy winced and took a step back. His frail shoulders shifted a few subtle inches upward. His gaze locked on the barn.

Gage wished Crystal had been gracious enough to keep her comments to herself. But kids didn't care. For years, Jeremy had endured rude remarks about his lack of height, and from kids who were more of a threat to him than an eight-year-old-girl. Why were children so cruel? Gage had never met one who couldn't open its little mouth and slice a person to ribbons, zinging insults as strong as sucker punches the second they let down their guard.

"He took karate lessons, too," Gage said. "Didn't you, sport?"

Jeremy stared at the barn.

"Well, that's good," Morgan said. "Karate builds muscle, and some guys need a little help until they get their growth spurts."

"What's a growth spurt?" Crystal asked. "Do I get one?"

"Well, sure," Morgan said. "But you'll get yours sooner because you're a girl. And if you take after your dad, Miss Chips Ahoy, you'll get drafted by a basketball team, and the stupid people will say things to you like, 'How's the weather up there?'"

"You're making it up," Jeremy said. "I've never read that in a book, and I read all the time. There's no such thing as a growth spurt."

"Yes, there is," Morgan said. "My brother didn't get his until he turned sixteen, then he shot up like a weed. We thought he'd sprinkled Miracle-Gro on his Cocoa Krispies." Morgan pointed to the barn. "See that door? He can't walk under it without ducking."

"Are you serious?" Jeremy whispered in awe.

"No," Morgan said, laughing. "But he is six-feet."

Jeremy grinned. Then looked at his feet and grinned again.

Gage couldn't believe what he'd witnessed. Morgan had actually managed to crack through Jeremy's shell and engage him in conversation. Only for a minute. But it had happened. After two long months, Gage had finally glimpsed the old Jeremy again, and his heart swelled with relief. His son was still in there. Below the surface.

He caught Morgan's eye and smiled. A lump of gratitude settled in his throat.

She didn't return the smile, but held his gaze for a full four seconds, clear and unwavering. Which was damned remarkable, since she didn't have a clue who he was. Most of the women he'd known in Atlanta were stingy with eye contact. They liked to keep their options open, keep a man guessing whether he was on the short list or the long. He frequented upscale bars, but rarely changed out of his undercover clothes. So, unless the women he preferred were angling for free top shelf margaritas or a post last-call tumble in the sack, his old jeans and faded shirts rendered him invisible.

"Let's go, sugar." Peach hustled her daughter off the porch. "Hey, Gage, if you're free tomorrow night, come on down to Bad Moon Rising. It's a little roadhouse near the creek. Morgan and I work there on weekends." She flashed him a wide smile. "First drink's on me."

"Thanks," Gage said. "I just might."

****

Gage looked at Peach. His eyes crinkled. His mouth curled into a grin.

Morgan could almost see the pheromones fly through the air.

But that's how Peach affected men. At first, none of them minded she was thirty pounds overweight and came with more baggage than a Norwegian Cruise Line. Baggage that included a taste for expensive bourbon and three children sired by three different men. All they saw was a warm, voluptuous, slightly bawdy Earth Mother who made them feel as if they were the center of the universe. Morgan had heard about some of her other talents. Talents that steamed up the windows of Peach's car and made it easier for the men on the receiving end to ignore the fact she was constantly on the prowl for someone to take care of her. The kinder women in Riverbirch called her "needy" or "sad", while others whispered behind her back that she was the worst kind of gold-digger, the kind who would hook up with anybody who offered to buy her a shot and pay last month's rent.

"Come on, Jeremy," Gage said. "We should leave, too."

"I have to use the bathroom again," Jeremy said. "It was that disgusting steak burrito you bought me after school. It tasted like dog food. Did you know those things have 390 calories, 1090 milligrams of sodium, and 14 grams of fat?"

"Way too much information." Morgan laughed. "Go on, kid. We don't charge extra for two trips."

"We ate at Maxie's," Gage said after he left.

"Then you're a brave, brave soul. Is Jeremy your only child?"

"Yes, but I'd like to have more someday. I don't want Jeremy to be an only child like I was. So, I guess a woman not wanting kids would pretty much be a deal breaker for me."

"I'll alert the media."

He glanced at the dried blood on the back of her hands.

"I need to wash up," she said. "There's a mud sink

in the barn. You can wait here."

"Or I can go with you."

She started up the sloped hill toward the barn, skirting the soggy edges of grass. She could feel his eyes boring into her back as she navigated the uneven path, and she fought the urge to smooth the flannel shirttail covering her bottom.

She stood at the sink and glanced at her reflection in the tiny mirror glued to the front of the paper towel dispenser. Strands of dark hair curled about her face, wild and unkempt. Her cheeks had flushed as pink as if she'd run to the top of Pip's Hill. Her eyes met her own eyes, and she quickly looked away. The time for soul-searching would come later. After he was gone. She turned on the tap, squirted a glob of heavy-duty hand cleaner into her palm, and began to scrub.

Gage leaned against the open barn door, watching her. When he spoke, his north Georgia accent caressed each word like warm honey. "This is a beautiful orchard. I bet you love it here."

"Not really. I've lived here most of my life, but I'm a city girl at heart."

He gestured past the cases of glass jars stacked in the corner to the rows of copper kettles lined neatly against the back wall. "So, your family makes apple butter?"

"No, we're witches. As soon as the eye of newt shipment arrives, we'll fire up these bad boys and brew some potions. You saw the *Maguire Orchard and Apple Butter Barn* sign by the road? It's a cover."

He chuckled softly and shook his head.

"Didn't buy it, huh?" She ripped off a brown paper towel. "We make apple butter, apple jelly, pressed cider, even a little apple wine on occasion. But keep that to yourself. Sean thinks we'd lose the Baptist business if anyone found out."

"This must be quite an operation. These kettles are enormous."

"The big one—around 300 gallons—is outside, built into a brick vessel. We heat it with propane. You could probably go swimming in it."

"But would you want to?" He gazed around the cavernous room. "I see the apple cider machine, but where's the farm equipment? Don't tell me you still pick apples by hand."

"We had an apple harvester and a hydraulic tree shaker, but we had to sell them to pay my grandfather's medical bills. It's a small operation, and not all the trees are ready to harvest. Sean thinks we can pick them by hand this year."

"Where are your pickers? The fruit on the trees looks like it's ready to drop."

"You know, Mr. Kirkland—"

"Gage."

"You don't have to stay and make small talk with me. I'm not exactly a small talk kind of girl. And I really don't care enough about the farm to discuss it with you. You can look around if you want. I'm not sure when Sean will be back."

"So, Sean is your brother?"

"He's my twin."

"Really? Does he look like you?"

"People say he does, but I can't see it. We're both tall, but his hair is stick-straight, and mine has a life of its own. His eyes are green, mine are blue. He's laidback and good-hearted, I'm cynical and mean.

Besides the same birthday, the only two things we have in common are a couple of freakishly long toes and the shared belief until the age of five that clowns were a race of people."

He threw back his head and laughed. His deep, rich baritone rumbled through the empty barn like thunder ricocheting off the mountain. A dimple slashed the left side of his face.

She hadn't expected him to laugh. Or for the sound of it to wrap around her heart like a steel band, squeezing it until the memories she'd buried clawed and scratched their way to the surface. She leaned against the door opposite him, to prop herself up more than anything else, and shoved her hands in the pockets of her jeans. She could feel them trembling against her thighs. She took a deep breath and lifted her gaze to meet his head-on.

His eyes had aged a bit, more hollow than she remembered and framed by a tiny web of lines that crinkled when he smiled. The searing intelligence was still there, and the flickering, mischievous gleam that had drawn her to him all those years ago. The dark, greenish brown irises seemed as bottomless as ever, but haunted now, as if the things they'd seen had stamped them with a melancholy imprint he couldn't quite erase. The last twelve years had taken their toll. But she had to admit, that standing this close and gazing into the same extraordinary eyes she had fallen into the day before she left Riverbirch to get married, still sent one hell of a shiver rocketing down her spine.

"You said you'd been here for...how long?"

"Two months," he said.

"Riverbirch is a small town. Funny I haven't run

into you before now."

"I'm living over the mountain in Cherokee Bluff. I've been busy settling in with Jeremy and planning the publicity campaign for In the Black. If I have spare time, I spend it working at my uncle's winery."

"I could use a glass of wine right now." She lifted her chin. "Can I ask you a question?"

"Sure." The muscle in his jaw clenched and released. "Ask me anything."

"All right. I would just like to know, strictly for the record."

"Know what?"

"Why the hell you never called me."

His dark eyes melted into hers. As the seconds ticked by, she couldn't look away.

"So," he said. "You do remember me."

"Well, yes. *Hell*, yes. I'm not brain dead. Yet."

She fought to keep her voice steady. Her insides were shaking like a freight train.

So far, she'd held it together. Getting out of the truck, seeing Gage Kirkland standing on her front porch like something that had materialized out of thin air. For one panicked moment, she'd thought she was hallucinating. Then her heart started beating again, and the breath she didn't realize she'd lost returned in short, silent bursts.

The man would still turn heads—lean, tall, well-built. His brown hair had been cut short, revealing a light swath of gray near the temples. Age had improved almost everything about him. Without the soft protective cushioning of early-twenties skin, his cheekbones looked more chiseled, the muscles in his arms downright powerful. Not the sculpted, twenty-hours-a-week-at-the-gym kind of powerful, but smooth and sinewy and strong. As if he actually used them. She looked at his clothes and stifled a laugh. His wardrobe choices hadn't changed. He was wearing the same thing he'd had on the last time she'd seen him—faded jeans and a blue Oxford shirt, sleeves rolled to his elbows. He looked more solid, more grounded. And sexier than ever.

He crossed his arms over his broad chest, ducked his head down, and peered up at her. Then he smiled his killer smile. "You look good, Morgan. Really good."

Her heart crashed against her ribs. "Thanks. So do you. You always did."

"Are you kidding? The last time you saw me, I was a twenty-two-year-old geek who thought he had all the moves. I was insufferable. I'm surprised you even spoke to me, much less let me—"

"—get to third base?"

He laughed again, a little nervously. "Something like that."

She took another breath and forced herself to push the sentiment aside. For her own self-preservation, she needed to look past his outer shell, attractive though it was, and see the real man underneath. The man who had shattered her heart.

The shock of having him near began to evaporate, leaving the bitterness she thought she'd liberated herself from simmering below the surface. Maybe time wasn't the great healer after all. Maybe it never wiped away the memories or the hurt. Not completely. Maybe she was destined to spend the rest of her life waking up after seeing his face in her dreams, then lying awake until dawn wondering how differently her life might have been if he hadn't been so quick to let her go.

She wasn't thinking clearly—he'd always had that effect on her—but questions kept slamming into her brain like little sonic booms. *Why was he here? What did he want? Why was he the small business consultant who had come to see Sean? What was he thinking, showing up at her house with a kid? Holy mother of— was there a wife somewhere?*

Her throat ached. *He has a child. A son.*

It wasn't fair. All those years ago, he hadn't lost anything. Not a damn thing, except her. She wanted to scream at him, demand to know why he was there, stirring everything up again—the hurt, the hope. Then she wanted to curl her hand into a fist and punch him in the face. Pain cut through her heart then blazed into anger. She welcomed it. Anger was safe. Anger was something she knew how to do.

"Let me get this straight," she said. "Your company—what's it called?"

"In the Black."

"In the Black. Out of the blue, In the Black sent my brother a letter saying he had won a two hour consultation to—how did you put it?—'help revitalize and reinforce small businesses in these exciting but uncertain times.'"

"Too wordy?"

"Too fishy. Is it true? Did Sean win a consultation?"

"Absolutely. I started In the Black last year. I helped my father-in-law save a friend's interior design business." *So, there was a wife.* "I didn't do much, just came up with some fresh ideas. But I was looking for a new line of work, and I seemed to have a knack for it.

Then I saved a cupcake bakery from going under, and an organic herb farm, and a landscaping business. Suddenly, I became the go-to guy in Atlanta if a small business was about to tank. Then I moved up here, and I'm having to start from scratch again. Giving away free consultations is great publicity and more cost effective than paying for ads in the newspaper."

"Oh, I've heard *The Riverbirch Gazette* is a goldmine when it comes to advertising. There are so many people here. So many small businesses to revitalize and reinforce."

"You're kidding, right?"

"Of course, I'm kidding. Do you really think you can make a go of business like that in a town this size? Riverbirch is a farming community, separated from Cherokee Bluff by a freakin' mountain. The nearest Wal-mart is thirty miles away. Who are you going to help? Maxie's Diner and Taco Bar? Spannagel's Feed and Seed?"

"Businesses everywhere are failing, no matter where they're located. I'm planning to expand, maybe as far as Knoxville and Asheville."

"How did you choose our orchard? Open the phonebook, close your eyes, and point?"

"Pretty much."

She leveled her gaze at him. "And you expect me to believe that?"

"Well...yes."

"You know what I think? I think you moved back here and got bored, then decided to contact my brother so you could get a look at me and make sure you did the right thing not calling me all those years ago. You went to a lot of trouble." She stepped back and held out her hands. "You wanted to see me? Well, here I am. Good old Morgan Maguire. Except for the extra fifteen pounds I've packed on—and I'm chalking that up to the fact I eat ice cream instead of screaming when I'm upset, which is *now*—I'm the same girl. I don't have my nose pierced, or a tongue stud, or sixteen butterflies tattooed on my ass. You'll have to trust me on that one."

"Morgan, I—"

"You know what stinks most about this? How cruel you've become. This orchard is my brother's life, and it's not exactly thriving. Sean was thrilled when he got your letter. For four days he's been floating around this farm in a bubble, believing the thing he cares about most in the world might actually have a chance to survive. Because of you."

"I didn't think—"

"No, you didn't. That much hasn't changed about you. Well, you know what? I want to thank you for not calling me twelve years ago. You did the right thing. You saved me from a life of...*you*." She turned and started down the path.

"Whoa!" he cried, following her. "Hold on. I have every intention of honoring my offer to Sean. I'll admit it's a little bogus. But I swear, it's sincere. When I heard Maguire Orchard was ready to fold, I wanted to use my skills to find a way to help without making it look like charity."

"That's ridiculous. Why would you want to help me? Because, after all this time, you've decided to feel guilty about dumping me? Well, *don't*. You don't owe me anything."

"I know," he said softly. "But I wanted to—" He took a step toward her. "Morgan, please. Okay, I'll admit I wondered what you were like now. But that's not the reason I set this up." He laughed. "Come on. Haven't you ever wondered about me?"

"Well, sure. Years ago. When I still gave a damn. Lately? Not so much."

Gage glanced up. His eyes caught the light. A spray of golden flecks shimmered near the dark green iris like sunlight scattered across the deep, clear water of Lacey's Pond. "I'm living in Cherokee Bluff now, and I would like it if we could be—"

"We can't be anything." She held his gaze without flinching. "You understand that, right?"

"I do now."

"Good. So, here's how we're going to do this. You can give your phony consultation prize to Sean. I want you to. He's counting on it. And it had better be good or I will sue you for false advertising. When you're done, I want you to slink back into oblivion and leave us alone. I'm sure it won't be too much of a stretch, since disappearing seems to be something you excel at. But I do not want you near my life."

A white Taurus with the word *Sheriff* painted on the side turned into the driveway.

"Excuse me. I have company." She turned and hurried down the path, grateful to put some physical distance between them.

Sheriff Teresa Stallard stepped out of the car and took off her sunglasses. The soft roll of flesh above her holster jiggled as she walked. A single salt and pepper braid, a proud tribute to her Cherokee heritage, hung down her back like a thick rope.

Morgan met her on the flagstone walk.

"How are you holding up?" the sheriff asked. "We

didn't find any vomit in the slaughterhouse. Most people get sick when they stumble on a grisly scene like that." She shook her head. "Lord, I've never seen so much blood in one place. If it had been me, I would've blown my cookies clear across the valley. I'd still be blowing them." Her gaze shifted to Morgan's left shoulder. "Hey, there. I'm Sheriff Stallard. I don't think we've met."

"Gage Kirkland." His deep baritone rumbled in Morgan's left ear.

"Bert Kirkland's nephew," Morgan said. "He was just leaving."

The sheriff nodded. "Honey, is Sean here? I need to talk to him."

"Not yet. He drove over to Barkerstown to see if he could line up some pickers. Everything's running late this year because of the bee situation. The Rome Beauties are in, but our regular pickers are working for Mr. Finch."

"For Lawrence Finch? Doing what?"

"Actually, he's paying them *not* to work here. Harlan was trying to work out a compromise, but now that he's gone—"

"Hey, there's a guitar in the house!" Jeremy cried, banging open the screen. "Does she give guitar lessons? Can I take them? *Please?*" He stopped short when he saw the sheriff.

The sheriff squinted at Gage. "You don't look like Bert Kirkland, but you do look familiar. Have I seen you around town?"

"My son and I have been here a few months. We moved to Cherokee Bluff after my ex-wife died."

"Sorry to hear it," the sheriff said. "What happened

to her?"

Jeremy's head jerked up. He stared to the left of his father's face. "Yeah, go ahead, asshole. Tell the sheriff how you killed my mother."

Gage opened his mouth to reply, then closed it again. Pain appeared in his eyes. The boy's words reverberated across the porch like the last jarring notes of a steel drum.

"Time to go," Gage whispered.

Jeremy jumped off the porch and raced across the yard to their car. He climbed in and slammed the door. Without another word, or glance, Gage turned and followed him.

Chapter 3

"Jeremy, son, we can't go on like this. You have to talk to me."

Jeremy turned his face away and stared out the side window of the car. His chin jutted forward. His small hands, one fist nestled tightly in the other, pressed together then released, as if he wanted to smash something. His father's face, maybe.

A car wasn't the best place to have it out with Jeremy. But the back roads were deserted, and unless the boy jumped out of a moving vehicle, he had no choice but to sit and listen.

"I know you're angry at me," Gage said. "Angrier than you've ever been in your life. I know I should tell you that you have every right to hate me for what I did, but I don't believe you do. The night your mother died, my only concern was for your safety."

"Shut up."

"I didn't know how bad things had gotten with her."

"Because you were never there, asshole."

"I wanted to be, but your mother wouldn't—" He stopped. The truth didn't matter. If he criticized Suzanne now, Jeremy would never forgive him. Gage took a breath and chose his words carefully. "I'm...I'm sorry about that, sport. Your mother...hid her condition from everyone but you. I thought she was getting better—we all did—and I didn't know how much she depended on you to look out for her." His voice caught. "But that night, I was only trying to protect you. When you were born, your mother and I agreed you would always come first. For both of us. No matter what. If the tables had been turned, she would have done the same thing."

The sudden appearance of a tear sliding down Jeremy's smooth cheek shook Gage to the core. Jeremy batted it away with the heel of his hand. "Shut up," he said evenly. "I don't want to talk about this with you. Ever."

"But you've got to talk about it. If not with me, then somebody. Dr. Lloyd says you won't talk to her either. What happened the night your mom died is eating you alive. If you'd just let me help you, and—"

"*No!*"

"Jeremy, please. I'd do anything for you. You know that, don't you?"

Jeremy twisted around and glared at his father with so much revulsion, Gage's blood ran cold.

What was Gage going to do now? What was left to do? Every time he talked to Jeremy, he made things worse. Jeremy was slipping away from him day by day, and he was helpless to stop it. He'd tried everything the psychologist had suggested, but nothing had worked. At some point, he was going to have to face the fact he might stumble through life never winning his son's forgiveness. And that was one life he didn't think he could endure.

Gage guided his '95 Mustang up the long drive to his uncle's winery. The guys at the agency had made fun of him for buying it. Especially his boss, Tyson, who drove a reliable Honda, and traded up every two years. But Gage didn't care. The old Mustang had kept him sane. He'd spent six months working nights and weekends to bring it back to life. More work than he'd ever imagined. But he hadn't given up. He'd replaced the split upholstery, put in new brakes, turbocharged the engine. He had refused to repair the scratches and dings on the black exterior, or have it painted. He liked the fact that it looked like it was ready for the trash heap. If he had to chase some bad guys, the expressions on their faces were priceless when the old beat-up car they were sure they could shake turned out to be hell on wheels.

He patted the dashboard, then glanced at his son. He wasn't giving up on Jeremy either. The boy was wrapped in grief. Drowning in it. And everyone told Gage nothing could be done except wait for it to subside.

Well, that wasn't good enough. There had to be something he could do. He just had to figure out what it was, then do it. He was in Jeremy's life to stay, whether Jeremy wanted him there or not. If it took the rest of his days, he would never stop trying to make his son love him again.

The second Gage stopped the car, Jeremy flung off his seatbelt, swung the low door open, and bolted. He ran up the stone walk, then disappeared around the side of the winery. *Probably looking for Bert,* Gage thought, fending off a stab of jealousy. Gage wasn't sure how Bert, scarcely the warmest human on the planet, had managed to forge such a special bond with Jeremy. Or why Jeremy worshiped the ground the old coot walked on.

Not nice, Gage chided himself. Although, *old coot* was one of the more savory descriptions that came to mind. If Jeremy got wind of how Gage felt about Bert, the boy would hate Gage even more. Like it or not, Bert was Gage's uncle. The same uncle he was forced to live with until he could climb out from under a mountain of debt. The same uncle who refused to help finance Jeremy's psychotherapy after the insurance money ran out because he thought child psychologists were as useless as tits on a tomcat.

Gage lifted his foot off the brake and leaned over the steering wheel. The sun had begun its slow drop behind the mountains.

Inertia. Not knowing what to do, so doing nothing. Hadn't that been his mantra for years? Hadn't Suzanne threatened to have it printed on a T-shirt for him? Why had she never understood that feeling helpless around the people he loved terrified him worse than hiding in the shadows with his gun drawn and his heart hammering in his throat?

He tapped the top of the steering wheel with the heel of his hand. Then struck it harder, and harder. What in blazes could he do for Jeremy that he hadn't already tried? If he could just think of one thing the kid liked, it would be a starting point. Something Jeremy wouldn't be able to resist. Something Gage, and only Gage, could offer him. A bridge he could forge between darkness and light. Gage rubbed the smarting, fleshy part of his palm. Outside, the winery lights popped on, nestled in long swags of grapevines wrapped around a split rail fence. His mind drifted off then back again, until the image of Morgan's face swam into view.

His cell phone buzzed in his pocket. He snapped

the cover open, read the caller's name, and cursed softly. *Tyson.* He took a deep breath and tried to sound upbeat. "Hey, Ty. How's it going?"

"I might ask you the same thing. What gives? I haven't heard from you in days."

"That doesn't mean I haven't been working. I've had to set things up, put things in motion. You know how important this case is. I don't want to blow it."

"I don't want you to blow it either. But I expect you to check in."

"I know. Sorry."

"So, what's the problem? This case is a piece of cake."

"Yeah, I've heard that one before. From you, as a matter of fact. Right before a 9mm bullet plowed its way through my shoulder."

"This recovery job should go by the book. Get in, grab the thing, and get out. You've done it before. You're the best I've got. Or had, until you quit two months ago."

"You know I don't like recovery work. It feels too much like stealing."

Tyson laughed. "Aw, hell, Gage. It ain't stealing if it's already stolen. The client's got proof of purchase. It's an open and shut case. And it's worth a bundle, that's why the recovery fee is so high. Hell, if I had time, I'd go after it myself. I only asked you because I knew you needed the money, and you live less than six miles from the client's daughter-in-law."

"Ex-daughter-in-law."

Dennis P. Quillen. Gage had wondered why that name sounded so familiar. Tyson said he was a high-powered politician moving through the ranks of public office, being groomed to be the next senator. Gage had never paid much attention to local politics. He didn't have the stomach for it. He made sure he voted in the presidential election, and maybe a primary or two, but that was as far as his patriotic duty took him. Apparently, Quillen's estranged son, Denny, had stolen a rare artifact from him. But before Quillen could get it back, Denny's ex-wife stole it from Denny. Gage got a chuckle out of that one. He could only imagine what Thanksgiving dinners at the Quillen house had been like.

Dennis P. Quillen couldn't afford to allow anything on his record that might tarnish his good name. Discretion was paramount, and going with a larger, more well-known firm might risk a media leak. If Gage recovered the artifact, and Quillen was satisfied with the outcome, chances were he'd recommend Ty's agency to other high-powered politicians in need of discretion. Tyson had definitely hit the big time with this client.

"Was she hard to track down?" Tyson asked. "I'm assuming you've found her."

"Morgan Maguire? Yeah, I found her."

"I downloaded a picture of her after you left. She sure is a looker."

"Well, you know what they say, 'Doesn't matter how good-looking a woman is, somewhere, somebody is tired of putting up with her shit.'"

Tyson laughed.

"Don't worry," Gage said. "I'm on it."

Gage had felt ill at ease accepting the job. After Suzanne died, he'd promised Jeremy he would quit the agency and stop running around like Magnum, PI on steroids craving the next big adrenaline rush. Then Tyson played the money card—a very large money card—and Gage had caved. That much cash could get Jeremy the help he needed to cope with his mother's death. It could pull Gage out from under his uncle's suffocating thumb. One week's work could free them both, give them a fresh start in a sweet little Tennessee town with a crime rate so low, the sheriff only worked part-time. The money could heal his son, make his child whole again. And that was the only thing he wanted.

The fact that the client's ex-daughter-in-law was the same woman who had disturbed his dreams for the last twelve years didn't enter into it at all. Running into Morgan Maguire again was one of those strange "small world" coincidences people amuse each other with at cocktail parties. An unexpected bone the universe had decided to toss his way. He didn't expect anything to come of it. The universe could be fickle as hell. One day Jupiter was aligning with Mars, and the next day, all the cards had been reshuffled and moved out of his reach.

"Anything else?" Gage asked. "Or is my lecture over for the day?"

"I called to warn you. Word on the street is Quillen's son Denny has gotten wind of his old man's intentions and is on his way up there. Denny is a loose cannon. And a doper. He got arrested for possession a few years ago, but Quillen pulled some strings and got his record expunged. If he's a pill head needing cash, and a good ol' boy from north Georgia with Daddy's pistol strapped to the back of his bike, I'd consider him armed and dangerous."

Gage's ears went on lockdown. Air roared through

his head like he'd jumped off a cliff. Was Morgan in danger from this man? Would her ex hurt her in order to get his hands on a Civil War flag worth a fortune? Gage wasn't one to brag, but he was Morgan's best protection. He tried to stay cool. If Tyson suspected he had known Morgan, and was willing to muddy the waters with a lot of personal clutter, he might as well kiss the job goodbye.

For her sake, and his son's sake, he couldn't let that happen.

"I'm sending Denny's picture to your phone," Tyson said. "How's the cell service?"

"Not great. Depends on which side of the mountain you're on."

"Call me tomorrow. Let me know what's happening."

"Sure thing, Tyson."

"Oh, and Gage? There's something you should know. The agency hasn't been doing so well since you left. Expenses are high. The client list is shrinking. Unless you come through for me on this, I might have to close the agency's doors in the next couple of months."

"Sorry, man. I didn't know things were so grim."

"Just get the job done, Gage. Make me proud. I'm counting on you. We all are."

Gage closed the phone and waited until Denny's image came through. He held it up and stared at it. So this was the man Morgan had married? Jeez Louise. She must have loved him at one time, although looking at the creep, Gage wondered how that was even remotely possible. Denny stood beside a black motorcycle, hippie-length hair pulled back into a thin ponytail, unfocused watery gray eyes resting on the backside of a hangover. He wore a faded work shirt and brown corduroy house shoes. House shoes? Who wore house shoes out in public, for Christ's sake? An escapee from the local asylum? Who would even be friends with the bum, much less marry him?

Gage sighed. Who the hell ever knew why a woman was attracted to a man? It could be something as simple as looking into her eyes instead of at her chest. Or listening to her as if she had something to say. Or letting it drop that he was the owner of a hedge fund portfolio and a fat, fluid bank account. Whatever the reasons—and there were a million of them—Gage had learned long ago that where women were concerned, there was no accounting for taste.

****

Morgan left her bloody jeans in the sink to soak. Thank God she had remembered to extricate Harlan's cell phone from the pocket before dunking them in the soapy water. She had meant to give it to the sheriff, but once the ambulance arrived, all hell had broken loose.

She lowered herself into the deep claw foot tub and let the warm scented water pool around her neck. The moment she relaxed, the tears she'd held at bay for the past two hours rolled off her cheeks and splashed into the water. Her thoughts scuttled from Harlan to Gage to Sean and back again. If the old people in town were right, and bad things came in threes, then it was time to crawl in bed and pull the covers over her head.

She rinsed a washcloth cold and pressed it against her swollen eyes. "Stop it," she said. "Just stop it."

It was no use crying about the choices she'd made. Or the ones that had been made for her. All that mattered was getting through the next few days with her pride and sanity intact. She dried her hands then punched in Sean's number on her cell phone. Still no signal. Phone service on the Riverbirch side of the mountain was about as reliable as a sundial at midnight. Hard to believe, since cell towers had sprung up everywhere, dotting the landscape like the metal structures in Sean's old erector set, spoiling perfect mountain views.

She leaned back and closed her eyes.

Let it go, she told herself. Even though the past seemed intent on hunting her down like a fugitive. *Don't look back. What's done is done. Spilt milk. Water under the bridge.* She wished she could take those words to heart. But the trouble with platitudes was they always seemed so soul strengthening in the morning, and so damned improbable in the wee hours of a long, lonely night.

Shake off the past and focus. How was that for a platitude? Her top priority was Sean. When he found out about Harlan's death, he would be devastated. He'd need all the strength she could muster, and even then, it might not be enough. She glanced at the clock above the pedestal sink. *7:43.* Where was he?

No telling how far he'd had to drive to find pickers. Maybe as far as Sevier County or the south side of Knoxville. Morgan wanted to be the one to break the news to him about Harlan, but if he had stopped at Bad Moon for a couple of tall ones before heading home across the valley, someone would have already told him.

If her grandpa were still alive he would have said, *"Harlan's number was up, child. And there ain't nothing you can do when your number is up."*

Morgan didn't agree. When somebody's number was up, there was a lot they could do. They could stay away from trees when lightning cut across the sky. They could run for the parking lot when a drunk started throwing punches at the bar. They could leave their strung-out husband in an Atlanta ER, sneak out the side door, and drive to Tennessee with fourteen bucks in their pocket. When somebody's number was up, they could fight like hell to get it deferred. Some people just didn't try hard enough.

Morgan pulled herself out of the tub and reached for a towel.

A loud thump sounded from the next room.

Her room.

She opened her mouth to call Sean's name, but a sudden wave of uncertainty stopped her. Was it Sean? Sean would have charged up the stairs calling her name. Sean's work boots would have thundered down the hall to his room. Sean would have never gone in her room without asking permission. Would he? She stood frozen, clutching the bath towel to her chest. The person in her room moved noisily across the floor.

She could hear the drawers in her antique dresser being jerked opened and shoved closed, old swollen drawers that were hard to manage. She had always meant to rub beeswax on the bottoms to keep them from sticking, and whoever was opening them, wasn't having an easy a time of it.

Another loud scrape sent her heart flying to her throat.

She dropped her bath towel in the sink, lifted her blue terrycloth robe off the hook, and slipped it on. She

breathe, don't—

The footsteps moved away from her room, then traveled the length of the creaky hall toward the staircase. Morgan glanced in the mirror over the sink at her chalk white face. A film of perspiration glistened on her temples, her eyes wide and paralyzed with fear. She recognized that person. She'd seen her once before in a rearview mirror, the night she drove out of Denny Quillen's life.

She sat on the side of the tub. The soft *tick-tick* of the round plastic wall clock whirred over her head. She waited for what seemed an eternity, until she finally heard the pulse and whine of a car motor start up near the front of the house. She opened the bathroom door and peeked out. Then she ran as fast as she could down the hall, across the upstairs parlor into Opal's old room. She hurried to the window and batted the thick velvet curtain to the side. A flash of black metal glinted in the afternoon sun as the tail of a car disappeared around the bend.

"Dammit!" she whispered.

She dropped on to the four-poster bed and stared out the window, willing the car to back up and identify itself. If only she'd been braver. Left the bathroom quicker. Run down the hall faster. Made it to the window sooner. If only. *If only.*

She hated those words.

She bounded off the bed and retraced her steps to her room. Her gaze flicked from the dressers to the bed to the closet. Everything looked the same. Nothing seemed out of place. If she hadn't been trapped in the bathroom, and heard someone rifling through her things, she would never have suspected anyone had been there.

Her gaze shot to the table beside the bed. She jerked opened the drawer and pulled out the tiny crowbar she kept wedged between the dividers. She scooted the wooden rocker away from the window, flipped back the blue and white rag rug, and with one expert twist, pried loose a small section of floorboard. She slipped her hand between the slats until she touched the plastic box, then lifted it out and opened the hinged top. Relief flooded through her as she stared at the flag.

The deafening sound of off-key chimes, courtesy of Opal's three-hundred dollar Westminster doorbell, ricocheted through the upstairs hall. *Bong, bong,* bong, *bong*. Every other note sharp or flat. As soon as Morgan had the money, she was ripping it out of the wall and replacing it with one that didn't make her want to tear her hair out.

She shoved the box back into its hiding place and rushed downstairs. Was the front door still locked? Why hadn't she checked it after the intruder had left? Why hadn't she put clothes on? All good questions. She wished she had answers for them. She glanced out the front window. A silver-white car she didn't recognize sat parked beside the fence. She pulled the robe lapels closer together and peered through the screen.

Lawrence Finch stood on the porch. His face always gave her a start. Pale green eyes bulged beneath a wide, protruding forehead. Wisps of graying blond hair fluffed across his scalp. A series of tiny scars spread like tentacles across his temple to his right cheek, twisting the shiny skin around his right eye as if it were covered with plastic wrap.

He saw her before she could draw back, and she had no choice but to open the door.

"Miss Maguire." His thin lips curled into a smile. She'd never been able to place his accent. New York? New Jersey? Some place up north, with enough of a sneering, patronizing edge to make the locals suspicious.

"Mr. Finch." She tightened the belt on her robe. His gaze dropped to her chest.

"I'm looking for Sean. Is he home?

"No, but I expect him any minute."

"We came to extend our condolences."

"We?"

Another man, shorter and stockier than Finch, stepped into view. "I don't think you've met my business associate, Peter Mendoza." Mendoza grinned. The glint off his gold front tooth sparkled in the waning light.

"I hear my friend Harlan Spannagel won't be working for you anymore," Finch said.

"Friend?" Morgan laughed. "You're kidding, right?"

Harlan had never made any bones about his dislike of Lawrence Finch. Finch had lured their apple pickers away with salaries Sean couldn't begin to match. The honeybee shortage, resulting in a severe lack of fruit tree pollination, had lowered the apple crop by over forty-percent, enough to sink even the most successful orchards. Without Harlan to run interference, Maguire Orchard couldn't hold on much longer. And Finch knew it.

"Well, thanks for the heartfelt sentiment," she said. "Now, if you'll excuse me."

She tried to close the door, but Finch's reflexes were swift. He held the screen open and jammed his foot in the gap.

"I think you'd better leave." Morgan tried to keep the tremor out of her voice.

Finch's steely gaze held hers. The scarred green eye quivered in its socket. "We'd like to talk to you, Miss Maguire."

Mendoza crossed a beefy arm over his chest. "Yeah, too bad about old Harlan. Now that your watchdog's permanently muzzled, and you can't find nobody to pick them apples, I reckon you'll have to think about selling."

"And I reckon you might want to think about replacing that gold tooth. It makes you look...greedy."

Finch shot Mendoza a warning glance, then smiled at Morgan. "I'm sure when your family's had a chance to get over the shock of Harlan's passing, you'll realize it would be in your best interest to reconsider my offer." He paused. "But take your time. I wouldn't want you to regret your decision."

"That sounds like a threat." Morgan looked at Mendoza. "That was a threat, right? Didn't it sound like a threat to you?"

Mendoza grinned.

"You're only postponing the inevitable," Finch said. "Before this is over—and one way or another, it *will* be over—you'll be on your knees begging me to buy this place." He smiled again, showing a long pair of incisors. "That's something I think I'd like to see—you on your knees."

"I'm sure you would," Morgan said. She reached behind the door. Her fingers skimmed past the flashlight hanging on a hook and curled around the metal baseball bat in the umbrella stand. "But right now, I'm asking you to leave."

"What if Mr. Finch don't want to?" Mendoza growled menacingly.

"Then I hope he's wearing steel toed shoes." She stepped back and positioned the bat over Finch's wedged foot. "You know, Lawrence—can I call you Lawrence? Or is it Larry? I mean, we're threatening each other, so we should be on a first name basis, don't you think? Anyway, Larry, you'd be surprised how strong my little arms are after stirring apple butter for twenty-five years. And how good my aim is. I bet I could break four or five toes with this thing."

Finch jerked his foot back. He smoothed the front of his navy sport coat and shot his cuffs. "You've had a trying day, Miss Maguire. I'll come back tomorrow when your brother is here."

"Suit yourself. But the answer will be the same."

Morgan closed the door and flipped the lock. She ducked through the kitchen to the laundry room and started pulling clothes out of the dryer. Standing half naked in front of Lawrence Finch had left her feeling vulnerable. And she hated feeling vulnerable. Almost as much as she hated bullies. Her husband had been a bully.

She dressed quickly in jeans and one of Sean's white T-shirts, then sat on the hall tree beside the front door, balancing the baseball bat across her knees like Granny Clampett's shotgun. She didn't know how long she sat gazing through the delicate lace curtains, watching a long bank of clouds steal across the darkening sky, but by the time the utility lamp in the

53

yard had come on, the hard wooden seat had rendered her rear end completely numb.

The sudden squeal of tires propelled Morgan to her feet. She grabbed the cordless phone off the desk and held her thumb over the 9, ready to call for help in case Finch and Mendoza were back for round two. She slunk into the shadows. A dark car backed over Opal's prized azaleas and came to a halt beside the fence. For one crazy moment she thought it might be Gage, and a ridiculous lump of hope rose in her throat. But when the door swung open, she realized it was Ethan.

Ethan stepped out and stretched his long legs. With his lanky frame silhouetted against the glow of the interior light, he looked like a younger version of his father.

She ran down the front steps. "Oh, God, Ethan. I'm so sorry about your dad."

Ethan's pale blue eyes filled with tears, and he blinked them back. "Thanks, Morgan. I'm sorry you were the one who had to find him."

"Who's in the car?"

"I've got Sean and Peach with me. Sean's passed out on the backseat. He promised he wouldn't throw up. I got the car detailed this afternoon."

"Sean's drunk? He never drinks more than two beers."

"Well, tonight he's hammered. Should we take him to Opal's guesthouse out back? I don't think we can get him up the stairs. He's dead weight."

"There's a daybed in the sunroom off the kitchen," Morgan said.

Peach pulled herself free, then helped them guide Sean, barely conscious and stumbling, up the porch steps to the sunroom. He flopped face first onto the iron bed.

"Someone might want to get a bucket," Peach said. "He's starting to turn green again." She placed her hands on the swell of her hips. "Better make it a big bucket."

Morgan lined a waste can with a plastic grocery bag and set it beside the bed. "Sean, can you hear me?" Sean groaned. He turned his face toward the lamp. A shaft of light cut across his gaunt cheekbones, making him look older than his thirty-four years. She looked at Peach. "I've never seen him this wasted."

Peach sat on the edge of the daybed. "When Jake Wheeler told him Harlan had died, he wouldn't believe it." She smoothed the quilted coverlet back from his shoulder then let her fingers glide over the strands of brown hair curling over his plaid shirt collar. "Poor baby. You mind if I sit here? Just to make sure he's okay?"

"Uh...no."

"Oh, sweetie," Peach murmured. "I'm so sorry." She stroked Sean's unshaven cheek with the back of her hand. "You just sleep now. Everything will be okay."

Morgan left quietly and joined Ethan in the living room. "You're right," she said. "He's hammered. Where'd you find him? Bad Moon?"

"In the back booth with the Wheeler twins, toasting Dad with Jaeger shots. Peach got Ralph to close for her. She insisted on coming with us. From the looks of things, Sean is her latest target. God help him."

"What were you doing at Bad Moon? I didn't think you liked bars."

Ethan sat on the wide ottoman. He blinked his pale

white-blue eyes. "I...I couldn't think of anywhere else to go. I sublet my apartment above the feed store to stay with Dad, and I was going crazy in his house. I kept walking from room to room."

"You should have called me." She put her hand on his shoulder. "No, I should have called you. I was going to, but I—"

"I keep seeing him lying in all that blood." Ethan shook his head. "I can't stop thinking about it."

She sat next to him. "I know. It doesn't seem real, does it? What happened to him, Ethan? He was walking toward the barn this morning after breakfast, and he looked fine."

Ethan raked a lock of brown hair back from his face. "I don't know. You know he's been taking a blood thinner since he had the clot in his leg last summer. The coroner said if the dosage had been too high, he could have died of hemorrhagic shock due to excessive bleeding. Maybe he screwed up and took too many pills. You know how distracted he's been. They're gonna—" He stopped and sucked in air. "They're gonna do an autopsy. Christ, Morgan, they're slicing him up like a slab of meat."

She couldn't help thinking what an ironic turn of events that was, since Harlan had spent most of his life doing the same thing to cows and pigs.

"I don't think I can stand it," he said.

Morgan put her arms around him. "They have to find out what happened. You want to know what happened, don't you?"

"Yes, but—"

He pulled back and looked at her. In the soft amber glow of the Tiffany lamp, he looked almost handsome.

Especially when he smiled. He had his father's smile, so wide and appealing, it lit up his whole face. His lips were a little puffy, and slightly out of proportion with his thin, narrow jaw. But nice. She had kissed those lips. More than once. But over the years, the memory had faded until it seemed as if it had happened to someone else. Even now, gazing into his eyes, she could barely believe the two fumbling teenagers in the cab of his father's Ford Ranger pickup had been them.

"Hey, girl," he murmured. "How come you're always around when I need you?"

"Because we're friends. Good friends."

"Best friends."

They hugged again, and this time he held her longer. His hands radiated a soothing warmth through her thin cotton shirt. Wouldn't life be simpler if she could fall in love with Ethan Spannagel, the sweet, mild-mannered owner of the local feed store? She could live out her days in the mountains, happy and content, the wife of a man who sold goat chow and fertilizer for a living. If he kept her picture in a drawer beside his bed, he might still feel something for her.

Sometimes she caught him looking at her shyly, longingly, as if he thought they could pick up where they'd left off the summer before her junior year at UT. They'd dated most of June and July, hanging out together, even parking on the south side of Chestnut Ridge for a few clumsy make out sessions. But the attraction had cooled quickly. At least for Morgan. Any budding romantic notions she might have felt for Ethan Spannagel evaporated the night they ran over a rabbit on Barkerstown Road, and he cleaned and served it for lunch the next day.

Peach tiptoed out of the sunroom and dropped onto the sofa. "I'm worn out."

"How is he?" Morgan asked.

"Fine." Peach leaned back and sighed. "God, I love that man. I'd do anything for him. Even if he is snoring like a buzz saw."

"Family trait," Morgan said. "I sound like the spin cycle on a washing machine."

"You do not," Ethan said softly.

"I've never seen Sean so sad," Peach said. "I wish I could comfort him. Sean's going to miss your dad, Ethan. We all are."

Ethan glanced at her from beneath his thick lashes. "Oh, I'm sure you're going to miss him, Peach. You and Dad were such good friends." He turned back to Morgan. "I hoped Dad could help get this place going again. What rotten luck for you and Sean."

"Oh, Sean won't give up," Morgan said. "No matter what happens."

"I don't believe in luck," Peach said. "I think people make their own luck. At least I do. I'm not gonna let Sean give up. I'm gonna help him through this." Her thick red lips pursed defiantly. "It looks like my job at the nursing home won't last much longer, so I'm gonna quit and help Sean with the orchard." She shot an accusing look at Morgan. "*Someone* has to."

"Oh, Peach," Morgan said. "I don't think—"

"The orchard is his life," Peach said. "And you'll never move away as long as Sean keeps asking you to stay. Don't you see, Morgan? This is your chance. You could go back to Nashville, and I could stay here with Sean." She bounced up and down, her idea gathering steam. "Oh, *please*, Morgan. He showed me how to run the cider press, and I'm good with numbers. I could keep the books. And I'd take real good care of him. If I helped him hang on to the orchard, he would realize we want the same things. Then he would finally see the real me."

"Oh, I think he's seen that already," Ethan said under his breath. "I think we all have."

For one selfish moment, Morgan wondered if it could work. Peach and Sean hung out together sometimes when she stopped by to pick up Crystal. Sean had never confided in Morgan about his love life—he was as private as she was—but maybe he had fallen for Peach. Sure, Peach had acquired baggage, with a capital *B*. But how many women in their mid-thirties didn't have a past? Sean was shy. Maybe an outgoing girl like Peach would be good for him. No one could accuse Peach of gold digging when Maguire Orchard was half a breath away from bankruptcy. If Sean truly loved Peach, Morgan could leave the farm with a clear conscience.

Peach was offering her a way out. Would it be so horrible if she took it?

Ethan stared at Morgan. "You can't seriously be considering this. What's the matter with you? Where's that reassuring cynicism I've come to rely on? Would you walk out on Sean and let him fend for himself with...*Peach*? Peach is a—"

"I'm a *what*, Ethan?"

"No offense, Peach," Ethan said. "I just don't think you're the right woman for the job."

A loud knock on the front door brought Morgan to her feet.

"Morgan?" Sheriff Stallard stood on the front

porch, squinting through the dusty screen. Kamikaze moths dive-bombed the globed porch light beside her head.

"I didn't hear you drive up," Morgan said.

"Deputy Nelson is in skulk mode tonight." Sheriff Stallard nodded to the six-foot-four man standing behind her.

Deputy Nelson grinned. "Hey, Morgan."

"Hey, Ron," Morgan said. "Come on in." Ron ducked his head under the doorframe. He hadn't changed much since he and Sean had graduated high school together. He still had the same shock of straight blond hair falling into his brown puppy dog eyes and the same sigh inducing, hard won muscles straining at the sleeves of his deputy uniform.

"Is Sean here?" Ron asked. "The guys at Bad Moon Rising said Ethan drove him home."

"He's here," Morgan said. "But he's passed out. He's taking Harlan's death pretty hard."

"Then we'd better get him sobered up," Sheriff Stallard said. "I'm going to have to take him down to the station, honey. I have a warrant for his arrest."

Peach catapulted off the couch. *"You what?"*

"No!" Morgan cried. "I don't understand. What are you arresting him for? He didn't drive drunk. Ethan brought him home."

"Calm down," Sheriff Stallard said. "And sit down. In fact, you'd all better sit down."

"We're not sitting down," Ethan said. "Not until you tell us what's going on." He slid his arm around Morgan protectively.

The sheriff nodded. "As it turns out, your father's death was a very nasty business." She and Deputy

Nelson exchanged looks. "Ethan, I know this will be a shock. But your father was stabbed on his left side. Repeatedly."

Ethan stared at her. "What do you mean, stabbed? I didn't see any stab wounds."

"Neither did the coroner. Not at first. Not with all the blood. Our department isn't used to handling things like this. The crime lab from Cherokee Bluff came over to help, and—"

"And you think Sean did it?" Morgan's mouth went dry. "That's ridiculous. What evidence do you have?"

"Sean may have been the last person to see Harlan alive. A witness noticed his truck parked in the Spannagel's driveway, then saw Sean and Harlan walk down the path to the slaughterhouse."

"Mrs. Cowden, right?" Morgan's voice cracked. "It was her, wasn't it? One word from that nosy old crone, and you're out here arresting my brother for murder? Come *on*, Teresa."

"Listen, Morgan," the sheriff said. "You'd better be grateful Mrs. Cowden spends her days looking out her upstairs window because she's your alibi. If she places Sean at the scene of the crime, near the approximate time of death, then I have to question him."

"Then question him here," Morgan said.

The sheriff glanced at Ethan and hesitated. "There's more. We found a knife smeared with blood in the slaughterhouse. A large pocket knife with the initials *SRM* and a four-leaf clover engraved on it. I'm pretty sure it belongs to Sean."

"Sean Robert Maguire," Peach whispered. "But you don't think—you *can't* think—"

"Everybody knows that knife belongs to Sean,"

Morgan said. "The 4-H Club presented it to him on Appreciation Day for donating part of the orchard for their mentoring program. The whole town saw them give it to him."

"Then you see why I have to take him in," Sheriff Stallard said. "It's classic probable cause. I have no choice."

"Sean's not an idiot," Morgan said. "If he stabbed Harlan with his own knife, a knife with his initials on it, he'd have the IQ of a wet sock."

"You think I killed Harlan?"

Morgan spun around. "*Sean!*"

Sean stood in the doorway, clutching the empty waste can in front of him like a feedbag.

"I heard wha' you said," Sean said, slurring his words. "I was at Harlan's house, but I din' hurt him." His eyes tried to focus on Morgan's face. "I couldn't hurt him. *I didn't.*" He looked at Peach. "*Wha'aryou* doin' here? I told you to leave me alone. Why are you here?" He turned to Morgan. "Why is she here?"

"He's definitely intoxicated," the sheriff said. "Anything he says while he's under the influence is inadmissible. When he sobers up tomorrow, we'll read him his rights."

"Screw that." Sean stumbled into the room. "Aren't any of you *listening* to me?"

"You were in the slaughterhouse with Dad?" Ethan said. "Why?"

"I followed him home because he was sick. He was alive when I left him. I swear." He fell forward. The waste can rolled across the floor and bounced off the side of the upright piano.

"Let's get him to the car," Sheriff Stallard said.

"I'll get my purse," Morgan said.

"There's no reason for you to come down tonight," the sheriff said. "We're just gonna put him in a room and let him sleep it off. We won't question him until tomorrow."

"When?" Morgan asked.

"Tomorrow, honey. As soon as he wakes up."

"Before eight o'clock?"

"More like nine," the sheriff said.

"I'll be there at eight."

Morgan collected Sean's shoes from the bedroom and handed them to Deputy Nelson. Her eyes filled with tears as he and Sheriff Stallard helped Sean to the car. Sean slid into the backseat and collapsed in the corner. His head lolled to the side.

"They're *taking* him *away!*" Peach wailed, sounding exactly like her daughter.

"Come on, Peach," Ethan said wearily. "We can't do anything about it tonight. I'll drop you off at Bad Moon to get your car."

Morgan caught his arm. "Look, I don't know what happened to your father. But I know Sean didn't have anything to do with it."

Ethan nodded, his eyes full of pity. "I'm sure he didn't."

"He didn't, Ethan." She stared at him. "He didn't. He *didn't!* "

"I believe you." He put his cool hands on either side of her face. "It'll be okay, Morgana."

"Morgana? You haven't called me that in a long time. Not since we were twelve."

"Morgana, half-sister to King Arthur. The most powerful enchantress in Avalon."

She smiled. "Spoken like a true video game geek."

"Well, you've always had me under a spell." He tilted her head down and kissed her forehead. "Now, go. Get some rest."

Morgan leaned against the porch railing while the two cars disappeared down the dark road. The cold night air coated her skin like a thin layer of frost. Fear pressed against her chest until it hurt to breathe. She couldn't think. Couldn't gather her wits. What mind she had left had turned to sludge. She paced the length of the huge wraparound porch, around and back again, until she wanted to scream.

She'd better hustle to move past the shock and get a grip on reality before her life came crashing down around her. There were decisions to be made, and she was the only one who could make them. Her step-grandmother was useless in a crisis. When disaster struck, Opal Maguire went to pieces, beautifully, and managed to snag the center of attention. She fluttered around like Aunt Pittypat, thumping her chest with a lavender hankie, pulling the blinds closed, knocking back crystal cordials of cream sherry until she fell asleep on the living room sofa. Opal coped by not coping. Then complained loudly how the chips fell.

With each lap around the porch, Morgan tried to shake some sense back into her brain. Sean was innocent. She knew that as well as she knew her own name. People loved Sean, admired him, wanted to be like him. He was sweet and kindhearted and good. And not just on the surface, like so many of the so-called God-fearing people who lived on the mountain. But in the deepest part of his soul where it counted.

A gust of air lashed against her neck. A shiver

swept across her shoulders, then down her spine to her toes. Someone walking over her grave, the old people called it.

The forgotten strings of the tiny white lights Sean had wrapped around the fence posts at Christmas twinkled softly, warmly, as if the people inside were standing by the fireplace, waiting for their holiday guests to arrive. Morgan walked to the end of the porch and yanked the electrical cord out of the socket, plunging the upper half of the driveway into darkness. As she stood, staring into the night, Opal's ceramic wind chimes jangled over her head.

She wrapped her arms around a post and gazed up at the stars. She should tell Opal about Sean's arrest before the Riverbirch grapevine reached Grace Church Village. She wasn't sure Opal really cared all that much about her or Sean, but it was the right thing to do. But what would she say? How could she explain what she didn't understand herself?

Fresh tears welled up in her eyes. *The world has gone batshit crazy.* First Harlan dying, then Gage Kirkland showing up out of the blue, and now...*this*? Her brother getting arrested for a crime he could not have committed? She'd looked after Sean for most of his life, taught herself how keep the big, bad ugly world at bay for him. How was she going to pull it off this time?

Morgan had arrived on the planet four minutes ahead of Sean, but she'd always felt years older. It was natural she should look out for him. She'd been born the tough one, the skeptical one, the one with the acid tongue who could drive the school bullies away. Even while their parents were alive, Sean had needed her protection. His tender, trusting heart was a flashing neon sign to the sharks and misfits of the world, a magnet for every lowlife with a hard luck story and an outstretched hand. Her brother gave everyone the benefit of the doubt, and she would never understand how he could continue to see the good in people she wouldn't trust as far as she could throw a piano.

How could she help him now? This wasn't as simple as reading Clyde Jenkins the Riot Act for throwing a Fourth of July sparkler at her brother. This was a murder charge. According to Sheriff Stallard, someone had deliberately killed Harlan Spannagel. But if Sean didn't do it, then who had? And why were they trying to pin it on her brother?

She glanced up at the sky. "I have to stay strong," she whispered. "No matter what happens, I cannot fall apart."

The soft roar of a car engine droned in the distance. Across the road, twin headlight beams flashed the side of the Jenkins' barn.

Morgan's heart picked up speed. She stood frozen, waiting. Would the car pass the entrance to the orchard or turn in at the gate? The sound drew closer, echoing off the side of the mountain until it burst into the open. A long black van turned into the driveway and cut its lights.

Her first instinct was to run for the front door and bathe herself in the brilliant rectangle of light spilling onto the porch.

Her second, more rational instinct was to slip into the shadows. Her left hand coiled around the cordless phone in her pocket. Her right hand picked up the garden trowel she'd left beside a concrete planter.

The van stopped a few feet from the utility pole.

The door opened. A man, shorter than Finch but taller than Mendoza, stepped out, unfolding his long legs one by one.

Chapter 4

"Stay where you are!" Morgan cried. "I have a weapon!"

Gage didn't move. Beneath the mercury vapor lamp, his shadow stretched across the ground in front of him like a dark crack in the earth.

"Morgan." His low baritone sounded distorted and gruff, as if his voice had pushed her name through the thick night air. "It's Gage."

"What are you doing here?"

He stepped forward and cupped his hand over his eyes to shield them from the glare. Beneath the light, all he could make out was her silhouette standing beside the porch swing. If her weapon of choice was a loaded gun, and it was pointed at him, he hoped she knew what she was doing.

"I asked you a question," she said.

"I'm here to beg a favor."

"Well, that's easy. The answer is no."

"Look," he said. "I get that you don't want to see me. I understand. More than you know, probably. But I can't change the past."

"Neither can I. Go away."

"I need—"

"I don't care what you need. Get back in your big black car and drive toward the mountain. Or off the mountain. Your choice."

"Not a good time to stop by, huh?"

A long, silent pause. "No, Gage, this isn't a good time. This is a terrible time. The only thing that could make this time any worse was if I was covered head-to-toe with poison oak and had scarfed down the Fried Clam Special at Maxie's Diner. I can't talk to you right now. I can't talk to anybody."

He reached out his hand as if he were approaching a skittish colt and edged closer. "I know you've had a bad day, but please, hear me out."

"*A bad day*? Are you serious?" She laughed harshly. "This just keeps getting better and better."

"It's about Jeremy. I'm here because of my son."

Another long, interminable pause. She glanced at the stars, sighed, looked back down. Then she moved out of the shadows and stood beside the porch railing. "Oh, what the hell," she said tiredly. "Come on up."

The night air, humid and cool at the same time, fueled his imagination. As he neared the house, he thought he could feel her heartbeat thrumming deep within his chest, pulling him toward her. But maybe it was his own heart flailing against his ribcage, hard enough to stall his breath, like something held captive inside him trying to break free.

He chided himself for not calling first. The last thing he wanted to do was scare her, or throw suspicion on himself. He was there to do a job. He shouldn't be hanging around her house at night while she was home. It was unprofessional and incompetent, and a gross conflict of interest. Something he'd never cared much about honoring before. But this time was different. This time he gave a damn.

He had solid reasons for saying yes to Tyson, but the cool impassivity he thought he could maintain long enough to satisfy his curiosity about Morgan had taken a dive. Right off the edge of the earth. One look at her and every screwed up fiber of his being knew that this time, if his heart stayed intact, it would be a bloody miracle.

"What about Jeremy? Is he all right?"

"He's fine." Gage glanced at the trowel and chuckled softly. "Is that your weapon? What were you going to do, plant one on me?"

"I still might." She set the trowel on the railing and crossed her arms over her chest, which every man who had ever tried to talk to an angry woman knew was Body Language 101 for *Stay the hell away from me.*

"Jeremy?" she prodded. "The reason you're here?"

It was too late to turn back. Gage swallowed hard. "Those things Jeremy said about his mother's death, I...I feel like I need to explain. When Suzanne, my ex-wife, died, we'd been divorced for five years."

"Please." Morgan held up her hands. "You do not have to tell me this."

"Yes, I do." Gage stepped up on the porch, barely missing a basket of raggedy geraniums.

She looked at him then glanced at the geraniums. "Then you'd better sit down before you brain yourself."

He sunk into the wicker armchair and tried to decide the best way to start. Why hadn't he planned what he was going to say before he jumped in the car and tore over the mountain to Riverbirch? Why hadn't he thought things through? He should know by now that spontaneity always got him into trouble.

He leaned forward with his elbows on his knees.

The words weren't exactly pouring out. He took a deep breath and clasped his hands in front of him, like a preacher signaling for the congregation to bow their heads. Then he took another breath. "Jeremy lost his mother two months ago, and he's a mess right now. He keeps lashing out at me, hoping to make me hurt as much as he does. I'm sure you've figured that out. But I want you to know I did not kill his mother."

"I didn't think you did."

"It was an accident. She pulled out of the driveway into the path of an oncoming car. There were extenuating circumstances which Jeremy blames me for. Actually, he blames me for all of it. But I did not— I could never—" He lifted his eyes and looked at her. "I don't want you to think badly of me."

"That's why you came back here tonight? So I won't think badly of you?"

"Yes. I mean, *no*. I just—"

"Well, I do think badly of you. I'll always think badly of you."

"You don't mean that."

"Why not? I can think badly of you if I want to. Most girls have a guy in their past they wish they'd never met. You're mine. Of course, most girls don't get to experience the thrill of having the guy show up out of the blue twelve years later. With his kid. On the worst day of their lives."

"If I'd known you were going to find a dead body today, I would have waited until tomorrow to show up."

She leveled her gaze at him. "I can't tell you how much better that makes me feel."

"Morgan, please. I wish you could—" He stopped. It was no use. Nothing he said would ever change her mind about him. He had set their destiny in motion. She hated him. He had to accept that and let her go. He would never deserve a second chance with her, and that couldn't have hurt more than a punch to his gut. Why did he care so much, after all this time, what she thought of him? Because seeing her again had awakened something deep inside he'd forgotten could even exist? Because the desire he'd felt for her the autumn he turned twenty-two was the elusive high he'd been chasing, and never come close to duplicating, with every woman who'd made a quick detour through his life?

"I could use a drink," she said. "Do you want a beer?"

"Sure."

"Then I'd like to hear more about Jeremy. He reminds me of a heartbroken kid I used to know."

"Who?"

"Me."

She turned to go inside, and as she stirred the air, he breathed in her faint, sweet scent. She crossed the porch, and he tried to burn the image of the woman she'd become into his brain, where it could ground itself in reality. Thick dark waves bounced against her shoulder blades. The narrow straps of a dark pink bra crisscrossed her back beneath her white T-shirt. Faded jeans hugged the contours of her thighs, sat low on her soft, rounded hips. He loved those hips. The memory of holding them as they moved against him blazed across his mind for an instant. He pushed it away.

If only he could...*no.* He couldn't. He was sitting on her porch, swallowing his pride for Jeremy. He'd plead his case and go away like she'd asked him to.

She'd made it clear she didn't want anything to do with him, and he'd respect that. Wondering what might have been didn't do anybody any good. His and Morgan's time had come and gone. Which, in theory, should make it easier for him to stomach deceiving her. But once she was out of his system, and he'd closed that chapter of his life forever, his new life, the responsible, grownup life he was determined to make with a son he barely knew, could finally begin.

And if he believed that, he was a bigger fool than he thought.

Christ, he was in trouble.

Big. Big. Trouble.

He and Tyson were friends, but if Tyson learned Gage had compromised this job, he would hand it over to Bobby Poole or that money-grubbing jerk, Cal Leonard. Neither one of those boys would give a damn about Morgan, or protect her if she got caught in the crossfire. If Tyson found out about his connection to Morgan, he'd tell Gage to get a grip or get the hell out. Then he'd tell him to go to a bar, find some hot little number to shake the cobwebs off his privates, and get back to work.

The screen door creaked. He looked up, and she was standing in front of him.

A little jolt ran through him. He still wasn't used to having her near enough to touch instead of hovering like an apparition at the edge of his dreams. In the world he was used to inhabiting with her, he'd be waking up right about now, squinting hard against the stark morning light, bracing himself for the mother of all hangovers.

She handed him a beer and sat across from him on

the frayed wicker loveseat. Her perfume, so quiet he wasn't even sure it belonged to her, roused his senses as it lingered in the air. She'd turned out the porch light, and the glow from the stained glass lamp in the living room caressed the soft planes of her face, making her look younger and more vulnerable than she had in the harsh light of day. She'd swept her long hair up and harnessed it into one of those plastic claw-things at the crown of her head. A few tendrils trailed against the nape of her neck. He remembered the long ago feel of it sweeping against his bare shoulder. Then later, after they lay tangled in each other's arms, the tickle as it draped across his chest. He had the urge to unclasp her hair and thread his fingers through it, then cradle her head in his hand.

"You could have asked me this big favor tomorrow, you know."

"I needed to get out and drive. I love driving. It clears my head."

"That's what I'm using the beer for." She took a healthy swallow. "Well, no. Actually, I'm using it as a sedative, but it's going to take a lot more than a bottle of Coors Light to make me forget this day." She rubbed the back of her neck. "I don't think it will ever be over."

"I don't think *we'll* ever be over," he whispered.

"What did you say?"

"I said I should have brought some wine."

"Well, you do live in a winery. Your uncle's winery."

"Blackstone Hollow Winery."

"Right." She took another swallow of beer. "So, tell me, how is dear old Uncle Bert? Has he calmed down since the night he caught us going at it on the bow of his catamaran? The night he called me—now, let me get this right—'a conniving little gold-digger, who's not getting one red cent out of this family if she gets herself knocked up.'"

"He was angry."

"Ya think?"

"I'm sorry for the things Bert said to you. If I could, I'd drag him down here and make him apologize. He can be an awful person."

"And yet, you're living with him."

"I'm living with him because my son needs stability. He needs someone he can count on, something familiar to hold on to. And right now, it's not me. After Jeremy's mother died, he wanted to go to Bert's house, and I couldn't deny him that. I can't deny him anything these days. He's fond of Bert, and believe it or not, Bert has a soft spot in his heart for Jeremy."

"Good to know. I wasn't sure he had one."

"A soft spot?"

"A heart."

Gage laughed softly. "Bert Kirkland can be a pain, but he's given Jeremy and me a home." He didn't mention the strings Bert had attached to the arrangement. Or the fact that on most days, Bert expected him to grovel at his feet out of gratitude, exactly as Bert had expected Gage's father to do."

"Are you a good father?"

"I'm trying to be. I have a lot of things to make up for. When Jeremy was growing up, I worked sixty hour weeks for the agency. I tried to stay connected to him, but Suzanne wouldn't—anyway, I ended up being more absent than present. It was my fault. And Jeremy's paid the price. Suzanne had some problems none of us were aware of."

"What kind of problems?"

"She was diagnosed with bipolar disorder. She refused to take her medication, drank too much. She and Jeremy became experts at hiding her condition. He's still incredibly protective of her. If I'd been around more, I might have realized how ill she'd become and taken the burden off him. It's not easy admitting how often I've failed him," he said around the stone in his throat. "But when Suzanne died, all my pride where Jeremy is concerned went out the window. I'll do whatever it takes to make him happy and whole again." He set his beer on the table and held her gaze with his. "If I promise to stay out of your life, and only see or talk to you when it's absolutely necessary, is there any chance you might consider—"

"—giving him guitar lessons?"

"Yes. How did you know?"

Her eyes softened. "Because I saw his face when he asked if he could take lessons. And then I saw your face. You were looking at him like he'd been lost, and you'd found him."

"It was like seeing the old Jeremy again."

"His mother is dead," she said. "I lost my parents when I was ten, so believe me when I tell you he will never be the old Jeremy again. Not completely."

"Maybe that's why the two of you seemed to connect. I think he trusts you."

"I only talked to the kid for five minutes."

Gage smiled. "Yeah, but you have a way of getting to people in a short amount of time. Jeremy is smart. I mean, *really* smart. Eleven-going-on-fifty smart. He doesn't suffer fools, and he doesn't pretend to like people when he doesn't. He's so sharp, half the people he insults, don't know they've been insulted. I know he likes you. If he didn't, I'd be standing here apologizing for the things he said today, not begging you for guitar lessons."

She took a long swallow of beer. Then she moved to the railing, wrapped her arms around her waist, and looked at him with her clear, haunted eyes until he forgot to breathe.

"I'm going to confide in you," she said. "Not because I trust you, or even like you very much. But because for some unknown reason—a rip in the space time continuum, perhaps—you're the person who showed up here tonight. If I don't tell someone, I'm going to explode. And you do not want to see that."

"What's wrong? Tell me."

Her eyes glistened. "My brother Sean has been arrested."

"Why?"

"They think the man I found dead today was murdered. Sean may have been the last person to see him alive. He's in custody, but he tied one on tonight, so they can't question him until tomorrow when he's sober."

"Did you or Sean know this man?"

"Oh, yeah. Harlan Spannagel worked here. He managed the orchard."

"I didn't realize." His brain snapped into work mode. He tried to keep the concern out of his voice. He didn't want to scare her until he had the facts. "What do they have on Sean? Exactly?"

"A witness placed him at the scene of the crime

and they found a bloody knife with his initials on it near the body."

Gage whistled through his teeth. "When is the autopsy?"

"I'm not sure. Soon, I guess. Tomorrow?"

"This is a small town. Cherokee Bluff may be able to handle it. If not, they'll probably have to send him to Knoxville or the county seat." He hesitated. He didn't want to destroy any illusions she'd created about her brother, but when a man went off the deep end and took another life, family members were usually the last to know. "Look," he said gently. "I don't know Sean. But we all do things in the heat of the moment we regret. Are you sure he couldn't have—"

"No! My brother is not guilty. He has a pure heart. I know people say that all the time, but if you spent two minutes with him, you'd understand it's true." She shook her head. "This is not right. Sean couldn't hurt another living soul, especially Harlan Spannagel. Harlan was like a father to him."

"Does Sean have a lawyer?"

"Not yet. Won't the court appoint one if they charge him?"

"Yes, but let me find you someone decent. I know a couple of high-powered attorneys in Atlanta. I'm sure they could recommend someone practicing in Tennessee."

"No, thanks. I appreciate the offer, but I should take care of it."

"If it's a question of money, most lawyers do a certain amount of pro bono work. I'm sure if I explained he was short of funds, they would be more than happy to—"

"Thanks, but we don't need your help. Financially, the farm has hit the skids. But I have a personal resource I can use if I have to. Something I can sell. Something that would bring in a lot of money if I found the right buyer."

"What is it?" he asked, knowing exactly what it was.

"A Civil War artifact—a battle flag in pristine condition. Very rare."

"Where did you get it?"

"It was a bribe from my ex-husband for not having him arrested."

"Do I want to know what for?"

"No. For years, this flag has been my secret security blanket. But I would sell it in a heartbeat to help Sean prove his innocence."

"Then let's hope it doesn't come to that."

She gave a little shrug. "If it does, then I'll handle it. In this family, if it rains, you can bet your sweet ass a monsoon is right around the corner. Most of the time, I try not to borrow trouble. It cuts down on stress."

"You sound very capable. I don't remember you being quite so—"

"Tough?"

"I was going to say resilient. But that sounds like I'm comparing you to vinyl flooring."

A smile played around her lips. "I wasn't always so tough. But I've had to learn a few survival skills along the way. I'm sure you have, too."

"Who looks out for you, Morgan?"

"Me?"

"Peach said you're the strong one in this family, the one who takes care of everybody else. I can't help but wonder who takes care of you?"

"I take care of me."

Her square chin jutted out in a soft declaration of defense, but he couldn't help notice the slight tremble in her bottom lip. His heart squeezed in his chest.

"Let me help you with Sean," he said. "We can pretend we don't know each other. I can be some guy who stopped by your farm to give Sean a free consultation and happened to have some information you might find useful."

"I can't screw this up. I've always been able to protect Sean, but this time I'm not sure I know how. If Sean is convicted for a murder he didn't commit, he'll sit in a jail cell for the rest of his life, still looking for the good in people, still believing that justice will prevail someday because he's innocent." Her eyes met his, and for the first time, the pure, unadulterated fear she'd been hiding surfaced on her face. "But it doesn't, does it? Justice doesn't always prevail."

"No, it doesn't. But we can do everything in our power to throw the odds in his favor."

"And find out the truth." Her eyes filled with tears. "Because he's innocent. He *is*. You believe me, don't you? Sean couldn't have hurt Harlan. Sean couldn't hurt anybody."

"Come here," he said huskily. He patted his chest and held out his hand, and suddenly she was in his arms, clinging to him, touching him, sliding her hands around his waist to draw him close. She stood with her head nestled into the hollow of his shoulder. Her warm, sweet breath fanned softly across his throat. He tried to remember if this was how it felt to hold her all those years ago, but he couldn't be sure. He didn't care. She was here, in his arms, where she wanted to be. At least for now. However long she could stand him for, he'd take it. The inexplicable joy of being near her assaulted his senses. It pounded him with awe. He'd felt so little for so long, it was almost too painful to endure.

"Is this where you tell me everything's going to be all right?" she murmured. When he didn't answer, she glanced up at him. "I'm talking about Sean."

"This is where I tell you not to lose it. Wait until the autopsy is over before you panic. You don't know what might turn up."

She pulled back. "But what if Sean's knife is the one that stabbed Harlan?"

"Well, if he didn't do it—"

"He didn't do it."

"Then someone is trying to frame him."

Gage wished he could say something to ease her mind, but this thing with her brother didn't look good. Maybe the guy was innocent. For her sake, he hoped he was. But that didn't always make a difference. Nine years working as a PI was long enough to know guilty people shifted the blame to innocent people all the time. And it almost always worked.

His hand brushed across Morgan's back. Miraculously, she didn't flinch. Through her thin cotton T-shirt, he could feel the sharp swell of her shoulder blades rise and fall with each breath. She let go of his shoulders, slid her fingers around the taut muscles in his upper arms, then dropped her head until her forehead rested against his chest.

"What the hell am I doing?" she whispered.

"I did call you," he said. "Twelve years ago. I said I would call, and I did." She lifted her head and stared at him. "Back then, neither one of us had a cell phone. When I called, a man answered. He said you'd gone to a fitting. For your wedding dress."

She pulled away and stepped back. "And you gave up? One lousy phone call, and that was it? What if the guy you talked to on the phone wanted you out of the picture? What if he was lying?"

"Was he?"

"No. But he could have been."

"You were going ahead with the wedding."

"Because you never called!"

He ran his hand back through his hair. "Jesus, Morgan. What was I supposed to do? We spent one night together. The next day, I went home to Atlanta, and you went back to UT. I was seeing someone. You were seeing someone. I know we promised each other we would find a way to be together. But when that guy—"

"Denny."

"When Denny answered the phone, he sounded so cocky, so sure of himself. I figured you'd chosen him over me, and didn't know how to tell me. Or didn't want to tell me."

Her eyes flashed. "You knew I wasn't married yet. If you wanted me so badly, you could have tracked me down, tried to change my mind. But you didn't."

"No. I didn't. I called to tell you I couldn't break it off with Suzanne."

"Why couldn't you break it off with Suzanne? It's a free country. You can marry a wombat if you want to. Well, not in the state of Tennessee. Or Georgia. But still. You didn't have a moral obligation to marry Suzanne unless she was—oh." She stopped. "Suzanne was pregnant. With Jeremy."

Gage nodded.

"And you married her because she was pregnant?"

"I'm not the first man to put his life on hold for nine months. I swear, Morgan, I thought that's how it would play out. I called to ask you to wait for me until after the baby was born, knowing it was a long shot you would say yes. We'd only known each other for one day, but meeting you felt like a miracle. I didn't love Suzanne, but I wanted to do right by her. I guess I was naïve enough to believe true love would win in the end."

"That only happens in books." She wouldn't meet his eyes. "And speaking of books..." Her tone had grown cold. She picked up *The Time Machine.* "I think your kid left this here."

"Thanks. He'll be glad to have it back. It keeps him from having to look me in the eye." He tucked the dog-eared paperback in his pocket. "About the guitar lessons. If you're having second thoughts, I can find someone else."

"No, I want to do it. I know what he's going through. When my parents died, there were times when nothing helped except banging out tunes on my mother's piano."

The light through the window bathed her face in a soft, amber glow. Regret scraped across his heart. "Can I say one more thing? And then I'll go."

"I don't think we—"

"I should never have let you go without a fight. I wanted to. Oh, God, how I wanted to—"

"Stop it."

"—fight for you. For us. I just didn't know how."

"It was a long time ago. We were kids then."

"We're not kids anymore." She glanced up at him. The pain that settled in her eyes cut him to the quick.

On impulse, he reached out and traced the smooth contour of her cheek. Slowly, tenderly, as if he were moving through one of his dreams. His fingers trembled. Their gazes locked. She leaned into his hand, grazing it with her lips, savoring the feel of it on her face. A low, involuntary groan rose from the back of his throat. The magic they could still conjure by looking into each other's eyes crackled between them.

"I can't do this," she rasped, stepping further away from him. "I'm sorry. But I can't."

"Okay."

A wall had gone up. The kind with spikes jutting from the parapets and snapping alligators circling the moat. A wall that would take everything in his arsenal to figure out how to scale.

She started down the porch steps, and he had no choice but to follow her.

"Let me to go to the sheriff station with you tomorrow. I'm used to dealing with cops and lawyers. I can run interference for you." He stopped. The fine hairs on the back of his neck bristled against his collar.

"What's wrong?"

"I thought I heard something."

He scanned the front of the house, the barn, the hydrangea hedge running along the fence. He looked behind him, then to the side. No movement. Nothing. His gaze flicked to the other side, then below the house. Neat rows of apple trees stretched across the valley in a wash of pale moonlight. The scent of freshly mulched flowerbeds pricked his nose. A slow, rolling chill traveled across his shoulders, down his arms.

Someone was watching them. He would bet his life on it.

He'd spent years sharpening the radar that had kept him alive, and whenever it started humming in his head like a mosquito looking for its next victim, he took it very seriously.

A noise near his car sent his reflexes into overdrive.

He shoved Morgan off the flagstone walk and dove into the yard. He pushed her to the ground, and into the shadows beneath the thick knobby limbs of a rhododendron bush. He clasped her to him. Then started counting backwards from five.

"What are you doing?" she said.

He held her closer, muffling her mouth against his chest. "*Shhhh,*" he whispered. "I'm counting."

"You're *what?*"

"It's a game I play. Keeps me on my toes."

He didn't have long to wait. He had barely made it to two when the first gunshot cracked the air.

Chapter 5

Gage roared up the gravel driveway, spewing an arc of tiny pebbles into the air. He drove past the tasting room and parked his Mustang beside the winery van. Shattered windshield glass fanned out around the four bullet holes like crystal spider webs, a grim reminder of the night before. After some yahoo had pumped a round of ammo into the winery van, Gage had stayed at Morgan's for over two hours, searching the yard, traipsing through the moonlit orchard like a ghost roaming a battlefield. Wishing like hell he still had a gun.

And every moment since, the fear he'd grappled with, worrying about Morgan, wrapped around his chest like a steel band.

He found Uncle Bert in the fermenting room, swirling dark red wine in a glass.

"Did he make it to school on time?" Bert asked.

"I got him there. When he gets out, he has an appointment with his therapist."

Bert frowned. "I thought we'd decided that sending a child his age to a therapist is an obscene waste of time and money."

"No, that's what you decided."

"Jeremy doesn't need a therapist. Getting over a death in the family takes time. In a few weeks, he'll be fine as frog's hair. Did he find the books I left for him in the kitchen?"

"He found them." Gage looked at his uncle and softened. "That is something nice you've done for him, Bert—giving him books. He loves to read. And now, he's hooked on sci-fi."

"It was always my favorite genre. Beats the crap out of those reference books he reads." Bert lifted his glass to his nose and inhaled deeply. "I think this cab's gonna do it for us. My company could use a boost like this."

"You're entering that contest again?"

"In October. The Wines of the South competition." He grinned at Gage, stretching his large jowls, reducing his shiny brown eyes to slits. "And this year, I plan to win."

Gage leaned against an oak barrel and stifled a laugh. Why had he not seen it before? Bert looked exactly like that big toad in the children's book he used to read to Jeremy. What was it called? *Something in the Willows?*

"I know you're angry about the van," Gage said. "But I promise to get the windshield replaced as soon as I can."

"Not your fault. I was a little ticked, but I'm over it now." He chuckled. "Jeremy called me an old blowhard this morning. I told him he was the only person in the world who could get away with that." He glanced at Gage and frowned again. "So, who was the target? You or the Maguire girl?"

"Not sure."

Gage didn't mention that Bert might have been the target as easily as Morgan. It was his company's car that had been vandalized. Blackstone Winery had begun as an expensive hobby Bert fashioned into a lucrative sideline. A savvy but ruthless real estate developer, he had made some serious money buying and selling prime commercial property to the rich and famous in Tennessee, Kentucky, and North Carolina. Even the stalled economy hadn't seemed to slow him down. But it was no secret his abrasive personality had garnered as many enemies over the years as Gage had made while working as a private investigator. Gage could handle the faceless convicts who still wanted him dead for bringing them to justice. It came with the territory. But Bert's enemies possessed the money and connections to take him down in style.

Bert took a sip of wine and rolled it around in his mouth, moving it from one plump cheek to the other. "*Ahhh,*" he said after swallowing. "A damn tasty finish."

"I'm here to ask a favor," Gage said, for the second time in two days. God, he hated feeling beholden to people. Especially Bert, who had spent years loaning Gage's father money to keep their family afloat, and never let any of them forget it.

Bert glanced up. His bushy gray eyebrows knitted together in one continuous strip of fur. "All right, son. What can I do for you?"

"The Maguires. They own Maguire Orchard."

"I know."

"Something shady is going on. A man named Lawrence Finch knows they're in financial trouble, and he's paying their apple pickers not to work for them. Some of the fruit is ready to drop, and there's no one to harvest it."

"What do you think I can do?"

"You still pick grapes by hand, don't you? You used to use the same pickers every year. Couldn't you get in touch with some of them and see if they'll—"

"Listen to you, boy." Bert snorted, then laughed. "When you came here, I knew it was only a matter of time before you started sniffing around that Maguire girl again. Why are you so all-fired anxious to help her family? Because you think it will gain you some Brownie points? Or are you looking for a one-way ticket back into her pants?"

"That wasn't very nice."

"Getting on her good side, then."

"Her name is Morgan. And getting on her good side has nothing to do with it," he lied. "I'm working for her brother." Another lie. After Morgan talked to Sean, the chances of Sean hiring him to save the orchard were about as likely as Jeremy forgiving him for not taking the car keys away from his mother. "I don't know who this guy Finch is, but he's sabotaging them."

"So?"

"So, I thought you might like to help your neighbors."

Bert set the wineglass on an upturned barrel and crossed his hulking arms. "The Maguires live in Riverbirch. We're on the other side of the mountain in Cherokee Bluff. They're hardly neighbors."

"No, but they're nice people. Like you could be. If you'd give yourself a chance."

"You're treading dangerous water, son. Don't forget the only reason you're here is because of Jeremy. That boy needs direction and a real home. You aren't capable of giving him either."

"Well, thanks for not sugarcoating it, Bert. I'm on a diet."

"Suzanne was the best thing that ever happened to you, and you threw her away."

"You know, your memory is getting more and more selective."

"You spent nights and weekends hustling for that two-bit detective agency, doing a job that could have gotten you killed. I was fond of Suzanne. While you were driving that heap around Atlanta carrying out a death wish, she was at home raising your son. That poor girl was so lonely, it's no wonder she dove into—"

"—a bottle of vodka?" The blood rushed to Gage's face. Arguing about Suzanne with Bert was like getting trapped in the devil's time warp, forced to relive the same painful memories over and over again. He wondered why Bert didn't realize how much it hurt him. Or maybe Bert didn't care. Gage shoved the anger down and kept going. "I'll admit I wasn't the most attentive husband in the world, but I'm sick of taking the blame for all of Suzanne's problems. She had those problems before we met, and no one knew about them. She was a master at hiding her illness, and her drinking, until they both spun out of control. One rainy night. At home. Alone with our son."

"You should have tried harder."

"To what? To love her? I never loved her. You knew that when you and my father bullied me into marrying her. And I doubt she ever loved me."

"Your father and I decided it was time you grew up and developed a backbone. Learned to do the right thing. You had a wonderful little family, and you destroyed it. If you'd had a real job, and stayed at home where you belonged, Suzanne wouldn't have started drinking."

"You...you don't know that." The sudden tremor in his voice betrayed his emotions. "When Jeremy was eight, Suzanne was re-diagnosed as bipolar, remember? When he turned nine, she threw away her medication. She said she missed the highs and lows. Said she felt dead inside."

"She didn't need those pills. She was fine. A little moody, maybe, but all women get like that. When your Aunt Vida's time of the month came around, she used to throw a fit when things didn't go her way. I used to mark it on my calendar in red ink so I would know when to lay low and keep my mouth shut."

"Don't you understand? Suzanne's troubles weren't hormonal. She had a chronic mental illness."

"That damned psychiatrist was her problem," Bert said. "What was he? Six months out of med school? If you'd only listened to me before you got the divorce, and—"

"And what? Waited for her little mood swings to stop swinging? Waited for her to look happy when I walked through the door? Waited for her to stop crying long enough to fix Jeremy a bowl of Hamburger Helper?" Gage took a slow, deep breath and let it out. "Suzanne needed more help than I could give her. That's why I found her a new doctor. She said she liked him. She swore she'd started taking her meds again. But she hadn't."

"And who should we blame for that?"

Gage sighed. "You and I have been over this a hundred times. We'll never agree on anything about Suzanne, so let's just agree to leave it alone. Let the past stay in the past. Try to move on. Suzanne's gone, and nothing will bring her back. Jeremy is the one we should be worrying about now."

"I've always worried about Jeremy. I've always wanted the best for him."

"And you never thought it was me, did you? You and Suzanne did everything you could to keep me away from him. But Jeremy is my son, and I will never, *ever* not be in his life."

Bert picked up his wineglass and took a hefty swallow. "Jeremy said you took him to that woman's house yesterday. Said he wanted to take guitar lessons from her. Do you think that's a good idea?"

"I think anything's a good idea if it helps Jeremy. He liked her. She made him smile. And before you start passing judgment on 'that woman', know that she agreed to give him lessons despite the fact she can barely look me in the eye. Despite the fact she dislikes me so much, she'd rather drown than accept a life preserver from me."

Bert waited a long moment before glancing up. "Jeremy smiled?"

"Twice."

Bert nodded. "All right. I'll see what I can do. But first, I need to talk to Finch."

"Thanks." Relief flooded through Gage. He hadn't expected Bert to agree so readily, but accepting a favor from his uncle came at a cost. Bert never gave anything away for free. Down the line, Gage would be expected to pay the price. But he didn't care. He was willing to do anything to help Morgan. "I'll track down Finch's number for you."

"I already have it."

"Why would you have the number of a bastard like Lawrence Finch?"

"Because the bastard works for me."

Gage stared at him. "Are you serious?"

"Yes. And I want you to promise to keep it to yourself."

Gage's head started pounding. He willed Bert's words to sink in and make sense. "Are you saying you hired Lawrence Finch to ruin the Maguire's harvest and force them into selling their land to you?"

"Why not? It's a unique piece of property. I'd do anything to get my hands on it. The Maguires own all the way down to Deer Creek. The stretch from Pip's Hill to the water is a large, northern-facing slope, less prone to frost, and perfect for Chambourcin grapes. Hell, boy, you can grow apples anywhere, but Chambourcin grapes are particular where they decide to thrive. Blackstone isn't doing as well as I'd hoped. If I don't do something to revive it, and fast, this place is going to die on the vine.

"I've been in touch with six nationally known wineries, and I could strike a deal with any one of them tomorrow to lease land to grow Chambourcin grapes. This could save us, pull us out of debt. Hell, boy, I'm trying to keep our heads above water. Don't look at me like I'm a monster."

"You haven't changed at all, have you?"

Bert blew out an exasperated sigh. "I only hired Finch as a go-between to work out a compromise. The Maguire girl hates me. Her family would never consider selling the land if they knew the offer came from me. Finch was a loose cannon. I should have kept him on a shorter leash."

Gage clenched his jaw. His hands squeezed into fists. He stepped back to put some distance between him and the man whose face he suddenly wanted to smash against a wine barrel. How could he have been so gullible? So trusting? How could he have believed Bert would help mend his son's broken heart? Morgan had been right. Bert didn't have a heart.

"I guess the thing that bothers me most," Gage said, trying to keep his fury under control, "is you don't think you did anything wrong."

"This isn't personal. It's business. If Robert Maguire were still alive, he would understand. When he got sick, he made some bad decisions. He handed everything over to his grandson and Harlan Spannagel, who know as much about running an orchard as I know about cake decorating. Before the poor man took his last breath, the two of them had run a four-generation family business straight into the ground. It wasn't my fault their orchard took a dive. The only mistake I made was trusting Lawrence Finch to handle things without screwing up."

Gage shook his head in disgust. "Listen to yourself. Do you even know what you're saying? You're playing with people's lives. Now that Spannagel is dead, and Maguire Orchard is vulnerable, you've decided to go for the kill? You said you'd do anything to get your hands on that property. Was getting rid of Spannagel and framing Sean Maguire for his murder part of the plan? It would be an easy way to make sure they're both out of the picture."

"I resent that." Bert poured himself another fingerful of wine and downed it. "You're just like you're father. So righteous. So bloody principled. You make me sick. My money put you through college. It paid for your son's life. You have no right to judge me."

"I have every right. You're someone my son loves and looks up to. I can't have him worshipping a man who takes advantage of decent people when they're down."

"Yes, but...*murder*?" Bert sputtered. "I'm not capable of murder."

"I'm beginning to think you're capable of anything. After Suzanne died, you took us in and gave Jeremy a place to heal. I'll always be grateful for that. But from this moment on, I cannot—I *will* not let my son live under your roof."

"You're going to move out? You don't have a pot to piss in. You can't afford to move out."

"Watch me."

Bert slammed the wineglass on the barrel, shattering the stem. "Why, you ungrateful little shit. If I hadn't promised your father on his deathbed I'd look out for you, I would've kicked you out of this family years ago. You're unreliable and self-centered, and the most irresponsible person I've ever known. If I hadn't paid for Jeremy's medical bills when he was born, that boy would be dead now."

"And you've never let me forget it."

"I ought to sue for custody. I may not be the moral compass you think I should to be, but at least I've always been in Jeremy's corner. Which is more than I can say for you. You've always done what you wanted, when you wanted, and to blazes with everyone else. If Suzanne hadn't pulled out in front of a truck and forced you to be a father to that boy, you'd still be working fourteen hour days for peanuts."

"I don't call running my own company—"

"Your own company?" Bert laughed. "Oh, right. You have a job resuscitating small businesses that can't afford to pay you. Unbelievable."

"At least I'm doing it on my own."

"On your own." Bert flicked a shard of broken glass onto the floor. "Where do you think you got the startup money for In the Black?"

"Oh, God," Gage whispered. "Please. No."

"That money came from me. For reasons I can't begin to fathom, Suzanne wanted you back, so she and her father put their heads together and found you a new career. Suzanne begged me to help you. And I could never say no to Suzanne."

Heat seared across the back of Gage's neck. Betrayal shot through his heart like a barb. For one dizzying second, he thought he might throw up. "So, that's how it is," he said. "Well, don't worry, Bert. You'll get your money back with interest. I won't be obligated to you for anything ever again. Now, if you'll excuse me, I've got packing to do."

"Where are you going? What are you going to tell the boy?"

"Where I'm going is none of your damned business." Gage held the old man's gaze without backing down. "But I'll tell you what I'm going to tell Jeremy, Bert. I'm telling him the truth."

Gage turned and walked out of the winery. He grabbed a few empty boxes as he passed the storage room, then ducked through the breezeway and went into the house.

Tell Jeremy the truth. About Bert? Or about

himself?

He dragged the large canvas bag out from under the bed and unzipped it with a flourish. He started grabbing clothes and tossing them in—clean, dirty, it didn't matter. All he wanted was get as far away from Bert as possible.

He raked rolls of antacids and change off the top of the dresser into his duffle bag, then glanced up and caught sight of himself in the mirror. The look on his face startled him. What was it? Liberation? Relief? More regret than he could handle? Did he even know who he was anymore? He'd been angry and empty for years. But when had he lost his soul?

Who was he to judge Bert? He was lying to everyone—Jeremy, Morgan, Tyson. Himself. He'd shaken hands with Tyson, a man he respected, and promised he would recover a stolen flag to help save the agency. Christ, did everything he came in contact with need saving? But the second he'd seen Morgan's name in the file, reason and logic had ceased to exist. He didn't care what consequences he might have to face or stopped to question if it would all be worth it. All he cared about was the fact that the gods, for whatever reason, had decided to lift the veil and show him a way back to her.

Taking Tyson's money, no matter how much he needed it, was beginning to feel like the biggest mistake of his life. Bigger than trusting a functioning bipolar alcoholic with his little boy. Bigger than the day he had hung up the phone and resigned himself to the fact that Morgan Maguire was lost to him forever. He'd lost his edge. But he didn't care. The moment he looked into Morgan's eyes again, the deepest part of his heart knew that stolen or not, he could never go through with the recovery, and if he bailed, Tyson would take the job away from him and send in the B team.

If he could buy more time until he gained her trust, he might be able to tell her the truth. If he could wait until she got to know him again, the best part of him, the part that could make her believe his intentions were true and honorable. Then maybe, just maybe, that little speck of trust would be enough to sustain him when the apple butter hit the fan.

Chapter 6

Opal pursed her carefully lipsticked mouth and frowned. "You might as well stop wearing a hole in the floor and sit down, missy. Pacing back and forth like an alley cat in heat won't get you in that room any sooner."

"I can't help it," Morgan said. "We've been here over an hour." She sat beside Opal on the wooden bench and pulled her denim jacket closer around her. Early morning light streamed through the glass door, shimmering across an arc of greasy handprints and dirt.

"Why can't you be more patient? You've always been antsy, never patient like your brother. Why don't you look at those pictures on the wanted posters? See if you know anybody." She peered over the rims of the half-glasses she kept perched on her nose. "Or you could tell me what Bert Kirkland's nephew was doing at the farm last night. And why somebody shot out the windshield of his car."

Morgan glanced at her sideways. "I think the Riverbirch grapevine has just broken its own record."

"Still, I'd like to know."

Every ounce of resentment Morgan forced herself to keep in check when she was around Opal rose in her throat. In Morgan's opinion, Opal had lost the right to know what went on at the farm the day she pulled more than her fair share out of the estate and left her stepgrandchildren scrambling to hang on to their heritage.

Sheriff Stallard opened the door.

Morgan jumped up. "What's going on? Where's Sean? Can I see him?"

"Calm down," the sheriff said. "We've finished questioning him, and we're transferring him to the police station in Cherokee Bluff. We're not equipped to handle a murder investigation here unless it's somebody's hog getting creamed by a neighbor's tractor."

Opal pushed herself off the bench and wagged a bent arthritic finger in the sheriff's face. "Are you charging him with Harlan's murder? Is that what you're doing?"

"Does he have a lawyer?" Morgan asked.

"Not yet," the sheriff said. "He's waived his Miranda rights. They'll hold him at the jail until they charge him."

"*Hold him?*" Opal cried. "*Charge him?* You've known that boy since he was in grade school. He didn't kill anyone. He's as sweet as pie. You're making a big mistake, Teresa, and everyone in this town knows it."

At seventy-seven, Opal Maguire could be a formidable woman if the spirit moved her. Her fine, closely cropped red curls had long since turned white. A swath of baby pink scalp cut its way across the side of her head like a crooked road. Her eyes, once a bright cornflower blue, had dulled beneath the cloudy film of cataracts. For some reason, she considered herself Riverbirch royalty, and had enjoyed spending her husband's money like a drunken sailor on shore leave. Now that he was dead, she was still spending it.

"I want to see Sean," Morgan said.

"Honey, we're not supposed to—"

"For God's sake, Teresa, he's her *twin*," Opal said, as if that were all the explanation anyone could ever need.

"All right." Sheriff Stallard sighed and nodded to the door across the hall. "Five minutes. Not a second more."

Morgan pushed her way into the room. Sean sat at a long table, holding his head in his hands. He glanced up when she closed the door behind her.

"How'd you get in?" he asked.

"Opal played the twin card."

"Works every time."

"How's your hangover?"

"Oh, is that what this is? I thought somebody backed over me with a threshing machine." His bloodshot eyes filled with tears. "Harlan's dead, Morgan. I can't believe he's gone. I keep thinking I should call him, and tell him what's happened. But he isn't there."

"I know."

"I'm gonna miss him so much—walking around the farm, whistling a tune wherever he went." Sean smiled and shook his head. "The man liked to whistle."

"Yes, he did."

"I can't believe somebody killed him. Who could've killed Harlan? They think I did it."

She pulled out a chair and sat opposite him. "Sean, where were you yesterday? You said you were going to look for pickers, then last night you said you followed Harlan home."

Sean clasped and unclasped his hands. He rubbed his knuckles against the fine brown stubble along his chin. "Harlan promised he'd have pickers at the orchard by yesterday morning."

"But I thought Finch—"

"Not the regular ones. Harlan found some itinerants driving across Barkerstown Bridge on their way to Kentucky to look for work. They said they'd pick for us, but then they never showed up. I asked Harlan what happened, and he didn't know what I was talking about."

"Harlan's mind was slipping. He hadn't been himself lately. You know that."

Sean rubbed his eyes with the heels of his hands, then shot her a panicked look. "The Rome Beauties are going soft. We cleared most of the windfall apples off the ground Wednesday, but the trees are still full. If we don't get them down soon, we'll lose the first crop. And if we lose that, we'll lose everything."

"According to Finch, we're going to lose everything anyway."

Sean's eyes narrowed. "You've talked to him?"

"Finch and some guy named Mendoza came to the house yesterday to see if we were ready to cave. They thought things might have changed now that Harlan is—"

"Dead?"

She reached across the table and touched his arm. "Sean, you've got to tell me what happened so I can help you."

He leaned back in the aluminum chair and wrapped his arms around his waist. His bloodshot eyes glistened.

"Sean?" she prodded.

"I had forgotten my cell phone and come back for it, even though it never does much good around here.

Harlan was getting ready to leave, but he looked...I don't know...weird. So I got worried and followed him home. He was all over the road. I thought he was gonna take out the Jenkins' fence. When he got out of the car, his nose was gushing blood. I knew he was taking a blood thinner. He was always complaining about how tired it made him feel, how afraid he was of cutting himself. So, I went inside with him. While he was in the bathroom, I noticed the orchard account folder lying on the table beside the computer. I opened it, and two copies of the August spreadsheet fell out. I thought it was odd there were two, so I picked them up and compared them. The numbers didn't match."

"What do you mean?"

"They were different. One spreadsheet showed the orchard making a profit. The other looked like we were completely in the red."

A loud knock rattled the door.

"Two more minutes!" Morgan shouted. "What else? *Hurry*."

"I asked him for an explanation, but he walked out the back door like he hadn't heard me. I followed him down the path to the slaughterhouse, and he started acting strange."

"Define strange."

"He'd wobble back and forth, then stop and hold his stomach. He told me to leave, and when I said no, he turned on me. Said I was a terrible person and a big disappointment to him. He said I'd ruined Maguire Orchard."

"You haven't ruined the orchard. It's not your fault the honeybees are trickling back. It's not your fault a creep like Lawrence Finch will do anything to get his hands on our land."

Two more raps on the door.

"Just a *minute!*" Morgan yelled. "That woman is beginning to get on my nerves. Go on. What did you do then?"

"I left. I tried to call Ethan to tell him his dad was acting crazy, but I couldn't get a signal. Then I got in the car and headed toward Cherokee Bluff, but before I got to the bridge, I met Finch and Mendoza driving toward me. They almost ran me off the road."

"What about your knife? How did it get in the slaughterhouse?"

"I don't know." He rubbed his temples with his fingers, hard, as if he were trying to push an explanation into his head. "I just...don't...know." The bewildered look in his eyes frightened her. She'd never seen him so lost and afraid. Not even the night their parents had left for a drive on their anniversary and never come back.

Sheriff Stallard opened the door. "Okay, that's it. Time to go, Sean."

Sean grabbed Morgan's arm. "The man from In the Black is coming over today. You have to meet with him."

"Sean, I don't think—"

"*Please*, Morgan. Harlan and I both believe he may be the only person who can help us turn things around. You have to be there. You have to let him help us." His gaze pleaded with her. "Promise me you'll see him. Promise you'll be nice to him."

"Okay, little brother. I'll be nice to him."

Sean managed a weak smile. "Only four minutes older, and you're still lording it over me."

"Damn straight."

He put his arms around her. "Thanks."

"For what?"

"For never thinking for one second I might be guilty."

Morgan hugged him tight. "Hang in there," she whispered.

"I will. I'm the half-full twin, remember?"

"You're going to need more on your side than luck."

"Stop being so pessimistic. It's like living with Eeyore." He grinned, and just like that, he was the old Sean again, the Sean who saw a silver lining behind every dark cloud. "Don't worry. If we have faith in the truth, everything will be fine. I believe that."

"I know you do." She hugged him again, then fought back tears as the sheriff escorted him out the back door to a waiting van. "I just wish I believed it, too."

****

Opal stood beside the water fountain in full flirt mode talking to Gage Kirkland. In spite of everything, Morgan's heart lurched at the sight of him. He'd swapped his formfitting jeans for a pair of pleated khakis and a blue long-sleeved shirt. The soft stubble on his chin had disappeared, replaced by smoother skin and two red shaving nicks. Damp tendrils of hair fringed over the back of his shirt collar. The crisp clean scent of his aftershave drifted toward her, a little pungent, as if he had spritzed himself only two minutes earlier in the car.

"How's your brother holding up?" he asked.

Morgan sighed. "Sean is such an irritating optimist.

If the world went up in flames tomorrow, he'd admire the pretty colors, then list five reasons why it could be a good thing."

"Looking on the bright side is a gift," Opal said reprovingly. "It wouldn't hurt you to try and stay positive, Miss Doom and Gloom." She batted her wrinkled eyes at Gage. "I've told her that for years, but it hasn't done a lick of good."

"How are you doing?" Gage asked Morgan.

"Me?" Morgan shook her head and laughed. "I'm a freakin' basket case."

Opal took out an embroidered handkerchief and dabbed at her temples. "Is it hot in here? My heart's going a mile a minute."

Gage slid his hand beneath Opal's elbow. "Let's get you ladies some coffee. The Wildflower Café next door looks good."

"No, I'm fine now." Opal fluttered her handkerchief in the air. "You two go on. I'm stopping by church to say a prayer for Sean. Something tells me my boy's gonna need all the help he can get."

"Her boy," Morgan said after Opal left. "What a joke. Do you know how many times she tried to ship us off to boarding school? Believe me, this is all for show. Don't let her fool you. She doesn't give a happy damn about either of us."

They walked to the Wildflower Café and sat at one of the round metal tables in the front courtyard.

"Your grandmother said her heart was racing. Will she be all right?"

"Step-grandmother. And yes, she'll be fine. Opal's always fine. She loves a good crisis as long as she isn't expected to do anything. Oh, she'll go to church, shed a few tears if anybody's watching, visit the Main Street shops to tell her troubles to whoever will listen, then go home, fix herself a gin and tonic, and watch *The Price is Right*."

"You sound bitter."

"And it doesn't become me, right?"

"Oh, you still look pretty good. But bitterness will give you frown lines and corrode your soul. Trust me on this."

She glanced up. A few of the leaves on the birch trees surrounding the town square had turned pale yellow-gold. The September sun shone through their branches, throwing mottled shadows on the sidewalk, caressing the center of town with its warmth. But Morgan couldn't feel it. Something cold and thick had seeped into her bones. Her troubles loomed in front of her like a wild horse bent on destruction, pawing the air with its hooves.

Gage signaled to the waitress for two coffees. He turned and gazed at Morgan with his dark, brown-green apologetic eyes, until she had to look away.

"I know you told me not to come," he said. "But you need someone in your corner. And frankly, after last night, I was worried about your safety."

"Don't call me Frankly," she murmured. She glanced his way but avoided eye contact. She wished he'd leave. The emotions he kept dredging up were keeping her in a constant state of exhaustion. She was running on fumes and two hours sleep, and she was scared. More scared than she'd ever been in her life. She needed some space to think. She couldn't think around Gage, and it was getting too damned hard to keep pushing him away.

"I've been instructed to be nice to you," she said. "But this thing with my brother and the farm is none of your business."

"Maybe not. But when somebody pumps six bullets into the windshield of my car, in your driveway, that makes it my business. Do you know who might not want me visiting you?"

"Besides me?"

"Yeah," he said softly. "Besides you."

"No."

The waitress set two steaming mugs of coffee in front of them. Gage stirred three packets of sugar into his and said, "I asked Stallard's secretary about the autopsy results."

"So did I, but she wouldn't tell me anything."

"That's because you didn't tell her she smelled like sunshine."

"No, I didn't." She looked at him. "Why didn't I think of that?"

"Not sure, but it worked. They should have the results back in four or five days."

"That long?"

"I know, but this is real life, not *CSI*. The county uses a contracted pathologist from Cherokee Bluff, and that takes time. She said it could be sooner, depending on their caseload."

"I hate sitting here helpless while Sean is in jail. What can I do?"

"Nothing until something happens. He'll either be charged or they'll let him go."

"I lied about Sean to Opal. If she knew how distraught he was, she would spread it all over town. Sean tried to put on a brave face, but I could tell he's terrified. He's grief-stricken over Harlan. It broke my heart."

"I found out something else."

"Because you told Deputy Nelson he smelled like rain?"

"No, did he?" Gage took a cautious sip of coffee. "Someone should tell the sheriff there's a sound tunnel running through the hallway from her office to the water fountain. I heard her talking to the lab on the phone. The knife they found had no fingerprints on it, so it had probably been wiped clean. Which is fairly normal. Not many weapons have fingerprints on them. But my point is they can't use that against him."

Morgan stared at him. "And you know this because..."

"I worked as a private investigator for nine years. Grunt work mostly—following cheating husbands and wives, investigating insurance fraud, getting the goods on a few corporate crooks. But sometimes, if the moon was full, and I'd been a very good boy, I got to hop in my tricked-out Mustang and tear through the streets of Atlanta chasing the scum of the earth."

"Define scum."

"Drug dealers, car thieves, deadbeat dads. I even tracked down a kidnapper once. Two of us worked that case, and we saved a little girl from—well, we got to her in time."

"I thought you were in pre-med."

"Turns out I can't stand to see people in pain."

"Wow. I never thought you'd end up doing something so dangerous."

"Me, either." He grinned. "But it seems I'm one if those guys who's addicted to adrenaline. The rush didn't come often, but when it did, it made me feel alive."

"Your wife and son didn't do that for you? "

"I—" He stopped and blinked. As if she'd slapped him.

"I'm sorry," she said. "I was out of line. I didn't mean to—"

"No," he said quietly. "It's a fair question. You're right. It was a crazy line of work for a family man. I took risks. I was fearless. But I had been systematically shut out of Jeremy's life, and nothing else did anything for me. For a lot of years, I was so angry at the cards I'd been dealt and the choices I'd been forced to make, I didn't care what happened to me."

"Are you talking about marrying Suzanne? What kind of shotgun did her father have?"

"It wasn't like that. My father and Bert encouraged me to marry her, but I could have said no. Suzanne had a difficult, high-risk pregnancy. A new crisis came up every month. She was bedridden for weeks. I couldn't leave her. Or tell her about you because of the stress it would cause. Jeremy was born two months premature, which is why he's always been physically smaller than normal. He's catching up, though.

"Suzanne and Bert teamed up against me. They didn't agree with my career choice. They thought it was dangerous and juvenile and selfish. They thought Jeremy would be better off if I wasn't in the picture. After our divorce, which Bert paid for, he helped her sue me for full custody. But somehow, by the grace of God, I got the only judge in Fulton county Bert couldn't bribe, and she ruled in my favor."

"But you're family. How could your Uncle Bert do

this to you?"

"There are layers and layers to that man. And most of them are made out of compost."

"So you got full custody of Jeremy?"

"Joint. Of course, when Suzanne realized she'd have to legally share our son with me, she did everything she could to sabotage the agreement—last minute changes of plans, trips to Disney World in the summer, skiing trips to Gatlinburg in the winter. All bankrolled by Bert, of course. But how could I say no? Jeremy loved doing those things."

"Weekend Father Syndrome."

"I tried to forge a relationship with Jeremy. I promised him I would quit my dangerous, juvenile job. I started In the Black. I pretended I was happy. And for a while, it all worked. Jeremy had gotten older, and I finally had some common ground with him. I'd begun to make real progress, feel like a real father. And then Suzanne died. And he blames me for it. He's in therapy now, and it seems to be helping. Dr. Arlene Lloyd. Do you know her? She seems very compassionate."

"Therapy is a good thing."

"Bert's right. I should have tried harder. Not being around when my son needed me is something I'll always regret. Something I'll spend the rest of my life trying to make up to him."

"You're there now," she said. "And he still needs you, whether he realizes it or not."

He smiled at her. It took his eyes a few extra moments to catch up.

"Bring him over today after school," Morgan said. "I don't have to be at Bad Moon until five. I can give him a lesson while you look around the farm. Sean believes in you, and I would really like for you to try to help him save the orchard."

"Okay. Thanks." He grinned, making her heart beat in slow, rolling thuds. "And I'm going to make some calls about finding Sean representation. If he goes up against a murder charge, he'll need the best lawyer we can find."

"We?"

"We."

He held her gaze with his while a current of electricity sliced a path through the center of her abdomen.

"I didn't want to leave you alone last night," he said.

"I was fine."

"Well, I wasn't."

"Oh, come on. A big, tough, adrenaline junkie PI like you?"

"Not so tough when the bullets are flying."

Memories of the night before slammed into Morgan's brain—the sound of gunshots cracking the air, Gage pushing her off the flagstone walk, lying stone still beside him in the wet grass with a broken rhododendron stob biting into her neck. If she closed her eyes, she could still feel his breath crashing across her shoulder, the strong, constant pulse at the base of his throat flicking against her cheek. How long had it been since she'd touched a man? Or been wrapped like his most cherished possession in the strong, shielding warmth of his arms? Had she ever felt so safe? Would she ever feel that safe again?

Maybe she should hold on to the memory. Bury it deep. Then, when she needed comfort, she could take it out and replay it over and over in her head to drive the unbearable loneliness away. Until something that felt like contentment trickled through her bloodstream, like a double shot of apple brandy on a cold, wintry night.

A shadow fell over the table.

She lifted her eyes and gasped softly. The last thing she expected to see were the pale, twisted, angry eyes of Lawrence Finch.

****

"Gage Kirkland?"

Gage followed Morgan's gaze to the man standing beside their table. He looked like an emaciated wolf. The scars around his eyes were disconcerting, but Gage suspected he used that to his advantage. He bared his teeth, more grimace than smile, and tucked a folded newspaper under his arm.

"I'm Gage Kirkland." Gage automatically stiffened. Strange men showing up out of the blue calling him by name was never a good sign.

"Morning, Miss Maguire," the man said.

Morgan nodded. "Mr. Finch."

"Your friend and I have some business to discuss."

Morgan glanced at Gage. "You know each other?"

"Only by reputation," Gage said.

Finch slammed the newspaper against the table. "You got me fired today, boy." His thin face morphed into a sneer, bunching his scars into a hard, fleshy knot. "I've worked for Bert Kirkland for two years, and today, because you moved your brat out of his house, he let me go. Cut me off. Told me he wouldn't be needing my services anymore."

"Your services?" Morgan's eyes narrowed suspiciously. "What are you talking about?"

"He works for Bert," Gage said. "As a front man. Bert wants your farm, so he thought he'd pay the Big Bad Wolf here to persuade you to sell."

"Oh, my God," she whispered. "Did you know about this?"

"Not until two hours ago," Gage said. "That's why I moved out."

Morgan jumped to her feet and faced Finch. "Why, you...you *snake*. I should have smashed your toes when I had the chance."

Finch took a step toward Morgan. Gage grabbed the table, ready to leap.

"It's okay," Morgan said. "This guy's not gonna hurt me. This guy's a sniveling little weasel. He's not so tough without Bert Kirkland's money in his pocket. Are ya, Larry?"

"You want to see tough?" Finch snarled. "I'll show you tough. The two of you just wait."

"Until you have some backup?" Morgan glanced around. "Where is Mr. Mendoza? Hiding in the bushes? I mean, that's what little weasels do, isn't it?"

"You'd better watch your mouth," Finch said.

"Leave her alone," Gage said. "If you have a beef getting fired, then take it up with me."

Finch smiled. "You know, I'd like to." His gaze darted between the two of them. "But I think the most efficient way to get back at you would be through her. It's never a good idea to wear your heart on your sleeve, boy."

Gage jumped to his feet and seized Finch by the arm. He shuffled him across the sidewalk to the parkway then flattened him against a telephone pole. The elderly couple at the next table huddled in fear. The man sitting behind them threw his cigarette on the ground and ran into the café.

"I can promise you one thing," Gage said evenly. His slow Georgia drawl liquefied each vowel. "If you go near Morgan again, I will personally see to it that you never bother another woman for *any* reason. Ever again. You get what I'm sayin'?"

"Threaten me all you want. But this is not over." He shook off Gage's grasp. "I have bills to pay, and the people I owe expect me to pay them on time."

"What people?" Gage asked. "People who'd just as soon see you dead as alive?" He turned to Morgan. "I think I've tracked down some of those people."

Finch glared at him. "I mean it, Kirkland. This is not over." He wiped the spittle off his mouth with the back of his hand and stalked away.

Gage turned to Morgan. She gave a quick backward glance to the patrons in the courtyard still staring and whispering, then calmly looped her purse strap over her shoulder and started down the street.

"Hey, wait a minute!" Gage threw a few bills on the table and hurried to catch up. "You can't leave now. Where are you going?"

She walked across the street and stood beside her old blue truck, rummaging in her leather purse for the keys. Gage stood in the grassy parkway. He was afraid she would slug him if he came too close.

"Morgan, talk to me. I swear I didn't know Bert was trying to force your family into selling. As soon as I found out, I packed up Jeremy and moved us out of Bert's house. Until today, I had no idea he was pulling the strings. I would have said something. I would have told you."

She opened the truck door and spun around to face him. "You know what? I don't have time for this. And I don't have time for you. One of these days, I'll learn to follow my instincts."

"Morgan."

"I'm so angry, I could spit." She threw her purse past the gearshift and put her foot on the running board. But instead of ducking inside the cab, she turned back to him, eyes flashing.

He caught his breath. Jesus, she was beautiful.

The morning light shimmered across her face, making the blue part of the gold-flecked iris look green. Her perfectly shaped lips clamped together in disgust. Her right hand balled into a fist. Gage had never seen her angry before. He'd imagined it enough times, but in his head, it had never looked quite like this. Passion and revulsion all mixed together, and directed at him.

"Here's the deal," she said. "I will give your son guitar lessons because I feel sorry for him. And I will let you give us your exalted opinion on whether or not the orchard can be saved, because my brother—God help him—believes you know what you're doing. But make no mistake. I want you and your uncle to stay as far away from me as possible. I don't want to see you. I don't want to hear your voice. I don't want to catch sight of your long, tall shadow slinking along the ground."

"Why not? That's all I am. Just a shadow on the ground. That's all any of us are."

"You say that like you believe it."

"I do believe it." He raked his hand back through his hair. "Come on, Morgan. Give me a break. I know you're angry about Bert, but you don't think I could condone the fact that he—"

"The hell I don't." She slid in and slammed the door, then sat staring at the steering wheel.

He waited for her to start the motor, thrust it into first gear and peel out of the parking spot. But she made no move to go. He stood in the parkway with his hands shoved deep in the pockets of his khaki pants. And waited. Finally, he pecked on the glass. "I'm not leaving," he said. "I'm never leaving. I'm going to stand here like Greyfriar's Bobby in the rain and the snow and the sleet until you talk to me. For as long as it takes."

She rolled the window down. "You really moved you and your son out of Bert's house?"

"Yes."

"And you swear you didn't know what Bert was up to?"

"I swear."

She sat for a few moments, then nodded. "All right. You get one chance." She started the motor, still looking straight ahead. "I'll see you at four."

"Yes, ma'am," he said. "Four o'clock. As soon as Jeremy gets out of his therapy session."

She leaned down. "Can you do me a favor?"

"Anything."

"Can you find out if Jeremy's therapist has an opening? I think I need to have my head examined."

Chapter 7

"My dad's outside looking around," Jeremy said. He shuffled into the living room and stood by the piano. "I hate piano. Piano sucks."

Morgan laughed. "Well, maybe you have the soul of an Eric Clapton or a Jimmy Page."

"Who's that?"

"Ever heard of Led Zeppelin?"

Jeremy's face brightened. "Sure. They're on my *Guitar Hero* game."

"Then you've heard Jimmy Page play guitar." She set his backpack on the sofa. "Are you hungry? Do you want a snack or something before we start?"

"My dad bought me a couple of burgers after therapy." He rolled his eyes. "Yeah, I'm in friggin' therapy. Just like all the kids in alternative school."

"Do you hate it?"

Jeremy shrugged. "Nah, it's okay. I thought it would suck, but I guess it's okay."

"I know you're the new kid at school. Do you ever get bullied? My brother did."

"Not much. I figure out ways around it." He grinned. "I may have inherited the shrimp gene, but I also got a few brains. Dr. Lloyd thinks I'm precocious."

"I'd have to agree. I wish I'd had someone to talk to when my parents died. I mean, I had my brother, but...you know, I couldn't tell him everything."

"You're parents died? Both of them? At the same time?"

"In a car wreck. When I was ten."

He glanced at the floor, then lifted his head. "Kinda like me, huh?"

"Kinda like you." She sat at the piano and patted the bench. "Come sit here. Pianos may suck, but they come in handy when you're tuning a guitar."

They spent the next thirty minutes lost in the sweet solace of music. In addition to being whip smart, it was clear Jeremy had inherited the same dry, self-deprecating sense of humor from his father that had first attracted Morgan to him. She wondered if Gage saw himself in his son. She did. And she wondered what Jeremy would have looked like if he'd been her child. Taller, maybe. With Gage's dark eyes and Sean's tall, lanky body.

When they finished, Jeremy said, "My fingers look like I've been hanging on a clothesline."

"They'll be sore tomorrow. It takes a while to build up calluses. I'm going to let you take my guitar with you to practice the four chords you learned. Just play around with them. Next time, we'll drag out some music and work on a real song." She smiled. "You did great today."

"Thanks."

"I hear you're a whiz at computers."

"I'm okay."

"I might need help from someone who knows his way around the Internet. Are you interested? If your dad says it's all right, I'd pay you for your time."

Jeremy grinned up at her, and for the first time she

noticed the tiny silver wires holding his retainer in place. "For real?"

"Absolutely. I own a Civil War artifact I might need to sell. There are people who would pay a lot of money for it, but I don't know how to go about finding them."

"What kind of artifact?"

"General Albert S. Johnston's personal battle flag." She reached behind the piano for the guitar case. "He was shot and killed the first day at the Battle of Shiloh. The poor guy bled to death because he'd sent all the doctors off to care for Union prisoners, and no one at the camp knew how to tie a tourniquet."

"Bummer."

Morgan laughed. "Definitely a bummer."

"What does the flag look like?"

"Like a Confederate flag, only smaller. It's about thirty-four inches square, made out of wool bunting. Each regiment had their own flag. Many of the soldiers' wives sewed the flags for their husbands and sons. Will you help me find a buyer?"

"Sure." He nodded vigorously.

She went to the roll top desk and wrote the information on a piece of notepaper. "I'm sadly lacking in computer skills, but I do I have an email address if you need to contact me. Here are my phone numbers. Call the house first. On this side of the mountain, cell service is iffy."

A man's shadow loomed in the doorway, blocking the low September sun.

"Dad's here." Jeremy turned around and stopped short. "Morgan?" he said in a small voice.

Morgan looked up. Her worst nightmare stood in

the doorway with his arms crossed, grinning at her. "Hello, Denny."

"Hey, girl." The screen door opened and banged shut. Denny Quillen stepped into the room, filling it up. His gaze skimmed the length of her body.

"You know, this isn't a good time, Denny. I'm giving a lesson."

"The boy won't mind." He looked at Jeremy. "Will you, boy?"

Jeremy's gaze jumped between Denny and Morgan. "I...I guess not."

"See?" Denny said. "He doesn't care. Go away, kid. Your teacher and I have some grownup talking to do."

"It's all right, Jeremy," Morgan said. "You can wait outside for your father."

"Down by the fence," Denny said. "What we have to say is private."

Jeremy hesitated, torn between not wanting to stay and afraid to leave her alone.

"It's okay, honey," Morgan said. "I'll be fine. Go on, now."

Denny stamped his foot. "*Go! Lesson's over!*"

Jeremy grabbed the huge guitar case and scuttled out the door.

Morgan waited until Jeremy had cleared the porch. "Still charming everyone you meet, I see."

"Only you, Morgan." He took a step toward her.

She always forgot what a big man Denny was, and how intimidating. A shiver traveled the length of her spine. Instinctively, she glanced around the room to determine her options.

"What's it been?" he said. "Two years?"

"Five. It just feels like two. Every five years, you show up like clockwork asking for a handout. Like I owe you something. Well, I don't owe you anything."

Time to curb her smart tongue. She knew better than to provoke him.

She went to stand behind the sofa, feeling safer with a barrier between them. If he wasn't too stoned, and still had a few muscles left from his track and field days, a sofa wouldn't be much protection. His watery gray eyes, magnified twice their size behind the lens in a pair of round wire-frames, regarded the move with amusement.

"Aren't you gonna ask me to sit down?"

"I don't think so."

He was thinner than he'd been the last time she'd seen him, although judging from the spongy bay window protruding from his midsection, he was still going through a twelve-pack of beer every night. For once, his prematurely gray goatee had been neatly trimmed, and he had pulled his straight gray hair into a ponytail. If he'd been wearing a tweed sport coat instead of a stained cotton work shirt, he could have passed for the seedy professor at some junior college.

"We were married once," he said. "Aren't you even gonna ask how I am?"

"We were married for two months. I've had relationships with cheese that lasted longer." Morgan clutched the crocheted afghan lying across the back of the sofa. "But okay. How are you, Denny? Still the light of your family's life?"

"Huh," he scoffed.

"Why are you here? Do you have some personal debts, quite possibly to someone named Guido, that you need to pay off?"

"Oh, ouch." Denny put a hand over his heart and stumbled backwards in mock agony. "Why do you always think the worst of me?"

"Because you always prove me right. If you're here to borrow money, I don't have any."

"No, but you have something else. Something that belongs to me."

"I don't know what you're talking about."

He walked toward her and stopped. The muscles in her arms tensed. A film of perspiration broke out across the back of her neck. "The flag, Morgan. I'm talking about the flag. My father knows you have it, and he wants it back."

"You gave it to me, remember?"

"I was drunk."

"I don't care if you were in a coma. You said it was payment for the grief you caused me. For making me lose the—for what you did to me. You said I could have it if I didn't report what you did to the police, remember? You didn't have to go to jail, remember?" She stared at him without cringing. Five years ago she might have backed down. But not now.

"It wasn't my fault you lost the baby. Shit, it wasn't even mine." He took another step toward her. "I want the flag back, Morgan. And I want it back now."

"I'm not afraid of you anymore."

He laughed coarsely. "You never were."

She used her peripheral vision to make sure the bat was still in the umbrella stand. She'd never been very successful using a weapon against him. The only time she'd needed one, he'd overpowered her before she could get to it. She cheated a few steps to the right and tried to gauge the distance she'd have to run if he came at her. He looked soft, out of shape. If he was still chain-smoking filterless Camels, she could probably outrun him.

She had to stay calm and *think*. Thinking had saved her before. By the time his rising exasperation crossed the line—and it always did—she had better have a plan in place.

Marrying Denny had been the worst mistake of her life. Or the second, if you counted falling in love with another man two weeks before their wedding. But she'd married Denny, in spite of the feeling of doom that had clutched her gut. In spite of pacing the church vestibule like a caged leopard, waiting for the call from Gage that never came.

Denny had hit her twice. The first time hadn't seemed completely unjustified after confessing she'd slept with another man. Although, it had left her wary and bewildered, with an unshakable mistrust of her own judgment where men were concerned. The second time, on the day he found out she was pregnant with Gage's child, changed her life forever, and sent her tearing out of his life for good.

"I only gave you that flag because I needed someplace safe to stash it," he said. "I knew you'd take good care of it for me, and I could get it back anytime I wanted. Well, I want it now."

Her gaze shot to the screen door. She hoped Jeremy had made it across the yard and was waiting for Gage at the road. She would never forgive herself if anything happened to him.

"The flag, Morgan." Denny started around the sofa. "Give me the goddamned flag."

She lunged to the right, but her timing was off. Before she could clear the sofa, Denny had blocked her path. He grabbed her upper arms and backed her into the front side of the upright piano. The keys banged, clanging in disharmony.

"You're hurting me!"

"I'll do more than that if you don't tell me where the flag is."

"Stop it!"

He lifted her off the piano, still holding her arms, and slammed her into the wall. The back of her head crashed into the framed picture of her grandfather. Denny's sour breath, a mixture of hard liquor and cigarettes, exhaled into her face. For a moment, she thought she might vomit. His gray eyes, so warm and gentle when she'd first met him, were glazed over and feverish, filled with the same bullying hatred that had manifested itself the day she'd lost the only child she might ever be able to have. Her hatred for him, and everything in her life he had caused her to lose, engulfed her. She stopped thinking and raised her knee. Then she smashed it into his groin.

Denny's grip loosened instantly. He doubled over, holding his crotch with both hands.

Morgan pushed past him and ran for the door, straight into Gage's arms.

"You okay?" Gage pulled back and searched her face until she nodded. "Let me deal with this." He strode across the room, hauled Denny to his feet, and spun him around. "Maybe it's time you picked on someone your own size." He pulled his fist back.

"No!" Morgan screamed. "No. Let it go."

"You sure?" Gage said. "I'll be glad to knock this

creep's teeth down his throat. Say the word, baby, and he'll be munching a mouthful of Chiclets."

"Just get him out of here," Morgan said.

"Hear that, mister?" Gage pulled Denny around the sofa and shoved him toward the door. "The lady wants you out."

Denny fell against the doorframe. One hand straightened his glasses, the other cupped the tender area between his legs. "I'm not finished with you," he yelled to Morgan.

"Wanna bet?" Gage said.

Denny turned and stumbled out the door, then down the steps to the front walk. Jeremy stood in the yard beside the rhododendron bush, watching him.

"What are you looking at?" Denny bellowed.

"Why are you still here?" Jeremy asked. "The stupid people left hours ago."

Denny lurched down the driveway to his motorcycle. He climbed on and revved the motor, then swerved into the road.

Morgan dropped onto the wicker loveseat. "I am so sorry."

"Who was that thug?" Gage asked.

"Denny Quillen. My ex-husband."

His gaze swept over her again and again, as if he were reassuring himself she was all right.

"I'm okay," she said.

"Please don't tell me he treated you like that when you were married to him."

"Only twice. The second time, I walked out. Well, actually, I ran."

"Bastard," Gage said. "And what was that monochromatic thing he had going—gray hair, gray eyes, gray beard? He looked like a Weimaraner."

Morgan rubbed the sore spot on the back of her head. "How did you know I needed help?"

Jeremy held up his cell phone. "I got it to work. I called Dad and told him two men were after you."

"What do you mean, two men? You saw two men?"

"Yeah," Jeremy said. "Two of them. The mean one you kicked in the junk and the skinny one watching through the window."

"Stay here." Gage jumped off the porch and ran around the side of the house.

"What did the other man look like?" Morgan asked. "Besides being skinny."

"Nerdy. Like my science teacher." Jeremy sat on the swing and kicked his foot against the floor. "He looked like Mr. Spock."

"Mr. Spock on *Star Trek?*"

"Yeah, but without the ears or the weird eyebrows."

Ethan? It couldn't be Ethan. Even though Jeremy's description sounded exactly like him. It didn't make sense. Why would Ethan and Denny be at her house at the same time? Had they come together? Ethan had met Denny once before at Bad Moon, but she didn't think the two men knew each other. How could they know each other?

"Where did the other man go? Did you see him leave?"

"He ran that way." Jeremy pointed to the brushy slope leading down to the orchard. "I don't think he saw me. I was hiding behind those bushes."

Gage loped toward them then stood with his hands

on his hips, gulping in air. "I checked behind the barn and the guesthouse. No sign of anyone," he puffed. "And yes, I am slightly out of shape."

"Slightly?" Jeremy looked at him sideways.

"Okay, more than slightly. It's been a while since I've had to go from zero to thirty in two seconds."

"Everything's fine now," Morgan said, as much for her own benefit as Jeremy's. "Why don't you go inside and get your dad a bottle of water from the fridge. Help yourself to some cookies." She waited until he left, then turned to Gage. "Jeremy just described Ethan Spannagel as the man who was watching through the window. Ethan is Harlan's son, and a good friend. The thought of him sneaking around like that is outrageous."

"I don't know what went on between you and your ex before I got here, but—"

"I have something he wants. He got loud and nasty when I wouldn't give it to him."

"Maybe Ethan came by for a visit and heard what was going on, so he…waited."

"Waited until my drunken ex-husband slammed me against a wall? He knows why I left the marriage. He knows Denny has a history of drug abuse and violence. He *knows* that. And yet, he did nothing?"

****

Gage wanted to tell her the man sounded like a hamster. Instead, he said, "He's probably still in shock over his father's death."

"That's a lot of shock. But why was he spying in my window?"

"Why don't you ask him?"

"I will." She nodded. "I will."

128

He pushed down the fear he realized was never going away as long as she was in danger, and forced a reassuring smile. He longed to put his arms around her, but she didn't seem to need comforting. She seemed to be handling things pretty well on her own. She'd—how had Jeremy put it?—kicked the guy in the junk. Gage chuckled. He would've liked to have seen that.

"Dad?" Jeremy handed him a bottle of water. "I'm sorry I got mad at you for moving all our stuff out of Uncle Bert's house. And I was thinking...."

"Where are you guys living now?" Morgan asked.

"We're checking into Taylor's Motor Lodge until we can find a place."

"No, Dad." Jeremy's square chin jutted out. "We can't go to a motel. Morgan needs us here. She's all alone."

"Oh, honey," Morgan said. "I'm fine."

"But what if the mean guy comes back?" Jeremy's eyes flashed accusingly at his father. "Someone has to watch out for her. I know karate. You know how to shoot a gun. You told me you used to sit outside apartment houses for hours, protecting the good people from the bad people. Morgan's our friend. Why can't you do it for her?"

"Jeremy," Morgan said, "I can take care of myself. I'll be okay."

"No, he's right," Gage said. "You shouldn't be here alone. At least not until things calm down. Do you have a friend you can stay with? What about Peach? Or Opal?"

"Why can't we stay here?" Jeremy asked. "She has a big house."

"Son, that's enough."

129

Jeremy ignored him. "Please, can we stay, Morgan? Because if we can't, I'll be so worried about you, I won't be able to sleep. Then my grades will go down. Then my therapist will get mad and say I need to focus. Only I won't be able to focus. Because I'll be worried about you."

"Oh, you're good." Morgan laughed. She glanced over his head at Gage. Apprehension hovered in her eyes. "I guess the kid has a point."

"That's why he's eleven going on fifty."

"Fifty-two," Jeremy corrected.

"You saw the little guesthouse beside the outbuilding. Opal made my grandpa build it to house her relatives when they came to visit. It's only three rooms, but it has a kitchenette and a fairly nice bathroom."

"Sounds good. That's all us guys need to be comfortable, right Jeremy?"

"Right."

Relief washed over Gage. He hadn't expected Jeremy to champion his cause, or to do it so eloquently, but he had a better chance of keeping Morgan safe if they stayed on the farm. When word got out she had two live-in bodyguards, no one would dare mess with her. He thrust away the ugly feeling that he was deceiving her. Jeremy was getting better day by day. He had Morgan and the therapist to thank for that. If he tried, he could find a way to finance Jeremy's therapy without relying on Tyson or Bert. He just needed to try harder.

As soon as he figured out how to resolve things, he would tell Tyson he couldn't go through with the recovery. He'd wriggled out of worse jams.

Somewhere. In a dream, maybe. But before he could call off the dogs, he needed to find out where she'd stashed the flag. If she discovered the real reason he was there, and what he'd agreed to do, she would never believe he had her best interests at heart. She would never believe anything about him again.

"We'll stay out of your way," Gage said. "You'll never know we're here. And it's just for a while. Just until Sean comes home." Gage tried to sound positive about Sean, even though he was skeptical everything would work out in his favor. "When your brother gets out, and you don't need your guardians anymore, Jeremy and I will leave."

"Her guardian angels. That's what we'll be, right Dad?" Jeremy looked directly into his father's eyes. "You and I will keep her safe."

A feeling, as close to pure happiness as he'd ever experienced, swept over Gage. He gazed at his son and swallowed the knot in his throat. He was afraid to breathe; the moment was so perfect.

Morgan laughed. "Now, that sounds like an offer I would be stupid to refuse."

"I know," Jeremy said, flashing her the easy smile Gage wasn't sure he would ever see again. "Because the stupid people left hours ago."

Chapter 8

"I know you've made a career out of using men, but I've never seen you use a dead one before."

"Shut the hell up," Peach said.

"Hello?" Morgan closed the feed store door. "Hey, you two."

"Hey, Morgan," Ethan said. "I didn't hear the bell."

"I'm not surprised." Morgan looked from Ethan's flushed face to Peach. "What's going on?"

"Nothing." Peach gathered up her huge purse. "I have to get to work."

"I'm right behind you," Morgan said. "I need to talk to Ethan."

"Yeah, well, good luck with that." She turned to Ethan. "We'll talk about this later." Peach slammed the door on her way out. The bell over the door tinkled wildly.

"What just happened here?" Morgan asked. "Why were you yelling at each other?"

Ethan wiped a streak of sawdust off the cash register. "I cannot stand that woman."

"So I noticed."

"Do you know she came on to me a few months ago? I didn't say anything because I was embarrassed. I mean, is that the kind of woman I attract? As long as

132

some guy's paying her way, she doesn't care whose lap she takes a spin on."

"I feel sorry for her."

"Why? Because she works two jobs and lives in a trailer with a kid? Or because she's a bitch who only bothers with people who can do something for her? She's slept with every man in town, and she still can't get one of them to marry her."

Morgan glanced around Spannagel's Feed and Seed Store. The air smelled sweet and earthy, like the booths at the farmer's market. Floor-to-ceiling display shelves filled with livestock feed and farm supplies lined the plank walls. A barrel of complimentary peanuts sat beside the front door, a tradition in parts of the South. Stray peanut shells lay scattered about the floor to crunch beneath the customers' feet.

"How's the feed store?"

"It's still a work in progress, but I can't complain. Dad never thought I'd make a go of this place, but I'm proving him wrong."

Morgan skimmed her fingers over a row of metal wind chime rods, setting off a sharp cacophony of clangs. "It always seemed strange to me that you sold food and supplies to care for animals while your father was busy slaughtering them less than a mile away."

"Haven't you ever heard of the circle of life?"

"It used to be one of my favorite songs. But I think I'm going to have to find a new one." She leaned her elbows on the counter. "I'm surprised you're working today."

"Where else would I be?"

"Ethan, your father just died," she said gently. "You're entitled to a day off."

"I don't want a day off."

She picked up a coupon for sheep manure and set it back down. What was she doing there? She had come to ask Ethan if he'd watched Denny throw her against a wall without lifting a finger to help, but the haunted look on his face kept her from saying anything. Ethan was grieving for his dad. It seemed callous to bring it up when he was in so much pain.

"I came to see how you were doing," she said. "This has got to be hard for you."

Ethan took her hand and held it to his chest. "I always wanted to walk through fire for you, Morgana." He managed a smile. "Be your knight in slightly tarnished armor."

"Well, thank you, kind sir."

"We used to be close, you know? Tell each other everything. I miss that. I miss you."

"Me, too." She fought the urge to pull her hand out of his sweaty palm. "When things settle down, we'll have to get together more often."

"You always say that, but we never do." He shook his head sadly. "I feel like I'm losing you. Like it's never going to be in the cards for us."

His emotions were raw. He had just lost his father. This wasn't the time to break out the cold hard truth that she would never love him in that way.

"Oh, come on." She tried to sound cheerful. "The old poker game isn't over yet." And then, because she was the real coward in the room, she said, "You know I love you, Eth. We're friends. *Great* friends. And I would never jeopardize something so dear to me."

He let her go. "You're right," he said, smiling. "The old poker game isn't over yet."

****

Morgan straightened the last two bar chairs and gave the counter a final swipe with her rag. "Are you done, J.D.? I don't owe you another one, do I?"

"Oh, no, ma'am." J.D. drained the last of his beer then wiped his graying blond mustache with his thumb and forefinger. "I allow this is all I'll be able to handle tonight." He smiled, crinkling his bright blue eyes, then adjusted the ever present blue bandana wrapped around his wide forehead. "I've gotta get home. I like to get there before my dad goes to sleep."

"How is your dad?"

"Ninety-three, half-blind, and mean as a striped snake."

"And you stay with him?"

"Oh, he's not so bad. I take care of him. He takes care of me."

Morgan dumped the container of lime and lemon slices in the trash. "You're a good man, J.D."

"No," he said softly. "I'm not worth much." He grinned at her and picked up his denim jacket. "But I'm happy."

After he left, Peach emptied the plastic tip jar onto the counter. "Why do you even talk to J.D.? He's nothing but a worn-out old hippie who still makes moonshine behind his garage and smokes anything he can get his hands on. I'd never waste my time on a loser like that."

"J.D. is a nice guy. He's a little lost. But half the people who come into this bar are lost souls."

"Listen to you. You want people to think you're tough, but inside you're a bleeding heart just like your brother. Get real, Morgan. J.D. is trailer trash."

Morgan looked at her incredulously. "You live in a trailer."

"So, what?" Peach swept a long strand of bleached hair over her broad shoulder. "I'm not gonna live in one forever. I have plans. I have dreams. J.D. will die in that airless little shack he lives in, and never know there's anything better out there. Like every other barfly who pisses away his paycheck in this dump."

"I thought you loved it here in Riverbirch. You said you always wanted to live on a farm."

Peach stopped counting one-dollar bills and glanced up. "I do. But unless you own one of these fine farms, you'll never get anywhere." She scraped a pile of coins into her hand. "Good thing I have my eye on a man who not only owns a farm, but treats me like a queen."

"Who?"

She shook her generous hips and laughed. "Well, Sean, of course." Her eyes closed halfway and unfocused dreamily. "He just hasn't realized it yet, but he's all about me. *Oh!* Guess who came into the bar this afternoon looking for you? *Denny.*"

"My ex-husband Denny?"

"I told him you didn't come in till five, and were probably still at home."

"He came by. Peach, I wish you'd called me. At least given me some warning."

"I didn't want to upset you. What did he want?" She bit her thick bottom lip. "I'd forgotten what a hunk he was. He looked good, Morgan. *Real* good."

Peach handed Morgan her share of the tips, then pulled a bottle of bourbon off the shelf. She poured a double shot and downed it, then cracked opened a beer.

Beneath the yellow bar light, her face looked puffy and sallow. And old. The amount of hard liquor she consumed on a daily basis was taking its toll.

"Andy's beginning to notice the bourbon is disappearing."

"Oh, I don't think he'll mind if I borrow a buzz. All I have to do is remind him I slept with him *after* he married Carol. He was all about me then, but Carol has always hated me. She thought I was having sex with him long before we actually did anything."

"How can you do that to another woman? How can you sleep with a married man?"

Peach shrugged. "He got me drunk and said he wanted to leave her. He said he'd heard I was the best." She grinned. "He paid my rent through June; I had to prove him right. That's why I still have a job here. That's why I'll *always* have a job here."

Morgan realized her mouth was hanging open, and closed it.

Poor, sad, delusional Peach. Did she really believe the men she latched onto gave a damn about her? Couldn't she see they were using her as badly as she used them? Her reputation was legendary. How many of these men, unless they were sober, and in strong, loving marriages, would turn her down if she came on to them? Riverbirch and Cherokee Bluff were small towns. By now, the local men knew what kind of woman she was. And after three drinks, most of them didn't care.

Peach poured herself another shot.

"Don't you think you've had enough?" Morgan chided gently. "You have to drive."

"Not for a while, Mother. I still have to make out

the schedule for next week." She fished a pack of cigarettes out of her purse. "Andy doesn't care if I smoke in the office, either. Another perk I've earned."

"I'm gonna head on home. Want me to lock up?"

"No, I'll do it." Peach pulled a bottle of cologne from her purse and spritzed some on her wrists. "Ethan said he might come by later. The two of us need to talk."

"What about?"

Peach hoisted her purse on to her shoulder. She picked up her shot glass. "I need to straighten some things out with him. For a few weeks, he was all about me, then he stopped calling. I really liked the guy. I thought we should talk it out, see where we went wrong."

"I didn't know you and Ethan were seeing each other."

Peach smiled. "Well, I guess he doesn't tell you everything, now, does he?"

Morgan crossed the empty bar and left by the back door. Was Ethan really meeting Peach tonight? Was he like some of the other men in town who trashed Peach behind her back then said yes to her the minute she invited them into her bed? Hard to tell with Ethan, though. Sometimes Morgan felt she didn't know him at all. If he *was* meeting Peach, she hoped he didn't mind paying a price. Nothing was ever free with Peach.

Halfway home, Morgan remembered she'd left her paycheck in the office. She banged her fist on the steering wheel and cursed. Of all the stupid-ass things to do. If, by some miracle, the pickers Harlan had talked to showed up, they would expect to be paid in cash. She had no choice but to turn around and go back.

She turned left into the abandoned Texaco station and made a U-turn, circling the only two pumps left standing. She braked at the road and waited for a car to pass. Her cell phone jangled to life beside her.

"Morgan here." She balanced the tiny phone between her ear and shoulder.

"Gage here." The low, familiar baritone sent a shiver skittering across her shoulders.

"Checking up on me?"

He laughed softly. "Well, I could lie and say Jeremy wanted to know why you're forty minutes late, but I'll take my chances and admit that yes, I was checking up on you."

"J.D., one of our regulars, hung around while we closed. It took forever. I just turned around on Barkerstown Road, and I'm on my way back to Bad Moon to pick up my paycheck. I can't believe I left it in the office. Hang on." She pulled on to the narrow, deserted road, then rolled the window down and breathed in the cool damp air. She switched her lights to bright and pushed the gear shift to second, then third. "Okay, I'm back."

"I wanted to say something about Jeremy and me moving into the guesthouse. I know it's the last thing you thought would happen today."

"You got that right." She glanced in the rearview mirror. "I'm still angry as hell at your uncle, but I'm willing to give you the benefit of the doubt." She didn't mention the warning bells clanging like a three-alarm fire in her head, or the voices screaming at her to run the other way.

"Good," he said. "I know having us around might seem like an intrusion. Jeremy and I discussed it, and we don't want to cramp your style."

"That would imply I have a style to cramp."

"What are you talking about? You have a lot of style."

"Oh, I'm stylish, all right. Jeans and a plaid flannel shirt, secondhand work boots, my grandpa's old straw hat. What do they call that, Early Barnyard?"

"Don't knock the farm girl dynamic. I've always had a soft spot in my heart for Mary Ann from *Gilligan's Island.*"

"Aren't you a little young for that show?"

"Reruns on cable. Every day after middle school. Mary Ann made puberty almost tolerable."

"I'm not going to ask what Ginger did for you."

He laughed. "I like this. You and me. Talking like normal people."

"I don't think normal people talk like this—oh, my God. Now, this is weird."

"What?"

"I'm turning into Bad Moon, driving around back where the employees park. All the lights are off, and Peach's car has a flat tire."

"Why is that weird?"

"Because I've only been gone fifteen minutes. Peach said she had work to do before Ethan stopped by. Maybe he got there early, and they decided to leave. I didn't notice her car had a flat before I left. You'd think Ethan would have stayed to help her change it, or called Triple-A."

Morgan switched off the ignition. She got out of the truck and climbed the rickety steps to the back door. She jiggled the doorknob. "Door's locked. That's a good sign."

"Morgan, I don't think you should be—are you by yourself?"

"Of course, I'm by myself. I'm unlocking the door. Not easy with a phone in one hand."

"Don't hang up. What are you doing now?"

"I'm walking down the back hallway. *Damn*, it's dark in here. Now, I'm reaching around the corner for the light switch. I can hear you breathing, Gage. This is starting to sound like an obscene call. Next thing I know, you'll be asking what color panties I'm wearing."

"I'm breathing hard because I don't have a good feeling about this."

"They're blue, by the way."

"Morgan, I hear something. What's that noise?"

"The door banged shut. Ah, good, the light came on. Well, that helped. One little light bulb dangling from a cord. I never realized how seedy this place looks. God, what's that?"

"What's what? Do you see something?"

"No, I smell it. What? It's smoke. I think I smell smoke. Peach's jacket is still hanging on the hook beside the door. She must still be here."

"Get out of there now!" Gage cried.

"Peach! Peach, are you in here?"

Morgan ran through the eating area, knocking tables and heavy wooden captain's chairs out of her way. She pushed open the kitchen door and flipped on the fluorescent light. The bitter stench of burning grease invaded her nostrils. She sniffed hard. "The air's beginning to fill with smoke, but I don't see a fire."

She sprinted down the hall to the office.

"Morgan!" Gage yelled. "Get out of there now! Hang up and call 911."

"I've got to find the key. If Peach is in the office, she's trapped." Morgan looked around frantically. "I don't know where the key is. Where's the key? *Where's the fucking key?"*

Then, she remembered. Andy always kept a spare under the money tray in the cash register. She ran back through the kitchen to the bar. She punched in her password, released the cash drawer, and lifted out the metal tray. Empty. Her fingers flew over the bottom of the drawer, felt in every corner. Still, nothing.

"Where is it?" she shrieked into the phone. *"Where is it?"*

She held the tray up to the light. The tiny halogen bulbs over the bar caught a quick glint of silver taped to the bottom of the tray. "Got it." She pried the key loose and ran back to the office. The acrid stench of smoke invaded her nostrils, burning them.

Wispy trails rolled from beneath the door like morning mist off a riverbank. Morgan held the phone under her chin. Her hands shook as she inserted the key into the lock. The key turned easily, and she pushed. And pushed. But the door would not budge.

"I've got the door unlocked," she cried. "But it won't open. Something's blocking it. I can't see what's in the way." She banged against the doorframe with her fist. "Peach! Are you in there? *Peach! Answer me!"*

"Morgan!" Gage yelled. "Get out of the building! I'm on my way. I'm hanging up to call 911, then I'll call you back. Just get out! *Now!"*

"The window on the door is painted. I can't see inside. The hallway is getting really smoky." Her lungs filled, and she coughed it out. "Oh, God, Gage, I think I hear her crying. She's in there. I hear her in there.

Peach! I don't know what else to do. I need both hands to do this. *Peach, where are you? Get away from the door! Move away from the door, Peach! I'm breaking the glass!"*

****

Gage's phone went silent.

He called 911, reported a fire at Bad Moon Rising, then called Morgan back. He paced the length of the guesthouse, his heart pounding, waiting for her to pick up. "Come on. Come *on.*" When her cell went to voicemail, he snapped his phone closed. He grabbed Jeremy's jacket off a nail and banged on the bedroom door. "Come on, son, we need to go. Morgan's in trouble."

Jeremy opened the door and stared at Gage, wide-eyed. "Seriously?"

"Seriously. Get in the car."

Gage sped down Milltown Road then turned onto Barkerstown, taking the treacherous hairpin turns as fast as he dared with a child in the car. Somewhere between making sure Jeremy was buckled in and starting the engine, he had switched to automatic, emptying his mind, concentrating on the crisis at hand, planning his next move. He had done it for so many years, it was second nature. It was also the only way he could hold the fear at bay without conjuring every worst-case scenario he could think of.

"Go faster, Dad," Jeremy said quietly. "I'm not scared."

He pulled into Bad Moon's parking lot, rumbling over the mud ruts and gravel, braking too fast and jolting the souped-up Mustang to a halt. A tall, thin man stood beside a dark blue sedan, staring at the front of the building.

"Stay here," he said to Jeremy. "Lock the doors and do not move." He got out, and for the second time that day, reached for his non-existent gun. He approached the man slowly. "Sir?"

The man turned around. He held a cell phone in his hand. "I just got here. I was getting ready to call for help."

"I've already called." Gage ran to the front door and jiggled the knob. "It's locked." He pushed hard against it with his hands, shoved it with his shoulder. "It feels like a wooden bar may be blocking it. You've got to help me break it down. Morgan Maguire is inside."

The man stared at him, then shook his head as if suddenly awakened from a fog. *"What did you say?"*

Gage kicked the wooden door frame. "Don't just stand there. Help me!"

The man thrust his foot at the door. One-two-three *kick*, like a boxer practicing his moves. The side of the pine frame splintered, but the thick door remained impenetrable.

"I thought Morgan went home," the man said, huffing out air. "I—I was supposed to meet Peach. Are you sure Morgan is in there?"

"She forgot something." *Kick.* "And had to—" *Kick.* "—come back for it." Gage stopped. His foot throbbed. The muscles in his thighs burned with exhaustion. But he'd be damned if he was going to bend over and hold them like the man standing next to him. He swallowed air then looked at the road. Panic clutched his throat. *"Where the hell is the fire truck? It should be here by now!"*

"I—I don't know." The man stood wringing his

hands. "I don't know what to do."

"Jesus." Gage pushed the man out of the way and picked up an aluminum bucket filled with sand and cigarette butts. He swung the bucket back.

"Are you going to throw a bucket at the door?"

"Do you have a better idea?"

The man shook his head.

Gage swung the bucket back like a discus and prepared to hurl it toward the wide door. He used the painted blue and white full moon logo as his target.

The front door crashed open. Plumes of gray smoke streamed into the night.

"Morgan!" the man beside him cried.

"Ethan! Gage! Help me!"

Gage threw the bucket on the ground and rushed past Ethan. Morgan held onto Peach, half dragging her across the threshold. Both of her arms wrapped around Peach's thick waist. Peach groaned loudly as they stumbled out the door.

"Morgan!" Jeremy was suddenly beside them. "Are you okay? Dad, is she okay? Her arm is bleeding."

Gage pulled Peach from Morgan's arms and helped her to a picnic table in the grassy area at the side.

The high-pitched whine of a siren wailed in the distance, louder and louder, until the bright swirl of red flashing lights appeared at the end of the road.

The next few minutes were a jumbled blur. Firemen in heavy black coats stormed the low slung building, carrying hoses the size of pythons. Two paramedics hovered over Peach. Morgan sat on the EMT truck's running board beside Jeremy, holding an oxygen mask to her face. She winced as she lifted her bandaged arm and slid it around Jeremy's shoulder. A slash of soot streaked across the right side of her face. Her jeans were shredded below the knees and spotted with fresh blood.

She looked up at Gage. Their gazes locked.

For one exquisite moment, the clamor of the firemen, the bitter stench of smoke, the red lights cutting across the black night sky—everything—all fell away. She smiled and waved her hand. His heart constricted with relief. She looked down and grinned at Jeremy, gently thumping the bill of his baseball hat to reassure him again she was all right. The kid wouldn't let her out of his sight. And Gage knew how he felt. The adrenaline that had pulsed through his veins like ice water the second he realized she was in trouble, and too far away for him to save, had only begun to subside. Whatever made him think an adrenaline rush was fun? Jesus. He never wanted to feel that wave of sheer helplessness again. Just thinking about it made him want to lean his head against a light pole and cry.

Morgan's friend Ethan stood beside Peach's cot with his hands shoved into his jacket pockets. He hadn't glanced down once at the woman splayed out on a stretcher, fighting her way back from respiratory distress. His tranquil gaze was riveted on Morgan's face. It never wavered. But the desperation in his eyes told the whole story.

Gage slowly shook his head. *He loves her. The poor sap is in love with her.*

So he and the Hamster weren't so different after all. In the relationship department, Ethan Spannagel wasn't any better or worse than the poor sap standing beside the EMS truck, keeping his distance, watching the woman who still owned his heart comfort his son.

Chapter 9

"I think you ought to call your step-grandmother," Gage said. "I know you don't like her, but she has a right to hear news like this from you." He tucked the chenille blanket around Morgan's legs, switched on the tiny shoji lamp beside her bed, and turned off the overhead light. Diffused blue light glimmered through the thin rice paper, caressing the angles of his rugged face. He'd claimed he wasn't tired, but the deeply etched lines at the corners of his eyes and the rigid tension around his mouth gave him away.

"It's too late. I'll tell her about the fire tomorrow. But I'll downplay my part in it. She doesn't need to know the grisly details."

"I'm not sure I know them." He stuffed another pillow behind her head.

"I'm fine. Stop fussing."

She pulled the covers up around her neck and shivered. "The sheriff said it looked like the filing cabinet had been rigged to fall in front of the door. Oily rags had been stuffed inside the trashcan beside the desk. Peach always smoked while she worked. She must have lit a cigarette and been thrown back when the rags exploded. One of the firemen said it was a miracle she wasn't killed."

"You'd think she would have smelled the oil."

"The whole kitchen smells like old grease. Peach probably didn't even notice."

"I can't believe you got her out."

"It wasn't easy. She isn't exactly petite." Morgan shivered again. "I ca-can't seem to get warm."

"You're still in shock." He picked up the crocheted afghan from the rocking chair and spread it on top of her.

"H-how's Jeremy?"

"Out like a light. I put him in Sean's room. I hope that's okay."

"Of course, that's okay." She leaned over and reached for the juice glass of brandy he had poured for her. The dark liquid burned a path down her throat.

"I still don't understand who would want to hurt Peach," he said. "She's a single parent. Could there be an ex-husband somewhere still holding a grudge? There seems to be a lot of that going around these days."

"Peach's ex lives in Cherokee Bluff with her two sons. She complains about him, but I think they're friendly."

Gage shook his head. "Then I don't know. It does seem like she was the intended target."

Morgan pulled her knees up, willing them to shop shaking. "It's crazy."

"Jeremy said he saw the guy who was looking in your window. What's his name—Ethan? He's a strange one, isn't he?"

"He's Ethan. I walked in on him and Peach arguing at his store today. Now, there's a story I'd like to hear. But they both clammed up."

"I got the impression she was after Sean. Romantically speaking."

"Peach is after any man who'll look at her twice. She has definite skank tendencies. I used to think Sean liked her, because he can be a terrible judge of character. But I'm sure now that he doesn't want her."

"Does Peach know that?"

"No. But I'm telling her when I stop by the hospital in the morning. They admitted her overnight for observation." She shivered again and handed him the brandy. "I can't stop shaking. You'd better take this unless you want to wear it."

He downed the rest of it then set the glass on the nightstand. He kicked off his athletic shoes and stood by the bed. "Scoot over. The only thing that will warm you is body heat."

She laughed. "I've heard that one before."

"I get the feeling you still don't trust me."

"I don't. But I'm really, *really* cold."

He peeled off his socks. "Just don't laugh at my feet. My toes look like they could swing me from tree to tree."

She moved to the middle of the double bed and watched as he smoothed the layers of blankets next to her and lay on top of them. He stuffed the lace covered sham pillow behind his head then gently pulled her toward him, shifting to the side so she could fit comfortably beside his hip.

She nestled into the crook of his shoulder and curled her arm across his chest. The world drifted out to sea and back. His steady heartbeat thudded against her cheek. His arms held her tight, surrounding her with the kind of bone melting warmth she'd forgotten existed. For the first time since she'd stumbled out of Bad Moon's door with Peach, she stopped shaking. She closed her eyes and breathed in his scent, spicy with a trace of sweetness that made her want to bury her face in the soft folds of his shirt. How could he smell so good after the day he'd spent? Moving Jeremy out of the winery? Fighting Finch? Handling Denny? Steadying her nerves on the phone like he was talking a jumper off a ledge? Then racing across the treacherous back roads at the foot of Blackstone Mountain to save her?

His chest rose and fell. She found herself matching the rhythm of each breath with her own. Her limbs turned to liquid. Her breasts betrayed her, and ached for him to touch them. This was the last thing in the world she should be doing. And the last person she should be doing it with. But she didn't care. Tonight, it was all she wanted. Maybe all she had ever wanted. She snuggled against him and tried not to think. If she turned off her brain, it could work. The nearness of him would block out every painful memory she could summon, every doubt she'd ever had. Lying with Gage Kirkland could systematically obliterate everything except the pocket of heat smoldering at the small of her back.

Why shouldn't she give in to it? He was there. In her bed. And as surreal as that felt, she knew better than to question a dream coming true, no matter how old and self serving it was.

He moved his fingers idly up and down her arm, leaving a trail of white-hot sensation in their wake. She shuddered and opened her eyes. His gaze was waiting for her to find his, and he smiled, deepening the dimple on the left side of his face.

"You look like you want to say something," he said.

"Thank you for tonight. On the phone, hearing your voice. Well, it got me through."

"Lady, I keep trying to rescue you, but you won't wait for me."

"I think they call that irony, don't they?" She laughed softly. "All those years ago, all I wanted was for you to rescue me. And now, you can't seem to stop doing it."

"Everything in its own time, I guess." He propped up on one elbow. The shadow from the shoji lamp moved across his face. "I used to say I believe things happen when they're supposed to. It kept me sane, helped me cope with disappointment." He lifted a stray curl and gently smoothed it back from her face. "But I don't think I really believed it until now."

"So, you're a PI *and* a philosopher?"

"No matter what happened—what we did, what we didn't do—it's all lead up to this moment. I've spent years thinking our time had come and gone. But I was wrong. Our time is here. It's now. And even though you don't believe it, or even want to believe it, I—"

She covered his lips with hers.

Her brain emptied like a spinning vortex. Every sensible thought she'd ever had flew out of her head, one by one, like demons unable to hold on to a revolving wheel.

Morgan had always prided herself on being cautious, the no-nonsense girl whose feathers few people could ruffle. But this man brought out something exotic in her. Something that fueled a streak of sexual desire that eclipsed her better judgment and caused her not to give a damn what she did, as long as she did it with him.

His hands stroked the contour of her cheeks. She moved her lips against his, sending her heartbeat into overdrive. Her tongue found his, and for a moment, she thought she was going to levitate. As the kiss deepened, he slid his fingers around the nape of her neck, then threaded them through the mass of thick curls suddenly loose from their clasp and cascading around her shoulders. "Very smooth," she murmured. "Where'd you learn to do that?"

"In my head. If you fantasize about something long enough, it becomes second nature."

His lips found hers again and again, teasing them, exploring them, claiming them with a hunger that took her breath away. She rubbed her cheek against the soft stubble along his jaw and moaned. "I'm not usually a moaner," she said, and moaned again. "But it's been a while. A really long while, and—*oh*, God, that feels good." She leaned her head back and laughed. "This is definitely taking the edge off the last two days."

"Maybe we shouldn't—"

"Don't start channeling the voice of reason now." She raked her mouth along the underside of his chin. "Later. Be reasonable later."

"But a lot has happened. Later, you might regret this, and—"

"I'm going to keep interrupting until you hush."

"You're feeling vulnerable right now, and—"

"Time to regroup." She pushed herself up, flung the covers back, and crossed her legs in a half-lotus. She pulled him to a sitting position, facing her. "Sometimes it's better with your head off the pillow and your eyes wide open. Keeps you from getting woozy and sentimental."

"I never could resist a woman in red flannel shorts."

"They're cranberry."

"Cranberry," he drawled. "I knew that."

He skimmed his lips inside the scooped neckline of her cotton t-shirt, then slowly trailed kisses along the column of her neck. Each one sent a shudder racing down her spine, across her abdomen, inside her thighs. She held onto his broad shoulders and arched her back as his lips traced a lazy path along her throat, hitting every nerve ending she possessed. Maybe sitting up hadn't been such a great idea. Two more minutes, and she would be reduced to a puddle in the middle of her great-grandmother's sleigh bed.

"Is this hurting your arm?" he asked.

"I don't feel anything." She kissed him. "And everything."

"Baby, are you sure you—"

"Stop overthinking this." She unbuttoned his cotton shirt and pulled it apart, then kissed the tiny indentation at the base of his throat, nuzzling the soft patch of dark hair curling against the collar. Her lips stopped at a circle of knotted flesh above his collarbone. "What's this?"

"A scar."

She ran her lips along the ridge. "This is one hell of a scar. How'd you get it? Bobcat bite?"

"Gunshot."

"Mom! *Mom!*"

Gage let go of her and bounded off the bed. In seconds, he was out the door and down the hall.

"Mom!" Jeremy shrieked. *"Mom! No!"*

"I'm here, son. Wake up, Jeremy. I'm right here."

Morgan pulled on her robe and stood in the doorway, listening.

"I want my Mom," Jeremy whimpered. "I want her here."

"I know you do," Gage said.

"I tried to stop her, but she wouldn't listen."

"You were dreaming," Gage said gently. "It was only a dream."

"She was mad I wouldn't give her the keys. Then she grabbed them out of my hands. I wanted you to stop her. You saw her. Why didn't you stop her?"

"I tried to, son. But I thought you needed me more."

"I started yelling, but you came to see what was wrong with me instead of going after her. It's my fault. It's my fault you came into my room instead of getting the keys from her."

"*Shhhh,*" Gage said. "It's not anybody's fault. Your mom wasn't herself that night. She hadn't been herself for a long, long time. Nothing she did could have ever been your fault."

Morgan quietly closed the door. She had already listened far too long. The words between Gage and his son were private, but the little she'd heard made her heart ache for both of them. Jeremy had been saddled with the kind of guilt no child should ever have to carry. She didn't have the power or the wisdom to ease his pain—nothing could do that—but there was one thing she could do for the kid. She could let him know he wasn't alone.

****

Gage rolled over and realized the fingers curled around Jeremy's arm were numb. He also realized the reason he had awakened so abruptly had nothing to do with the bright sunlight streaming through the windows. His cell phone was ringing.

He fished it out of his pants pocket and eased himself off the bed. Then he unlocked the phone with his thumb, staggered into the hall, and pulled the door closed behind him. He looked at the name on the screen. "Shit," he whispered, his low baritone cracking. He cleared his throat and said, "Morning, boss."

"So, you're alive," Tyson said. "I was beginning to wonder."

"Hold on." Gage hurried past Morgan's closed bedroom door and went downstairs. He snaked his way through the living room and dining room, then let himself out the back door. Cold from the concrete stoop seeped into the soles of his bare feet. "Okay, Tyson. Shoot."

"What's up? Did you get the flag?"

"Not yet."

"Then what the hell are you waiting for? Does she have it or not?"

"She has it."

"So, what's the holdup? Is she on to you?"

"No, but there have been…extenuating circumstances."

"Christ, Gage. Speak English."

"Something funny's going on. Last night, the bar she works at caught fire. The day before, she found a dead body on a neighbor's farm. Then Quillen's son showed up and threatened her if she didn't give *him* the flag. And her brother's in jail because—"

"I don't give a rat's ass where her brother is. Or if she even has a brother. Just get the godammed job done or I'll find someone who can. I gave you this job as a favor."

"Bullshit. You gave me this job because it's six miles from where I'm living, and you don't have to pay travel expenses."

"Listen Gage, I can't sit around waiting for the full moon. This thing isn't open-ended. I have a client breathing down my neck. If you can't come through for me, he'll take his business elsewhere."

"I know, I know."

Gage rubbed his forehead and stared at the beds of purple asters on either side of the guesthouse. A wide slash of early morning sun fell across the backyard. The sharp scent of fresh mulch and fertilizer jabbed at his nose.

What the hell was he going to do? He couldn't take the flag from Morgan, but if he didn't find it and deliver it to its rightful owner, Tyson would send some punk who would. Either way, Morgan was in trouble. He had to find out where the flag was hidden. For her sake, he hoped it wasn't in the house.

Should he talk to her? Confess he'd shown up with a hidden agenda the size of Montana? She didn't trust him. Or any man, as far as he could tell. But she seemed to be trying. The night before had been incredible—holding her, touching her. More than he'd had a right to ever hope for. If she found out he'd lied to her, she would never trust him again. Not that she was going to anyway.

The sound of a car door slamming brought him scrambling to his feet. He edged to the corner of the house just in time to see Morgan unlatching the gate.

"Gage?" Tyson said. "You there?"

He couldn't risk telling her. And he couldn't take the flag. The best he could do was buy himself more time until he had a plan. He sat on the steps. "Tyson, man, please. Give me two more days—until Monday. By then, I should—"

"Tomorrow. I'll give you until tomorrow. But I'm putting the word out that a job paying big bucks just opened up. Some of these guys are champing at the bit to make some fast cash."

"I understand. But if I can't—" The screen door hinge screeched behind him. "Gotta go."

Morgan stuck her head out. "Everything okay?"

"Yeah," Gage said, closing his phone. "My old boss called. He hadn't heard from me in a while, and he wondered how I was doing. I came out here because I didn't want to wake you."

"I've been up for hours. I went to the hospital to see Peach, then stopped by the grocery store. I hope you like eggs. It's one of the four things I know how to cook."

"Eggs will work."

She sat beside him on the stoop. Why did women always look so damned appealing when they weren't trying to? Her oversized white shirt—probably her brother's—fell open at the neck, revealing enough creamy cleavage to drive him back into her arms. Her faded jeans hugged her curves in all the right places. She'd harnessed her long hair into a high ponytail, and smelled of some kind of scented soap that made him lightheaded. And that neck. That long silky neck. It was all he could do to keep from leaning over and pressing his lips against it, then letting them trail down it, lazy and slow. It had turned her on the night before. Big time. Sent shivers of excitement pulsing through her, then through him. Knowing he was capable of giving her that kind of pleasure had tripled his own.

"So, how are you doing?" she asked.

"Not bad." He smiled at her. "It was a long night. Thanks for letting us bunk inside."

"I wouldn't have wanted to stay in the house alone. Not after the fire."

He glanced at her tiny bandaged wrist. "How's your arm?"

"Not bad."

"Oh, I see how this is going," he said, laughing. "How's Peach?"

Morgan wrapped her arms around her knees. "Something's going on with her. We've never been close, but she seemed guarded. Peach is a bucket mouth. She'll tell anybody anything, whether it's true or not. She didn't even ask about Sean, and two days ago she was planning to quit her job and move in here to help him run the orchard."

"Maybe she's found someone else. You said her turnover time was faster than a bell clapper in a goose's ass."

She looked at him sideways. "I don't even know what that means."

"Me, either."

"Anyway, I was standing by the elevator, waiting to leave, and I heard one of the nurses say, 'I sure am glad the man visiting Peach Davison is gone. He made me nervous.' Then, she described Denny. Exactly. Down to the corduroy house shoes. It had to have been Denny. How many guys in Riverbirch look like forty-year-old drug addicts in corduroy slippers?"

"Why would your ex-husband go see Peach? Do they know each other?"

"Just from the bar, I think. The thing is, I went back to Peach's room to ask her if Denny had been there, and she was gone."

"What do you mean gone?"

"Gone, vanished, not there. Her hospital gown was lying on the bed, and her closet was empty."

He thought for a minute. "Let me see what I can find out. I do have some skills in that area."

She smiled. "And other areas."

"I wish I could get hold of her cell phone. Those things can be enlightening"

"Oh. Oh, my God. I have Harlan's phone. I put it in my pocket after I found him, and it's still there. I meant to take it to Sheriff Stallard yesterday, but I was so upset about Sean, I forgot."

"Mind if I look at it?"

"Dad?" Jeremy stood behind them, peering through the screen. "I'm hungry."

Gage laughed. "You're always hungry. I'll check out the phone after breakfast."

"Guess the Maguire Diner is open for business," Morgan said. "Eggs or waffles, kid?"

"Both."

"Let me make them," Gage said. "If you don't mind me cooking."

"I would welcome your cooking," Morgan said. "I would welcome anybody's cooking."

Morgan made coffee, then sat on a kitchen stool while Gage and Jeremy fixed breakfast. The mood was unexpectedly light, and Morgan wondered if Jeremy and Gage's talk the night before had cleared the air.

Their easy banter seemed natural and spontaneous. The look of relief that kept crossing Gage's face whenever he looked at his son touched her heart. Between the laughter and the new-found circle of warmth that enveloped the three of them at the sun-drenched table, no one seemed to mind that the waffles were a little soggy and the eggs a trifle overcooked.

After breakfast, Morgan gave Harlan's phone to Gage.

"Are you going to see Sean today?" he asked.

"They said I could come at two. They still haven't charged him with anything. How long they can hold him without charging him?"

"Not sure," Gage said. "It varies from state to state. I have a call in to a lawyer I know in Atlanta. His secretary said he'd get back to me."

"Thanks," Morgan said. She turned to Jeremy. "Aren't you late for school?"

"It's Saturday," Jeremy said.

"You're right," Morgan said. "Hey, I need to stretch my legs. You want to take a walk with me while your father looks around our sad little bankrupt farm?"

"Sure." Jeremy's face broke into a wide grin. "I'll get my shoes." He slid across the polished dining room floor in his sock feet, then raced upstairs.

"That's some kid you've got there." The rasp in her voice deepened.

He reached out and took her hand. "I'm not going to let anything happen to you."

She nodded.

"If you don't mind, I'd like to look at the books, too."

"Sure. According to Sean, there are two sets—one

in the red, and one in the black. No pun intended. The printouts were on the desk beside Harlan's computer the day he died."

"Interesting."

"I think so, too. Sean's computer is in the office. The password is *apple42*."

"Forty-two apples in a bottle of apple wine?"

"Forty-two pounds in a bushel. I'll be back in five. I need to run upstairs and put on my face."

"The one you keep in a jar by the door?" The grin spreading across his face was identical to his son's.

"No. The one that keeps me from frightening small children and animals."

She started for the door, and he reached for her. He slid his fingers down her arm to her hand, clasped it in his, and wrapped it around his waist, pulling her close. His lips were inches from hers. "I think your face is perfect the way it is."

"Spoken like a true face connoisseur."

He nuzzled the spot between her shoulder and her neck. "Are you regretting last night?"

"Of course not. There's nothing I like better than a good old-fashioned case of arson. And wrapping dishtowels around my hands to break glass is a skill I don't get to use often enough."

He chuckled. "I mean us. You and me."

"We didn't do anything."

"We did enough. Enough for me to realize you're still the smartest, sexiest, most beautiful woman I've ever met."

"Well, that beats pleasant and polite, I guess."

"You're anything but polite."

She caught her breath as he grazed his lips against

the slope of her jaw. "I don't know what you're talking about. Didn't you hear me say 'thanks'?"

His laughter, sexy and low, rumbled in her hear. Warm breath drifted across her neck, sending a shaft of need rushing to her solar plexus. Her hands slid around his neck. She rubbed the side of her chin against his and breathed in the heady scent of his skin. She ran her fingers along the curved neckline of his white T-shirt, then bunched the soft cotton into her fist and held it tight.

Gage glanced at her beneath half-closed lids. His lashes, black, and longer than hers, swept against the lean angle of his cheek. The memory of his mouth moving against hers the night before hadn't been out of her head since she'd opened her eyes that morning. So when his lips found hers, she tried to prepare herself for the tremors of pure sensation that would soon be rocketing down her spine.

His tongue slid against hers. The bones in her legs began to dissolve. He let go of her hand and wrapped his arm around her shoulders, pressing her against him, deepening their kiss. Her mind coasted along, soaring down a mountain somewhere with the wind tearing through her hair and the sun hot against her face. She held on to the back of his neck and his T-shirt as if they were anchors keeping her rooted to the earth.

"I can't find my shoes," Jeremy called from upstairs.

Morgan stepped back and laughed. "Look in the bathroom," she yelled.

"Come back here," Gage said, pulling her to him. "I don't want to let you go yet. Maybe not ever."

"Things are zipping along a little too fast." She

traced the outline of his collarbone with her fingertips. "There's still a lot we don't know about the people we are now. Like this scar you don't want to talk about. How'd you get it? And if you say from a gun, I will brain you with a waffle."

He absently rubbed the scar with his right hand. "I misjudged a situation because I was in a hurry, and hadn't done my homework. It's always the easy cases, the ones where you let your guard down, that screw you over. I'd been following a man whose wife thought he was cheating on him, something I'd done a hundred times. I was leaning over the edge of a hotel balcony, trying to get a clear shot with the camera, and he looked up and saw me. He didn't care if I'd caught him with another woman, but he sure as hell wasn't about to let me photograph the four-hundred G's worth of crystal meth spread across his king-size bed. He pulled out a gun and shot me before I could focus my eyes, much less the camera. The bullet hit two inches from my heart. The last image I saw before the world turned black was my son's face."

"So you quit your job."

"No. I healed up, and went back to work. I only quit after Suzanne died. It wasn't a hard decision. Jeremy needed me. When I told him I wasn't going to work for the agency anymore, he said, 'I don't care what you do.' But as he was turning around, he couldn't hide the look of relief on his face, and I knew I'd done the right thing."

His dark green eyes held hers. A sudden flash of regret was replaced almost immediately by cold determination, a look he'd probably practiced for Jeremy's sake to hide the fact that giving up the job he loved was one of the hardest things he'd ever had to do.

Gunshot wound or not, Gage Kirkland's passion was going after the bad guys.

For years, she'd wondered what his life was like, if he was happy, if he had a family, if he had followed his bliss and was living quietly, practicing medicine somewhere in a Georgia hospital, charming nurses and patients alike. It had never occurred to her he would choose a life living on the edge, where dodging bullets and bringing dangerous criminals to justice were part of his everyday routine. Replacing the image of him she'd carried in her head with the real one was mind boggling. But she had to admit, that this side of Gage, a side she could never have imagined existed, seemed thrilling to her. It was like falling in love with Clark Kent one day and discovering twelve years later he was Superman.

Chapter 10

Morgan found Jeremy slouching in the front porch swing, reading. The kid always seemed to be reading. "Are you ready? I want to show you something seriously cool."

"What is it?"

"A secret place."

"It's not a garden, is it? That movie sucked."

"It's bigger than a garden." She pointed to the hill behind the barn. "That's called Pip's Hill, but for slovenly, out-of-shape people like me, it's a mountain. Are you up for it?"

He didn't hesitate. "Sure. We can always roll back down if it gets too strenuous."

Morgan laughed. "I like the way you think, kid. And you're the only eleven-year-old I know who can use the word *strenuous* in a sentence."

"I read a lot."

"I talk a lot."

They walked behind the barn, then hiked to the top and cut across the ridge to the woods.

"Jeez!" Jeremy said when they stopped to rest. "Is everything around here on a friggin' mountain?"

"Haven't you heard of the hills of Tennessee? Well, you just walked up one." She pulled a bottle of water out of her jacket pocket and handed it to him. "Here.

Save half for me."

"I'm a kid, remember? I should get more than half."

"You're not a kid. You're a con artist."

They followed the path through the dense hardwood forest until they came to a section of trees covered with kudzu vine. It dripped from the branches, wound around the trunks like green ribbon snakes, smothered the unlucky ones like dark, leafy shrouds. The air smelled mossy and damp. Shafts of golden sunlight cut through the green canopy, illuminating the tamped down dirt and grass. For a while, the only sounds they heard were the crunch of brittle sticks beneath their feet and the distant solitary cry of a bird.

Morgan cleared her throat. "Jeremy, you remember when I told you my parents died?"

"Yeah."

"Their car was hit by a sweet little old man who had gotten confused and didn't realize he was driving on the wrong side of the road. He didn't mean to kill them. It just happened." Jeremy thrashed through a tall patch of weeds. "All I'm saying is that sometimes things happen, things we don't have any control over."

Jeremy picked up a stick and knocked it against a stump. He squinted at the treetops. "Didn't it make you mad?"

"Sure. For a long time. But one day, when I was missing them so much, I could barely speak, I remembered something my mom had given me."

"What?"

"She loved quotes. She taped them on the fridge, left them on my pillow, put them in library books for others to find. This one was from Gandhi. Do you know who Gandhi was?"

"Another movie that sucked?"

"Gandhi was a wise man who said, 'There are no goodbyes for us. Wherever you are, you will always be in my heart.'"

Jeremy turned to her. His eyes filled with tears. "I didn't get to say goodbye to my mom. I don't even know where she is. They wouldn't let me go to the funeral."

"Oh, sweetie," Morgan said.

"Can you find out where she is? Can you ask my dad or something? I don't talk to him about her."

"Not talking about something doesn't make it go away."

He blinked up at her. "You sound like my therapist."

Morgan playfully bonked him on the head. "I'm going to take that as a compliment. Unless she looks like Sigmund Freud in drag."

"Who?"

"Never mind." The forest had opened into a small, flat meadow. "See those trees?" Morgan pointed to a row of ancient chestnuts growing in a straight line along the upper edge. "We're going to count down five trees, and turn left."

Jeremy counted as they walked. After the turn, she said, "Now, look back where we came." She placed her hands on his thin shoulders. "See the huge knothole at the top of the fifth tree? If you ever come here and get lost, use that as a marker to lead you out."

"Where's the secret place?"

"Behind that big rock. But be careful. I've always heard there are sinkholes and caves down there, but

Sean and I could never locate them." She looked at the vine covered trees. "I don't think I've ever seen so much kudzu. It loves it here."

"Kudzu loves it everywhere," Jeremy said. "It's all over Georgia, too. I read that it came from Japan, and the government got farmers to plant it to stop soil erosion. Then it took over."

"Like green wildfire."

"It's cool, though. The trees look like giant alien families. Aliens who live in the ocean. The arms grow down like seaweed, then sway in the wind." He pointed behind him. "See, the biggest one is the dad. And the mom's beside him. The little trees are the kids, I guess."

"Or maybe they're alien soldiers getting ready to attack."

"Or maybe they used to be ordinary people like us—"

"—until they danced around the forest one night during a full moon, and got beamed aboard the Giant Alien Kudzu Ship."

Jeremy laughed. "You're weirder than me, Morgan."

"We're here." She stopped. "Do you see anything? Take your time. Look around."

Jeremy turned completely around, craning his neck. "Nope."

"Follow me." Morgan waded through the thick underbrush. She climbed around a large rock and stood beside a mound of kudzu slightly shorter than her head. Then she leaned down, put her hand through a thick web of vines, and pulled. A door opened.

"It's a car!" Jeremy squealed. "A car's hidden

under there! Are we the only ones who know about it?"

"I'm sure someone else knows. It would be easy to see in winter. Kudzu turns brown and dies after the first hard frost. Want to climb inside? You're not afraid of spiders, are you?"

Jeremy grinned and shook his head no. The elated expression on his face warmed her heart, a heart that had long ago hung up a "Closed for Business" sign where children were concerned. This must be what Gage had talked about missing with his son. This is what he'd been grieving for. It would take time for Jeremy to trust that his world was secure again, but she could already see a change in him.

The kid had been forced to grow up too soon, covering for a mentally ill mother who used him as an instrument of revenge against her ex-husband. If Jeremy had been Morgan's son—and, oh, God, she wished he had been—she would have done everything humanly possible to safeguard his innocence. She would have put him first, protected him at all costs, loved him more than— She stopped and put her hand on her heart. The old familiar pain raked across it like broken glass, stabbing it until she couldn't take a breath.

What was she thinking? She'd had a child growing inside her. Gage's child.

And she hadn't been able to protect it at all.

Jeremy crawled into the abandoned Ford Fairlane. He clambered over the split upholstered seat, then cleared away a trailing cluster of vines until he could scoot beneath the steering wheel.

Another wide grin spread across his face. "You're right, Morgan. This is seriously cool."

****

Gage stood in the middle of Morgan's dining room, gazing from one end to the other. *Where the hell could it be?* He had searched everywhere, and one thing was clear—he had lost his edge. There was a time when he would have been in and out, recovered object in hand, in a matter of minutes. But his instincts had officially become defunct. Old houses were full of hiding places. A flag could be rolled up or folded. It could be anywhere. He closed his eyes and tried to channel Morgan. If he could think like her, maybe he could figure out where she'd stashed the thing.

He slipped Harlan's cell phone in his back pocket and tromped upstairs again to her bedroom. Women liked to keep the things they treasured near them. He stood in the doorway. His gaze flicked across her now familiar belongings—from the calico skirted dressing table to the colored glass bottles lining the window sill to the collection of dulcimers hanging on the pale blue wall. She was everywhere. He could feel her watching him, sensing he was violating her trust.

Traces of her perfume—the sweet, soapy, vanilla-spice thing that drove him to distraction—wafted through the air. He glanced at the unmade bed. Images from the night before flooded his brain—Morgan's eyes, half-closed with desire, her soft hands roaming across his back, setting his nerve endings on fire, her sweet lips seeking his with a hunger that matched his own. Christ, he'd wanted her more than he'd ever wanted anyone. He'd never stopped wanting her, or wishing he could make love to her again. Last night, on that sweet-smelling tumble of sheets, his wish had almost come true.

"*Enough*," he said, shaking his head. "Focus, dammit."

He opened her drawers for the second time, one by one, running his hands around the perimeters, feeling for false backs. He forced himself to stay detached and not let his gaze linger any longer than it had to on her things. He propelled it along, skimming over her books, the neatly folded clothes, the framed photographs of her family forever locked in her young embrace. He rummaged through her closet, moving things aside, putting them back, careful to leave no trace anyone had been there.

Tyson always said Gage had been born with the gift of ransacking someone's property without leaving footprints. Not exactly something to make your parents proud, but he had no parents. Never had, really. His mother died of a stroke giving birth to him. After that, his father had wasted away grieving for her, then spent years drifting from one failed business venture to another until a swift and deadly bout of pancreatic cancer took him out in a week.

Gage lifted the flowered dust ruffle and peered under the bed. Not even a respectable collection of dust bunnies. He glanced at the clock on the bedside table. Morgan and Jeremy had been gone for almost two hours. They would be back soon. He was running out of time.

He opened the bedside table drawer and inspected it thoroughly. "Bingo," he whispered, withdrawing the tiny crowbar like a miniature sword. He glanced around the room, then scooted her rocking chair aside, and flipped the rug back. He ran his hands over the polished wood floor. Not a mark on it. Oh, she was good. Better

171

than she knew, in fact.

He inspected the grooves between the wooden slats with his index finger, slowly and methodically, until a sharp ridge scraped against his fingertip pad. He inserted the crowbar and carefully pried up a small section of attached floorboard pieces. He lifted out the Lucite box, opened it, and rubbed his hand against the rough cotton flag. He wanted to unfold it, see what all the fuss was about. But he had no time to waste. He returned the box to its hiding place, smoothed out the rug, and replaced the rocker.

He would talk to her this evening after Jeremy was in bed. Tell her to get the flag out of the house before someone came looking for it. If she became suspicious, and asked him straight-out why moving the flag was so all fired important, he would have to come clean with her. It was the only way he could protect her.

The front doorbell jangled above him.

He went downstairs and flung the door open. Ethan Spannagel's hand, poised to knock, froze in midair. Ethan's gaze traveled from Gage's unbuttoned shirt to his bare feet.

"Hello," Gage said, enjoying the shocked look on the man's face. He didn't like Ethan Spannagel, and he didn't know why. Jealousy, maybe. Ethan and Morgan seemed to have a special bond that went way back. He crossed his arms over his chest like Mr. Clean, then reconsidered trying to intimidate the guy and held his hand out. "I'm Gage Kirkland. I don't think we've officially met. Thanks for helping me get Morgan and Peach away from the fire last night."

"Is Morgan—"

"Not here."

"But you are."

"My son Jeremy and I are staying in the guesthouse."

Ethan's eyes narrowed. "Last time I looked, it was behind the main house, not in it."

Gage shrugged. "Well, the soaking tub is in here."

"Where's Morgan?"

"She's with Jeremy. They walked up Pip's Hill. Do you want to wait?"

"No, thanks." Ethan shoved his hands in his pockets, but made no move to go. "You know, this is a small town. People like to talk. You might want to think about that the next time you show up at Morgan's front door half-dressed."

"You're right. Next time, I'll put my shoes on."

"Or you could stay somewhere else."

"I could." Gage shifted his weight to the other foot. "But I'm not."

"Morgan and I have known each other since grade school."

"She told me," Gage said. "What's it like growing up with a slaughterhouse in your backyard?"

"I'm a vegetarian."

"Umm. Well." Gage nodded. "I...uh...heard about your father. I'm sorry. Is there anything I can do?"

"Do?" He looked at Gage incredulously. "What would you do?"

"Maybe help find the person who killed him?"

"What I think you should do is stay away from Morgan." Ethan squinted.

"Yeah, well. I don't always do what people tell me to." He smiled brightly. "Are you sure you won't wait?"

Ethan glared at him.

"I guess not. Well, have a nice day." Ethan shot him one last look with his pale, watery eyes then shuffled off the porch. Gage waited until Ethan cleared the end of the walk before going back inside. He stood behind the lace curtain and watched Ethan lumber down the drive. "She'll never love you," he whispered. "And I'll never deserve her."

Chapter 11

At first Morgan thought she'd imagined it. The faint crackle of breaking twigs, the swoosh of air too close to identify. But as she and Jeremy made their way through the forest, it was clear something was tracking them.

They lapsed into an uneasy silence, matching their gait as they tramped along the path. Jeremy hadn't said much, and Morgan wondered if he realized they weren't the only ones walking through the dense woods. She dropped back and glanced at her watch. They'd been gone two hours. Longer than she'd anticipated, but hardly long enough to cause Gage worry.

Another *crack*. This time followed by the soft rustling of leaves.

Jeremy glanced behind him. She didn't want to worry the kid. Common sense told her it was probably an animal scurrying through the thick brush, scavenging for food. Raccoons or squirrels, wild turkeys, deer, even a bear or two had been spotted roaming the woods from time to time. Especially during the drought, when food and water were scarce.

Jeremy picked up his pace and threw another worried glanced behind him.

"It's all right," she said, trying to sound calm. "If

an animal is following us, it's probably wondering what we're doing in its forest. Or it's looking for food."

"I didn't bring anything to give them." A trace of panic colored his voice. "Did you?"

"No, but they won't bother us." God, she hoped that was true. September was late for bear sightings, but it had happened before.

"Are you afraid?"

"Of course not," she lied. "I've played in these woods since I was ten. Here. Hold my hand. We can make better time as a unit." *And I can stop watching you to make sure you're okay.* She fought to think of something to distract him. "Hey, did you know your Dad and I knew each other years ago?"

"Really?"

"Back before he married your mother. We met at the Riverbirch Harvest Festival. I was stirring apple butter beside a big tent. I looked up, and he was laughing at me."

"Why?"

"Because I was muttering under my breath and cursing a blue streak. Stirring apple butter was the last thing I wanted to do that day, and I didn't care who knew it. He thought it was funny."

"And you became friends?"

"Yeah."

"Then how come I never saw you before the other day?"

"Well, he lived in Atlanta, and I live here. We didn't keep in touch."

A loud *crunch* sounded beside them. Jeremy squeezed her hand and froze.

Morgan whirled around. *"Okay!"* she yelled.

"Whoever is there, just stop it! You're scaring us!"

She scanned the trees, the piles of dead leaves, the jagged stacks of rock sprouting tiny scrub cedars from their crevices. She held her breath and tried to think. Bears could be sneaky unless they were hungry. A wild boar would still be moving toward them, crashing fearlessly through the underbrush. Squirrels and raccoons would have lost interest by now. Deer would have disappeared the minute she'd made the first noise. If someone like Finch was following them for sport, she'd never be able to outrun him with a kid in tow. Another crackle of leaves, this time nearer. She put her arm around Jeremy and drew him close. "This is not funny!" she yelled. "I know you're there, so you might as well show yourself. I mean it! Come on out, you piece-of-shit coward!"

Ethan Spannagel slowly emerged from behind the thick dead limbs of a felled oak.

"*Ethan!* What are you—Jesus, Ethan, you scared me half to death! What are you doing here?"

"I didn't mean to frighten you," Ethan said. "I stopped by the house, and Gage said the two of you had walked up Pip's Hill. I was worried about you being up here alone."

"So you decided to follow us?"

"Stalking is more like it." Jeremy pushed his baseball cap back from his forehead. "If you were looking for Morgan, why didn't you yell out her name?"

"I thought I saw someone watching you." Ethan pushed his glasses up on his nose. He regarded Jeremy solemnly. "I didn't want them to see me in case I needed to go for help."

"You're weird," Jeremy said. "And I don't believe

you."

"Did you see someone?" Morgan asked. "Who was it? Finch? Mendoza? Bert?"

"I said I *thought* I saw someone. It must have been my imagination."

"Or Bigfoot," Jeremy said.

The three of them started walking. "Have you talked to Peach?" Morgan asked. "I went to see her, but she didn't have much to say. She didn't hang around the hospital very long either."

"I wouldn't worry about Peach. She's a survivor."

"Did the two of you get a chance to talk last night? She said you hadn't been getting along, and she wanted to clear the air."

"Is that what she called it?"

"Well, not specifically, but—"

"I knew I shouldn't have gone to Bad Moon. But she won't leave me alone. I thought if I talked to her, I could convince her there can never be anything between us. She's not my type. And even if she was, I couldn't afford her." He pushed a branch aside to let Morgan go ahead of him. "I stopped by the farm to make sure you were all right. I was planning to give you a ride home last night after the fire, but by the time I'd finished giving my statement to the sheriff, you'd already left with Gage."

"He and Jeremy are staying with me until Sean comes home."

"Do you think that's a good idea? I mean, what will people think? The two of you staying alone, out here in the middle of nowhere? It doesn't look good."

Morgan chuckled. "Why, Ethan, what a prude you are. They're sleeping in the guesthouse. It's all perfectly respectable. Since when do I give a flip what other people think?"

Ethan moved up beside her, leaving Jeremy to bring up the rear. "Have you made any plans about leaving? Peach said you wanted to get back to Nashville as soon as possible. Are you going soon?"

Morgan stared at him. "How can you ask that? My brother's in jail. I can't think about leaving now."

"Your brother's in jail?" Jeremy asked. "Cool. What'd he do?"

"He didn't do anything," Morgan snapped. She looked at Ethan. "As long as Sean's in trouble, or this farm's in trouble, I'm not goin' anywhere."

"I understand," Ethan said, nodding. "Listen, Dad's funeral is Sunday—tomorrow."

"So soon?"

"I'm having him cremated, and I just want to get it over with. But I was wondering if you could play something on the piano. I don't know who else to ask."

"Of course, I'll play."

"Thanks," Ethan said. "I have to meet with Pastor Byrd at three to go over the details. You can choose whatever you want. Dad didn't care for hymns much. He won't care what you play. The Higher Ground Baptist Church might. But he won't."

"So, no Def Leppard or the B-52's?"

Ethan smiled shyly. "Better not."

"Does this mean they've finished the autopsy?"

"I guess. Somebody from the sheriff's department called and said they were releasing the body later today."

They came to the end of the path and took a sharp right out of the woods. The brilliant sunlight warmed

Morgan's face and arms. She started down the steep hill, picking her way around gopher holes and rocks.

"I've seen you before," Jeremy said to Ethan.

"I don't think so. I mean, you were at the fire last night, but we've never actually met."

"I was hiding in the bushes when that man yelled at Morgan. You were on the porch, looking through her window. Then my dad came, and you ran away. I saw you."

The blood drained from Ethan's face. He looked at Morgan. "I—I was going to tell you, but I didn't want you to think I was a—"

"—pussy?" Jeremy said.

"I thought it would be better if I went for help. I've met Denny. He's a loose cannon." He laughed self-consciously. "He could do some serious damage, Morgan. You know that."

"Better than anyone," Morgan said. "Don't worry about it."

"Yeah, don't worry about it," Jeremy said. "My dad wasn't afraid to kick his ass."

Morgan opened her mouth to reprimand him, then closed it. The kid had a point.

Halfway down the hill, the sheriff's car pulled into the driveway. When it stopped in front of the fence, a tall, sandy-haired man got out of the back seat and stretched.

"Oh, my God," she said. "It's Sean." She jumped up and down, waving both arms. *"Sean!"* She scooped up Jeremy and swung him around, laughing and crying, "Sean's home! He's home! My brother's home!"

"Before we go running down the hill, I need tell you something," Jeremy said.

She set him down. "What, honey? What is it?"

"I don't think 'piece-of-shit' is an adjective."

Morgan laughed. "In my world it is. And as long as you're staying here, you can use it anytime you want."

Jeremy grinned, looking exactly like his father. Something tightened in her chest. She grabbed his hand, and they galloped to the bottom of the hill, laughing and whooping, as if the weight of the world had been lifted off them both. She took the porch steps two at a time, threw her arms around Sean, then did something she'd only done twice in her life:she burst into tears. It was only later that she realized she'd left Ethan behind without a single thought or glance, standing alone on the top of Pip's Hill, watching them go.

****

Sean sat perched on a kitchen stool, freshly showered and shaved, wolfing down the last of the bacon, egg, and cheese sandwich Gage had made for him. "What are my plans? The only plans I have are finding some pickers and getting those apples off the trees. At this point I'd hire the 4-H Club, if I thought they'd do it."

"Not a bad idea," Gage said.

"Forget the damned apples," Morgan said. "I want to know more about the sheriff letting you go." She refilled Sean's coffee cup. "How do they know you didn't stab Harlan?"

"They don't," Gage said. "Unless they turn up more prints. What they do know is Sean didn't stab him while he was alive. Once a person is dead, their heart stops pumping, and they can't bleed."

"Well, somebody stabbed him," Morgan said.

"True," Gage said. "But if they can prove Sean

stabbed Harlan after he died, the most they can get him for would be mutilation of a dead body. Which is no small thing, but it's not murder. No one killed Harlan with a knife. He was already dead. His blood was so thin, he hemorrhaged, which probably muddied the waters for the autopsy but in no way changed the outcome. Whoever tried to frame your brother for Harlan's death wasn't very smart. But then, most criminals aren't smart. Most criminals are idiots."

Sean leaned back against the wall. "And you know this because...."

"He's an ex-PI," Jeremy said proudly. "You should've seen him throw that creep against Morgan's piano. It was *awesome!*"

"What creep?" Sean looked from Gage to Morgan. "What happened? What are you not telling me?'

"Denny showed up the day after you were arrested," Morgan said

"Oh, Lord," Sean said. "What did he want?"

"He wanted to take back the flag he gave her," Jeremy said. "You know, the one that real famous general used in the Civil War? The one she's gonna sell for a lot of money?"

Sean looked at Morgan. "No. I don't."

"Come on, Jeremy," Gage said quickly, as if he recognized a storm blowing in when he saw one. "Let's go pack. Now that Sean's here, our bodyguard services are no longer needed."

"No," Sean said. "Stay until you find a place. You've both been great to watch out for Morgan. The guesthouse is sitting there empty. You might as well use it."

"That okay with you, Morgan?" Gage asked.

She nodded.

"Okay, then. Thanks," Gage said. He raised his eyebrows and gave her a little bolstering smile. He placed his hands on Jeremy's shoulders and turned him toward the door. "Okay, sport. Let's go *un*pack."

After they'd left, Sean said, "Okay, twin of mine. Spill it. What was the kid talking about?"

"Denny gave me an old Civil War battle flag that had belonged to his father. It's supposed to be very rare and worth a lot of money."

"What are we talking here? Hundreds of dollars? Thousands?"

"Hundreds of thousands," Morgan said quietly.

Sean whistled through his teeth. "And this is the first I've heard of it?"

"I wanted to tell you. But I was afraid you'd—"

"Want you to share it with me?"

"I was afraid you'd find out why Denny gave it to me."

"I think I have an idea."

She crossed her arms across her chest and leaned against the counter for support. "The flag was a bribe not to press charges when he—when he hit me."

"I figured as much." He walked to the sink and poured the rest of his coffee down the drain. Then he turned and looked at Morgan with her father's eyes. "Do you think I didn't suspect something? You couldn't hide the bruises on your arms. I heard you crying in the middle of the night. We knew you'd had a miscarriage."

"How?"

"You know what this town is like. Doc Branson let it slip to Opal at church. He wanted to put you on the

183

prayer list."

"Why am I not surprised?"

"I wanted to help you, but whenever I brought up the subject of your life with Denny, you didn't want to talk about it. So I left you alone. I knew Denny was bad news the first time I laid eyes on him. But I never thought he would hurt you." He curled his fingers into a fist. "If I'd known, I swear, I would have—"

"What? Come after him?"

"I'd have come after you."

"I thought I could handle it myself."

"Why am I not surprised?" He shook his head sadly. "You've always been the one who's handled everything—Grandpa, me, Opal. Even those damned dogs of hers. And I've let you do it. I was glad when you moved to Nashville because I thought you'd finally have a life of your own, and not have to worry about anyone else's happiness. Then Grandpa got sick, and you had to come back. I'm sorry I had to ask you to stay until I get the farm up and running. But I didn't know what else to do."

"It isn't your fault Opal threatened to contest the will, and we gave in. We didn't have a choice." She looked at him, her heart ravaged with guilt. "But it is my fault I didn't tell you I had the means to save the orchard. It was selfish of me. And I am so sorry."

He smiled at her. The same sweet, crooked smile her father used to give her. "I'm glad Denny gave you that flag, and you have a nest egg to fall back on. Don't you dare give it back to him. You deserve it."

"Sean, I—"

"Stop it, Morgan. Turn your brain off and stop thinking. You're my twin, remember? And you may think I don't know you better than anybody else. But I do."

"And I know you." She sighed. "You're dying to say something. Let's have it, then."

"Here's what I know. I know you're not as cynical as you pretend to be. I know you love me. And I know you don't want to get rid of the orchard because you're sick of the smell of rotten apples and cow manure. You're afraid the stress of running this place will end up killing me like it did our grandfather. He had cancer, but we all know how stress can lower your resistance."

"I hadn't even thought of that." Tears welled up in Morgan's eyes.

"Hadn't you?" he asked gently.

She shook her head no, then slowly nodded yes.

"I also know that one of the reasons you hate Riverbirch is because you think you don't belong here. But you do. You belong here as much as any of us. This farm has been in our family for four generations. It's in your blood."

"But it's not in my heart."

"I'll get to your heart in a minute. Stop being so tough. You've got a hard shell around you, like one of those snapping turtles on the banks of Deer Creek. And you're just as stubborn. You won't let anybody make things easier for you."

"You're the one who needs help. Somebody's trying to frame you for murder."

"You have to start trusting people, Morgan. And you can start with the sheriff. Teresa will solve this case. I have faith in her." He cocked his head and smiled. "It's not hard to have faith. All you have to do is swing out over the lake, let go of the rope, and jump in. You can swim. I've seen you."

"I wish I was more like you. But I can't stop being me."

Sean shook his head. "The guy who finally gets you is gonna have his hands full."

"So, who do you think killed Harlan?" she asked, shifting the subject away from her.

He set his coffee cup in the sink. "This may sound completely off the wall, but I wouldn't write off Opal."

"Seriously? You think our step-grandmother killed Harlan Spannagel?"

"You know what she's like. She has a mean streak, especially when she doesn't get her way. If we hadn't backed down from her lawsuit, she would have kept the estate tied up in court for years, until she'd drained it dry. I knew she had her eye on Harlan. I even caught them kissing once. I came in from the barn, and Harlan had lip prints all over his face, like Barney making out with Thelma Lou. For a while, I thought they might get together, but then things seemed to go sour. The last few weeks, I've heard them arguing. They fought the day before Harlan died."

"You think she could have slipped something into all those cakes and pies she's been taking him that would thin his blood? Why would she take him a cake if they'd argued the night before?"

Sean shrugged. "I don't know. Maybe at their age, eating cake is the equivalent of makeup sex. I also think that Lawrence Finch framed me. I believe he went to Harlan's to convince him we should sell, found him dead in the slaughterhouse, then found my knife in Harlan's toolbox and couldn't pass up a chance to get me out of the picture."

"But Finch wasn't after the farm. He was working for Bert Kirkland. That's why Gage and Jeremy moved out of Bert's house."

"And into our house?"

"They thought I needed protecting."

"Uh huh."

"Sean!"

He laughed. "You've got a bigger problem than I thought."

"What?"

"Your heart. I said I'd get back to it."

"What's wrong with my heart?"

"It's a little misguided. It may not be into running an orchard with apples no one wants to pick. Or making apple butter no one wants to buy. Or living in the country where, if you're lucky, you might get two piano students a year. But your heart's not in Nashville either."

"Then, where is it?"

"Well." Sean raised his eyebrows and grinned. "Judging from the electricity flying back and forth across this room every time you and Gage looked at each other, I'd say your heart, and his son, just walked out that door."

Chapter 12

Gage stomped up the path to the barn. If Morgan wasn't there, he was sending out a search party.

Christ, the woman could be stubborn! He'd asked her—no, *told* her—to let Sean or him know exactly where she was at all times. They couldn't be too careful with Harlan's killer on the loose and a drugged up ex-husband lurking around. But then she'd disappeared. So, when he found her on the other side of the barn, loading wooden boxes into the back of a truck bed, he didn't know whether to chew her out or take her in his arms.

"I thought we had a deal," he said.

"You and Sean and Jeremy had a deal. No one asked me how I felt about having three full-time bodyguards."

"All right. How do you feel?"

"Claustrophobic."

She glanced at him from beneath the tattered brim of her straw hat but kept working. Her sleeveless denim shirt lay open at the neck, giving him a bird's eye view of some of the most thigh-hardening cleavage he'd ever seen. The muscles in her upper arms were tanned golden, and sculpted just enough to make him realize that the reason she hadn't asked for help moving the heavy boxes was because she hadn't needed any.

"I take it you're going apple picking," he said.

"Yep." She lifted her hat and wiped her forehead with the back of her wrist. "I know it's ridiculous to think I can even make a dent in those damned apples, but I can't sit around doing nothing."

He started rolling up his sleeves. "Okay if I go with you? Jeremy and I could help."

"Sure. But I've got to warn you, it gets old. Real fast."

"I don't scare that easily."

"So I've noticed." Amusement flickered behind her eyes. And something that looked so much like a promise, it made him want to give in to the merciless tightening in his groin and pull her to him.

Ten minutes later, the three of them were bumping down the long, uneven slope to the orchard. She hadn't been too keen on letting him drive, but had relented after he confessed he'd always wanted to rappel a hill in a pickup. Jeremy and Morgan hung on to their seatbelts as the pickup rumbled over the rough terrain, bucking and squealing its way from one gear to the next.

"If y'all don't stop yelling, I'm gonna make you get out and walk," Gage said, laughing.

"I've had smoother rides on a runaway mule," Morgan said.

"Go faster, Dad!"

Morgan held onto her hat. "Like father, like son?"

Gage grinned. "I think I'm exhibiting admirable restraint. And that's a hard row to hoe with you sitting this close."

"You can park now," Morgan said. "If you can remember where the brake is."

Gage guided the truck between two rows of apple

trees. They got out and threaded the wide canvas bags over their shoulders.

Morgan showed Jeremy how to twist and pull an apple from the branch. "Gently. Like this," she said. "When the bag gets heavy, dump them into those padded boxes. But slowly, so they won't bruise. Nobody wants to buy a bruised apple."

They worked side by side in amiable silence, filling up bags, transferring them to the wooden boxes. Jeremy worked hard, without complaint, and after an hour or so, Morgan suggested he take a break. He didn't argue and was soon settled beneath the shade of a tree with a cold soda and his book.

"He's starting to come around, isn't he?" Morgan said.

"Thanks to you."

"Me? I didn't do anything."

Gage smiled. "More than you know, Morgan Maguire." He stood looking out across the meadow. "Look at this place. Mountains in the distance, horses grazing in a field of goldenrod, Lacey's Pond sparkling in the sun. How can you leave something this magnificent?"

"Easy. I pack my little suitcase and throw it in the car."

"But how can you leave Riverbirch? Isn't this place a part of your soul?"

She shifted the apple bag on her hip. "I can leave because I've never fit in here."

"I can't believe that."

"Why not?" She pulled off her hat and shook out her hair. "I may have been born here, but I am not a Riverbirch girl. I always wanted to be someone else, somewhere else."

"Sometimes it takes leaving a place, then coming back to appreciate it." He handed her a bottle of water.

"Riverbirch, Tennessee, is about as rural as it gets. Any girl who doesn't know how to drive a tractor, or saddle and foal a mare, or cook up a mess of creasy greens and a skillet of cornbread is considered uneducated. If a Riverbirch girl doesn't have a framed photo of her prizewinning 4-H cow on the mantel by age six and a ring on her finger by eighteen, her parents are either prayed for or pitied. In my case, both."

"Okay. I get that. But I think you like the country more than you let on. I think you love it here." He took a deep, satisfying breath. "I know I do. I'll never live in a big city again. I want a quiet life, a safe life for my son. The air is bigger here, and cleaner. It's easier to breathe in a place like this. And right now, I need to breathe."

She took a long swallow of water and leaned against the stepladder.

"Jeremy said Ethan surprised you in the woods. He stopped by the house, you know. I don't think he liked me being there." Gage shook his head. "I'm sorry, but that guy seems a little off."

"Who, Ethan? He's harmless. A bit intense at times. And very serious. But harmless."

"Thinking someone is harmless when they're not can come back and bite you on the ass."

"Mild-mannered, then. Sweet. He's...soulful."

"And those eyes of his. They remind me of those weird children's eyes from *Village of the Damned*. When he looks at me, all I want to do is think of a brick wall."

"He can be a little strange. But he's had a hard life. His mother killed herself, and I think Harlan blamed him for it, though I'm not sure why. Harlan's always been distant toward him. The Spannagels are a dysfunctional family. I liked Harlan, but I don't think he was much of a father. Ethan had to grow up on his own without a lot of guidance."

"He's got the hots for you, you know."

"No, he doesn't. We're friends." She laughed softly. "Like you and me."

"Uh, huh. Then I *am* worried."

Morgan laughed.

Gage sat on the ground opposite her. "You know, there's something else I've been worrying about ever since Denny tried to bully you into giving him that flag. You don't keep it in the house, do you?"

"Yes."

"Wouldn't it be safer for you, and the flag, if you locked it in a safety deposit box?"

"Don't worry. It's safe." She gave a little half-shrug. "But you're probably right. With Denny sneaking around, the smart thing to do would be to take it to the bank on Monday."

Gage swung around. "*What the*—do you hear that?"

A black Cadillac came barreling down Milltown Road, followed by an open bed truck. They pulled into the Maguire driveway and turned down the hill toward the orchard. Jeremy came to stand beside his father. For the first time in months, he didn't flinch when Gage placed his hands on his shoulders. As the vehicles came closer, their horns blew. Wild cheering broke out, much of it in Spanish.

"Uncle Bert!" Jeremy cried, jumping up and down. "Hey, it's Uncle Bert!"

"The man never ceases to amaze me," Gage said. "I think he's brought some workmen to help pick the apples. And brother, does he know how to make an entrance."

"Yeah," Morgan said. "Like Darth Vader."

****

Gage leaned against the door and watched Morgan process apples, a task he found both hypnotic and sexy. Of course, she could stand on a stool in a potato sack reading the phone book, and he would find it sexy.

She lifted a clean apple from the water bath, pushed it into a metal food mill, and pulled the lever. Pieces of apple shot through the sieve. Seeds and core went one way, soft apple pulp another.

"I know you're not happy about Bert showing up with the pickers," he said.

She scooped up another apple, shoved it in the mill. "Bert Kirkland is not someone I want our family to be obligated to. I understand he's trying to make amends for what he did, but having him pay their salaries doesn't feel right."

"The pickers seem happy. They're getting double the pay."

"I know, but you've seen the orchard. It would take two pickers weeks to bring in this harvest. By then, the apples will be unsalable."

"What does Sean say?"

"Oh, Sean's looking on the bright side. He thinks it's fine and dandy as long as the apples are coming off the trees. To him, all is forgiven." She dumped the apple pulp into a large plastic bucket. "But I'm not as forgiving as Sean."

"You were last night."

She lifted her head and stared at him. Her eyes sparkled. The corners of her mouth twitched, causing the little dimples beside it to appear, then disappear. "Last night I was cold."

"Not for long."

He held up Harlan's cell phone.

"Oh, my God," she whispered. "Did you do it? Did you figure out the password?"

He nodded slowly and grinned. "Wasn't too hard once I found out his birthday. There are some very interesting voicemails on it. Three from Ethan. Sixteen from Peach. And one from your step-grandmother."

She wiped her hands on a dishtowel. "What did they say?"

"Ethan seemed a little panicked, and wanted to know why Harlan had ditched his doctor's appointment. But the sixteen messages from Peach were very informative. Seems your old friends Peach and Harlan were having an affair. Although, technically, I don't guess you can call it an affair, since neither one of them were married, but—"

"Tell me."

"—it sounds like Harlan was King of the Silver Foxes. Or King of The Little Blue Pill." He laughed. "And judging from the dazed look on your face, this is a fact you did not know."

"No. I didn't know he and Peach were sleeping together."

"Well, I'm not sure how much sleeping was involved, but they were definitely doing things together. Fun things, as it turns out. Until Peach decided that if Harlan wouldn't let her move into his house and play house, she could at least make a tidy profit blackmailing him. Of course, in order for her to collect, he had to be dead first."

"What do you mean?"

"Seems Harlan was a little strapped for cash, so instead of paying Peach to keep her mouth shut about the fun things they were doing, and not blab the sordid details to the Cherokee Bluff Chamber of Commerce and the Higher Ground Baptist Church, where Harlan served as a deacon *and* a charter member of the ethics committee, he promised to change his will to include her."

"I'll bet that's what she and Ethan were arguing about."

"No doubt. Which brings me to the last voicemail sent the morning of his death."

"From Opal."

"Opal was a little more discreet than Peach, but I think she was benefitting from the old guy's Viagra prescription, too." He laughed again. "Close your mouth, honey, before a fly lands on your tongue."

"I can't believe it. Sean suspected their relationship had crossed the *friends* line. But not me. How naïve am I?"

"Geezer sex, and lots of it, is one of the best kept secrets of the Senior Citizen Brigade. One of the things I loved most about being a PI was all those fascinating secret lives I got to unearth."

"What did Opal say? Exactly?"

"She said she'd been praying about it, and had decided to forgive Harlan for—and I quote—'having relations with that slut I paid to take care of my husband.' She also reminded him that he'd promised they would be together as soon as she was a widow, and even though he'd strayed with said slut, she expected him to honor that promise or she would make him damned sorry he didn't. She also said she was bringing him his favorite cake."

"Jam cake with caramel icing. It was on the kitchen counter."

"Had he eaten any of it?"

"I don't think so. It was still in the cake carrier. I recognized it has hers the minute I saw it. Sean and I wondered if she accidentally put something in the cake to make him hemorrhage?"

"Accidentally? Well, maybe. He was taking a blood thinner. All kinds of things can thin somebody's blood: over-the-counter supplements, fish oil, alcohol. I don't know what she could have slipped into the cake batter to make him hemorrhage that fast, though, do you?" Morgan stared at the bucket of apple pulp. "Morgan?"

She looked up. "I'm still trying to wrap my head around the image of Opal and Harlan going at it like a couple of squirrels."

"Squirrels?"

"Don't ask."

Gage laughed. "Well, all I can say is, hats off, Harlan! And thank God for glucosamine. I could have used some last night." He lowered his head and smiled. "You do remember last night, don't you?"

"I was wondering when you were going to bring that up."

"You mean the way you lured me into your bed? Nice trick—pulling Peach out of a burning building, then going into shock so I'd have to crawl in and warm you up."

"You didn't crawl in my bed. You crawled *on* my bed." Her eyes widened in mock disbelief. "Did you say I lured you? What the hell are you talking about?" She kicked an apple peel at him with the toe of her boot. "*Lured* you? You wish."

"I do wish," he said softly. He took the bucket out of her hand and placed it on the worktable. Then he slid one arm around her waist and pulled her to him, never letting his gaze waver from hers. "I wish it with all my heart."

"Gage, I—"

"*Shhhh*," he whispered, smoothing the dark waves back from her face. He pressed his lips against her forehead, kissed the side of her face, the top of her cheek. "I think it's time to use those lips of yours for something besides talking."

"You want me to whistle?"

He captured her mouth with his. Exactly the same way she'd done to him the night before.

Morgan wrapped her arms around his neck and drew him close. The sweet scent of apples permeated the air, clung to her clothes and skin. Her lips tasted of cider. "You've been sampling the goods." he said, kissing her again. He could feel her lips curl into a smile.

"Damn straight," she murmured, opening her mouth, letting him inside. Her eyes blinked, then opened halfway, watching him like a cat planning its next move. He backed her across the floor and leaned her against the plank worktable, then ran his hands down the side of her cotton shirt until he found the waistband of her jeans. He encircled it with his hands and, in one swift motion, lifted her up and deposited her, sitting, on the edge of the table. Her rear end hit the plywood with a *plop*. A low, rasping giggle burbled up from her throat.

She was thawing.

He could feel it.

Since she'd let him in her bed for a convenient blast of body heat, an easiness had developed between them. He could hear it in her voice when she teased him, see it in the suggestive gleam in her eyes. The banter between them had become effortless and exciting. Her wit kept him on his toes. He'd never had to work so hard to keep up his end of a conversation, or had so much fun doing it. Believing she had let down her guard enough to be comfortable with him melted his heart. It gave him hope. And it had been a long time since his heart had dared to hope for much of anything.

Morgan pulled her mouth from his and tilted her head back. He took it as a cue to nuzzle the tender spot below her ear, then slowly trail kisses down her throat. First on one side then the other. She groaned and arched her back.

In Gage's opinion, men who ignored a woman's neck were in too big of a hurry to hit pay dirt. He couldn't say it was his favorite body part, but after his divorce, when he'd sampled as many different women as he could, searching for the one who could turn his brain into a blank slate, all of them, except the one freaked out by vampires, loved having their necks kissed. Spending a few extra minutes kissing a girl's throat could raise the heat level ten-fold.

Buttons were a different animal. He'd never been

adept at managing them. His hands were too big, and when he could see second base slide into focus, nerves and impatience always got the better of him. He usually regressed into a skinny, hormone powered teenager who could shoot the moon just by looking at a bra, much less going spelunking for one. He fumbled with her shirt buttons and let his mouth slide across hers to distract her from his clumsiness. He slid open her collar and let his thumbs skim their way down the placket, across the flesh colored lace, to the soft swell of her breasts.

God, they were exquisite—white and creamy and yielding. Just as he'd remembered, only more voluptuous. A delicate sprinkling of freckles formed a subtle V at the base of her throat where her collar had spent the summer curled back, open to the sun. He raked his lips along the tops of her breasts and fought the urge to bury his face in them. He longed to release them, feel their weight in his hands as he stroked them, feel her nipples harden against his fingertips. Instead, he said, "You know that fifteen pounds you said you gained?"

"Yes." She froze in his arms. Her hands loosened their grip on his shoulders.

"Well, don't ever lose them. You are the most beautiful, the most perfect—"

"Don't say anymore. You're throwing ice water on a fire."

"It's true. Even if you never let me near you again, it's still true."

"You're making me crazy," she murmured before her lips found his again. "Gage, we're in a barn. This isn't a good place to...."

"*Dad!*" Jeremy shrieked. *"Dad, hurry!"*

Gage spun around. Morgan grabbed the plastic bucket and held it in front of her chest.

"What's wrong?" Gage asked. "What's happened?"

"It's Uncle Bert," Jeremy cried. "Two guys are trying to beat the shit out of him."

Chapter 13

The orchard looked like a scene from *The Good, the Bad and the Ugly.*

Sean held Mendoza against the front grille of the pickup like a young Clint Eastwood, calmly listening to him spew obscenities in two languages. Finch lay sprawled on the ground beside Bert. The two Hispanic pickers stood over them, hands poised to hold them back if they went at each other again.

Finch wiped his bloody nose and scrambled to his feet. "Get out of my way," he snarled, pushing one of the pickers aside.

"*Owww,*" Bert sniveled. "I think you broke my hand."

"Get up, you fat slob, and fight like a man," Finch shouted. "You owe me money. *Big* money. And I'm not leaving here until you give it to me."

"I don't owe you anything," Bert said. "You've botched job after job for me, so you can forget about getting paid."

"We had a deal!" Finch said. "I need that money."

"Nothing is in writing," Bert said. "There were no witnesses. The terms we discussed will be my word against yours. You're not getting another red cent from me. Ever. "

Finch paused. He squinted briefly at the sun,

flicked an apple leaf off his dirt-streaked jacket, and shot his muddy cuffs. Then he let out a bloodcurdling scream and ran at Bert as if he were storming a castle. The pickers grabbed him midflight. "Let go of me!" Finch cried. "I want my money!"

"It's time for you and your friend to leave," Gage said. "Unless you want me to have you arrested for assault and fraud. I can do that. I would *love* to do that."

Finch pointed to Bert. "He's the fraud."

"Can it," Bert said.

"Morgan, don't you and Sean understand?" Finch pleaded. "*I'm* not the bad guy here. Bert's been planning this for months. He wants to steal your land. He wants to plant a vineyard on the north slope and grow Chambourcin grapes. He thinks he can make millions."

"It doesn't matter," Morgan said. "You need to grind your axe with Bert on his property. Go to the winery and fight him. Just leave us alone. You know, Larry, in some twisted way, I admire you. You've got a giant pair of brass balls showing up at our farm like this. But I'd say the chances of you collecting money from a man who tried to cheat his neighbors out of land that's been in their family for four generations are slim to none. In the future, you might want to choose your employers more carefully."

Finch glared at her. Then he nodded to Mendoza, and Sean let him go. "I've always liked you, Miss Maguire." He smiled, showing a row of tiny yellowed teeth. "Not only are you easy on the eyes, especially in a bathrobe, but you're a cut above the other hicks in this town. Up until now, I've been nice. But I'm through being nice." He smiled again. "I'm going to let you in on a little secret." His triumphant gaze shifted to Bert. "Harlan Spannagel was not the good friend you thought he was."

"Stop right there," Sean said. "I won't have you talking trash about a man who—"

"Who what?" Finch scoffed. "Lied to you? Tried to destroy your business?"

"That's not true," Sean said. "Harlan was like a father to me. He was my grandfather's best friend. He cared about our family. He would never have done anything to hurt us." He looked at Morgan. The sorrow on his face broke her heart. Maybe it was the twin-thing connecting her to his wavelength, but she was sure he was thinking of the day he'd found the two sets of accounts for Maguire Orchard beside Harlan's computer.

Finch looked at Bert cowering on the ground. "Tell them, you sniveling bag of muck. Tell them how much Harlan cared about them. They're going to find out anyway. Tell them or I'll break your other hand."

Bert pushed himself up and staggered to his feet. "Harlan was working for me, too. I was paying him to miss loan payments for the orchard, to siphon off capital, to let things slide into bankruptcy. To run your business into the ground. I'm begging you to forgive me, Gage. All I want is for you and Jeremy to come back and—"

"Get out," Gage said. The knot in his jaw tightened. His fists clinched, and for a moment, Morgan thought he was going to smash them into Bert's face. "You ruin lives, Bert. You tried to ruin mine, and my father's, and the Maguire's. But you are not going to ruin my son's life. That is something you are not going to do."

"No, Dad!" Jeremy cried. "Don't make him go! He didn't mean it. Please, Dad, let him stay. He's sorry. Aren't you, Uncle Bert? Aren't you sorry?"

Bert gazed at the boy sadly. "Yes, I am, Jeremy. I'm very sorry. But sometimes being sorry doesn't quite cut it. Right, Gage?"

Gage took Jeremy's hand.

"Dad, no!" Jeremy tried pull away. "Let me go. I hate you! I want to go back to Uncle Bert's. Let go of me! *I hate you!*"

Without a word, Gage led the boy through the orchard gate and back up the hill.

Finch bunched a handful of Bert's sleeve. "I meant what I said, old man. This isn't over."

"It is for me," Bert said.

Bert waited until Gage and Jeremy disappeared behind the house, then turned to Morgan. "Why aren't you going after my nephew? He wants you. He's always wanted you. I'm sure you're the reason he divorced Suzanne. If it hadn't been for you, he might have made that girl happy. Then she wouldn't have gone off the deep end. Then she'd still be alive."

"Why are you blaming me?" Morgan asked. "Gage and I only spent one day together."

"But you made one hell of an impression," Bert sneered. "You thought you could trap him into marriage. But the funny part was he'd already been trapped by Suzanne, and didn't know it. Suzanne beat you to the punch. That girl was a go-getter."

"What are you saying? That you admired Suzanne because she got pregnant first?"

"Don't feel bad. I heard you got somebody else to

marry you a week later." He laughed harshly. "I knew you'd survive without getting your claws into my nephew. I knew it that night in the boathouse, and I know it now. Women like you always survive."

"*Enough!*" Sean shouted. "I'm not a violent man, Mr. Kirkland, but if I ever hear you speak to my sister like that—or any woman—I will find you, and I will make an exception."

Morgan stared at her brother. She hardly recognized him. The sweet, soft-spoken guy who couldn't bring himself to raise his voice to one of Opal's unruly dogs was gone. In his place stood a man with a steadfast code of ethics and a set of sinewy muscles straining against his T-shirt sleeves to back them up. Sean pulled himself to his full height and towered over the three astonished men like a warrior set in stone. His gaze held Bert's, razor-sharp and unwavering. Meek, peace loving Sean Maguire had become a force to be reckoned with. And everyone in the orchard that day knew it.

He glanced at Morgan. "You can go on up to the house, sis. These three scumbags are leaving." He stomped his foot as if he were shooing raccoons off the porch. *"Now."*

****

Gage sat at the table with his head in his hands. He tried to rein in his temper and ignore the banging and cursing in the next room. He wasn't sure what Jeremy was doing, but it was a safe bet the closet door would never be the same. He opened his mouth to yell for him to stop, then closed it again. Why add fuel to the fire? The boy had every right to express his anger. Gage had deprived him of everything he loved—his home, his

205

friends, his uncle, his mother.

Another loud *thud*, then a *crash* reverberated from the bedroom. Probably Jeremy's school backpack slamming against the bedside table. Gage should devise a point system. Two points for correctly identifying the thing being thrown. Five for identifying the target.

A knock on the door brought Gage to his feet.

Morgan stood on the tiny porch with her arms crossed over her chest. "What's going on? I can hear that racket clear across the yard."

"Jeremy's still upset," Gage said. "He's blowing off a little steam."

"Yeah, well, we're all upset. But we're not all acting like three-year-olds."

"I didn't want to make things worse. I don't know what to say to him."

"Mind if I try?"

"Sure." He swept his hand toward the bedroom. "Have at it."

Morgan walked inside. She rapped hard on Jeremy's door. "Jeremy, honey, it's Morgan. *Cut it out!*"

The banging stopped abruptly.

"Gee, why didn't I think of that?" Gage said.

"Because you're too busy blaming yourself, and it's time you—"

"Cut it out?"

"Exactly. By the way, your uncle left. I don't think he'll be back anytime soon. I'm not inviting him for Christmas dinner."

"You can see why he's the last person I'd want to take a handout from. I'd convinced myself that moving in with him was the best thing for Jeremy." He looked at her helplessly. "But I don't know what's best for

Jeremy anymore. He's so angry."

"That will pass. You just have to be patient."

"Everything comes with a catch, doesn't it?"

"Only the good things." She sighed. "I finished listening to the voicemails Peach left on Harlan's phone. Unbelievable."

"That girl's a piece of work."

"She's a piece of something. Gage, there's something I need to say."

He looked at her expectantly. "Okay."

"Let's get some air." Gage followed her outside and sat beside her on the low porch stoop. "If you don't like what I'm about to say, then...don't like it. But I believe part of Jeremy's problem—a huge part, actually—is the fact that he doesn't have closure for his mother's death. He can't begin to heal or move on with his life until you help him find it."

"How do you give a child his age closure? It's not like he has a full life to get back to."

"But he does." She picked up a yellow birch leaf and started shredding it. "Where is she? Where is Suzanne?"

"Her ashes are at her parents' house in Atlanta. Why?"

"Because Jeremy doesn't know that. He doesn't know where his mother is. He didn't get to say goodbye to her, and no one's told him anything. It's left him heartbroken and adrift. To him, she grabbed the car keys, ran out the door, and never came back. Part of him believes she might still be out there somewhere, and we both know, she's not. Jeremy needs resolution."

"I'll fix it," he said hoarsely. "I'll take him to scatter her ashes somewhere. We'll do something special in her honor. I'll help him say goodbye." He reached out and took Morgan's hand. "Thank you." He brought it to his lips. When he looked at her, his eyes blurred with tears. "So many good things have happened to me and my son since I met you again. Jeremy has turned a full one-eighty, something I thought would take months of therapy to accomplish. And it's all because of you. No matter what happens, I'll never forget what you've done for us."

He slid his arm around her and pulled her to him. Her head nestled into the crook of his shoulder. She seemed to melt into him. He hadn't felt this happy since the day Jeremy was born. Or safe. Was it weird to think a woman he'd only spent a total of four days with had the power to make him feel safe? Where would he ever find that again?

Time was running out.

He had to tell her about the flag. The longer he waited, the worse his chances were of making her understand he never meant to hurt her. Not then. Not now. He had to find a way to tell her the truth without destroying the future they might have together. If that was even possible. And he had to do it soon.

The door opened, and Jeremy came out. "Sorry, Morgan. Sorry, Dad."

Morgan moved away from Gage. She motioned for Jeremy to sit between them. "You know, kid, I've always believed people are who they are, and no matter how hard you try, you can't change them. But if they can't always be the people you want them to be, it doesn't mean you love them any less."

"Uncle Bert should say he's sorry," Jeremy said. "And mean it."

"I know," Gage said gently. "Maybe he will one day."

Sean roared up the hill in his Jeep. He swung out of the seat, strode across the yard, and handed Morgan his cell phone. "Here. Of course, I can get a signal when the Wicked Witch of the South calls. And you're the only one who's had enough sleep to deal with her."

Morgan sighed. "Opal." She took the phone. "Morgan here."

"I don't know what to do!" Opal wailed. "I've been assaulted! Should I call the sheriff?"

"*What?* Who?"

"Denny Quillen. That horrible man you were married to. He hurt my wrists. Oh, Morgan, please come help me. They look terrible. They're already turning blue. I wanted to wear my blue chiffon dress to Harlan's funeral, but now, I just don't know. The blues might clash."

"On my way." Morgan snapped the phone closed. "Denny paid Opal a visit."

"I'm going with you," Gage said.

"I hear you're pretty good with computers," Sean said to Jeremy. "Is that true?"

"I know my grades two minutes after the teacher enters them." Jeremy shot a quick look at Gage. "Not that I'd ever change them or anything. I mean, I guess I could, but—"

Sean laughed. "I don't want you to change my grades, I want you to help me find some files I'm not sure even exist."

"*Yeah,*" Jeremy said. "Can I stay here, Dad? And help Sean?"

"You sure you're okay with this?" Sean asked

Gage. "If unwanted visitors show up, I'll call the sheriff. But I don't think there'll be any more trouble today."

"I hope you're right. It's just—"

"I'll keep a close eye on him," Sean said.

"Okay, then," Gage said. "You guys be careful."

Sean tossed his keys to Morgan. "Take the Jeep. It'll get you over the mountain faster than the truck. And do yourselves a favor. After the two of you check on Opal, go to dinner. Get away from this farm for a while. I'll pick up some burgers and sugar for the apples, then after we eat, Jeremy can help me fire up the outside kettle. I think I have enough propane."

"You're going to start a batch now?" Morgan asked. "It takes five hours to cook apple butter. By the time the apples boil, it'll take you all night."

"I read where you drop a silver dollar in the kettle to keep the apples from sticking," Jeremy said. "Is that true?"

"Absolutely," Sean said. "The Harvest Festival is two weeks away, and I want to have something to sell. Two nights on a cement mattress without sleep reset my body clock. If I'm gonna be awake anyway, I might as well be doing something productive."

And as long as Sean's awake, Gage thought. *He'll be standing guard over my son.*

"I...I wanted to tell you how sorry I am about Harlan," Gage said.

"Thanks," Sean said.

"After Morgan and I make sure Opal's all right, I think we should go to the Spannagel's house and ask Ethan for the accounting files. Finch said Harlan was working for Bert, and you need to see those files in hand as soon as possible. Before they're compromised."

"I'm not sure I believe Finch was telling the truth," Sean said.

"Still," Gage said, "you should know what you're dealing with. If Harlan was embezzling from Maguire Orchard, and you can prove it, you can prosecute Harlan's estate and demand restitution. The court would freeze the estate until the heirs are able to pay you back."

"You mean Ethan," Morgan said. "He's the only heir."

"You know what's been bothering me?" Sean said. "The accounting files were in folders sitting on Harlan's dining room table in full view of anyone who walked by. He liked to work from printouts, said it helped him see the big picture. But Ethan had been living at his dad's house for over a week. He had to have seen them."

"Oh, I'm sure he saw them," Morgan said. "But he would never mention it. Appearances are everything to Ethan. His father was a well-respected man in this community. If Ethan knew what Harlan had been hired to do by Bert, he would take every precaution he could to hide it."

"I wonder how much Bert really knew about this," Gage said.

"And Finch," Morgan said. "And Mendoza. Sean met them on the road after he left Harlan, driving toward Harlan's house."

"They weren't driving," Sean said. "They were flying."

"Maybe I'm wrong," Morgan said. "Maybe Ethan didn't notice the files. I don't pay any attention to the files in Sean's office."

Gage cocked one eyebrow. "This is different. This is your orchard. I think Ethan would keep tabs on anything that belonged to you. If he was aware of what was going on, he wouldn't have wanted you to find out because it would blow his chances with you. That man is more into you than you realize."

Morgan glanced at her watch. "Ethan's meeting the pastor at the church at three. If we hurry, we'll have enough time to check on Opal then get to the Spannagel's house."

"But Ethan would be gone by then," Sean said.

"I think that's the idea," Gage said.

"Don't look so worried, little brother. Gage is an ex-PI. I'm in good hands. Let me grab my purse, and we'll go."

Gage turned to Sean. "I guess it's time to get back on the horse. God, I love PI work. I can already feel the adrenaline beginning to shoot through me. I'm used to going it alone, though."

"Then convince my sister that breaking into Ethan's house is too dangerous."

"It was her idea." Gage smiled appreciatively as Morgan climbed into the Jeep. "She's not boring, is she?"

"No, she's not."

"She has guts."

"And you hate gutsy women, right?"

Gage grinned. "Only if they clean fish for a living."

Chapter 14

The last thing Morgan expected to see in Opal's kitchen was Peach standing at the sink, wringing out a washcloth.

Morgan set her purse on the counter. "What are you doing here?"

"I was visiting Edith Duncan down the hall—she used to be one of my patients at the nursing home—and on my way out, I heard someone crying in here. I knocked on the door, and it was Opal." Peach opened the freezer and took out two ice cubes. She wrapped them in the washcloth. "This is for her bruised wrists. Vinegar helps, too, but I couldn't find any."

"Opal doesn't cook," Morgan said. "She heats up."

"What are you two talking about out there?" Opal hollered. "I can't hear you!"

"Nothing." Morgan lowered her voice. "She said Denny grabbed her. Did you see him?"

Peach's blue eyes widened. "No, but I'm sure he didn't mean to hurt her. She's taking a blood thinner—warfarin. You can breathe on her wrists, and they'll bruise."

"I didn't know she was on warfarin. Is everybody on warfarin?"

"Everybody over seventy. Half the people at the nursing home take it. I found it in her medicine cabinet when I was looking for an icepack. She said she'd had a mini-stroke after your grandpa died, and she didn't want anyone to know."

"That's not like her," Morgan said. "If anything's wrong, Opal blabs it to the world."

Gage stuck his head around the door. "Everything okay? I hear major whispering."

"Opal's on a blood thinner," Morgan said. "Just like Harlan. Isn't that dangerous?"

"Not if she's monitored by a doctor," Peach said. "A lot of things can affect her Pro Time."

"Her what?"

"Prothrombin Time. It's a blood test to measure how fast the blood clots."

"What can affect it?" Gage asked.

"Diet," Peach said. "Foods with large amounts of Vitamin K in them like spinach, broccoli, parsley, collards. All those will thicken the blood. Certain OTC supplements like fish oil and Vitamin E can thin it. So can aspirin."

Gage leaned against the windowsill. "So, if a person took too many blood-thinning supplements, it could cause them to hemorrhage spontaneously?"

"Oh, sure," Peach said. "If they were on a high enough dosage, over time, it could do a lot of damage. They could be fine one minute, then start bleeding out the next."

"Morgan!" Opal trilled from the living room. "Peach! What's going on in there?"

"I'll get this." Gage took the makeshift icepacks from Peach.

"Hold them on her wrists," Peach said. "She'll be fine."

After Gage left, Morgan said, "Damn that Denny! What's the matter with him? Scaring an old woman. I should have him arrested for assault."

"Why are you always so hard on him?" Peach rinsed her hands and pulled a paper towel from the dispenser. "He's not doing drugs. He's almost stopped drinking. He's trying to turn his life around. He wants to sell the flag you're keeping for him so he can put a down payment on a house." She clutched the wet paper towel in front of her like a bouquet. Her eyes shone. "Oh, Morgan, it's the most beautiful place. He showed me a picture of it—a little one-story ranch, right on the golf course. He said he's gonna take me there sometime and we'll—"

"You came with him here, didn't you?"

Peach stared at Morgan. A slow blush crept up the fleshy folds in her neck.

"How did you know about the flag, Peach? Did Denny tell you about it when he came to the bar? Or did he tell you today when he brought you here to help frighten Opal into telling him where it was? What did you do? Keep watch in the hall so you could warn him in case someone heard an old lady screaming?"

"That flag belongs to Denny, and you know it. All he did was ask Opal where it was, and she flew mad—I mean, *crazy* mad. She said she was tired of you and Sean hiding parts of the estate from her. Then she went at him like a banshee. He had to hold her wrists to keep her from choking him."

"She's a seventy-seven-year-old woman. She can't open a jar of pickles without help. How do you think she could choke him? Put him in a headlock and use her knees?"

"Denny said you wouldn't believe him."

"Honey, Denny will say anything, *do* anything to get what he wants. You don't need that kind of man in your life."

"You don't know what I need."

"Peach, he hit me once—twice, actually. When he's drinking, he can't control his temper. I know firsthand he hasn't changed." She softened her tone. "I don't want you to get hurt."

"You don't want me to have Denny." Peach pushed a coil of brassy blond hair back from her forehead. "You're so selfish, Morgan. You've had everything handed to you since the day you were born: a big house in Riverbirch, a fancy college education, a husband, money."

"I worked hard for the money I made."

"Oh, right. Giving piano lessons. How hard is that?"

"You'd be surprised. It isn't easy scraping bubblegum off ivory."

"Oh, please." Peach's plump face twisted in disgust. "You don't care about Denny. You just don't want me to be with him because you can't stand to see other people happy. You've been alone for so long, you can't remember what it's like to fall for someone."

"Like you fell for Sean? And Andy? And Ethan? And Harlan Spannagel? You'll fall for anyone who'll buy you a shot of bourbon. Anyone you can use."

"You're just like your brother. You think you're so high and mighty, but you don't have a clue what the real world is like. You don't know what it feels like to be desperate. I've had to work every day of my life doing things for money you wouldn't last two hours doing, *and* raising three kids. And now I'm getting laid off again." She glowered at Morgan, her eyes wet with tears. "Denny could be the man I've been waiting for. If he'd just—so, where *did* you hide the flag? I looked everywhere. I—" She stopped. Her mouth opened and closed like a stranded carp.

Morgan's eyes narrowed. "Does everywhere include my bedroom?"

"I...I—"

"It was you, wasn't it? You broke into my house and snooped through my things. I was in the next room. I heard you. Hell, Peach, not many people would have the nerve to sneak in while I was at home. I've gotta say, I'm a little impressed."

"Oh, shut up. You have no right to judge me. You have no idea what my life is like. I work and work, and never get anywhere. I would do anything—*anything*—to get out of that rat infested trailer and give Crystal a decent life."

"Even blackmailing Harlan Spannagel into changing his will?"

Peach's blue eyes flashed.

"You and Ethan were arguing about it yesterday, weren't you?"

"Harlan promised me that money. He *promised*. And believe me, I earned every penny."

"Oh, I'm sure Harlan was flattered that a young, if slightly used woman found him attractive. He was a man, after all. But he was a smart man, and I doubt if he changed his will for you, no matter what you did for him. Or to him. What concerns me most, besides your extensive knowledge of blood thinners and your easy access to them, is the fact that you left threatening messages on Harlan's voicemail, and he died the next day. What did you do, Peach? Slip some warfarin into his moonshine and wait for him to bleed to death? Didn't take long, did it?"

For a woman of considerable heft, Peach moved like a ninja. Her hand whizzed through the air and struck the side of Morgan's face before Morgan had time to blink, much less duck.

Morgan's hand flew to her cheek. Her eyes smarted with tears.

Gage rounded the doorway. "I heard a—" His gaze flicked from Peach to Morgan. "What the—did she hit you? Morgan? Are you all right?"

"I'm fine," Morgan said.

"Morgan, I didn't mean to," Peach said.

"Yeah, you did," Morgan said. "And you know what? You can have Denny. The two of you are perfect for each other." She picked up Peach's faux leather clutch and walked into the living room, still holding her stinging cheek. She opened the door and sailed it down the hall like a Frisbee. "Peach was just leaving," she said to Opal. "And she won't be coming back."

"Floozy!" Opal spat. She held her wrists in the air like she had a gun at her back. "That woman is nothing but a floozy! Harlan didn't have a chance. She snatched him away from me while I was nursing my dying husband. Snatched him right out from under my nose. Like a common...*Floozy!*" she hollered one last time. Gage closed the door behind Peach.

Gage gently pulled Morgan's hand away and inspected her face. "Looks like we may need more ice."

"I deserved it," Morgan said. "I can't seem to keep my mouth shut."

"I'm very fond of that mouth," Gage said. "Open or shut."

"I accused her of poisoning Harlan."

He whistled through his teeth. "Not exactly the way I would have handled it, but...she is a legitimate suspect. She had access to prescription blood thinners and she thought Harlan had changed his will to include her. That's one hell of a motive."

"But she was at work when he died."

"She said she left work early. She was already at your house, waiting for you and Crystal when I arrived. I have no idea how long she'd been there." He opened the freezer and pulled out a frozen bag of breaded okra. "If she'd given Harlan a lethal dose of warfarin, she couldn't know the exact time he was going to hemorrhage. We don't know what Harlan's time of death was, but she might have had time to stop by his place before you got there, find him dead, and stab him with your brother's knife. Do you think she did that? Why would she do that?"

"I don't know." Morgan said. "Payback, maybe?"

"For what?"

"I think Sean rejected her. When he was passed out, she was all over him, patting his arm, stroking his hair, comforting him as if they were a couple. But when the sheriff came to arrest him, he looked straight at Peach and said, 'What are you doing here? I told you to leave me alone.' Of course, he was smashed at the time."

"Sounds like he was sober enough to know he didn't want her around. We need to talk to Sean, find out if he did reject her and when. She's at your house five days a week picking up Crystal. If she wanted to frame Sean for Harlan's murder, she could have found his knife, then held on to it and waited for Harlan to hemorrhage, then—" He stopped. "Okay, that could take forever. This theory is a little farfetched, even for me."

"Come on. We need to hurry. I thought of something else we need to look for at Harlan's besides the files."

"What?"

"When I was at his house, I noticed some pill bottles lined up on his dresser. I don't know what they were for, but there were a lot of them. I wonder if the sheriff confiscated them."

"Hard to tell. But if he took too many pills, then he did it of his own volition. You said they were already on his dresser, so no one forced him to take them."

"No, but he may not have known how harmful they could be. He was always medicating himself. He'd do anything to keep from going to the doctor. But he wasn't stupid, and he knew how to use a computer, so I can't believe he would take a bunch of drugs and supplements unless he'd researched possible interactions."

"Unless someone suggested he take them. Someone he trusted."

They got in the Jeep.

"Is this a good idea?" Gage asked. "It's a quarter to three. By the time we get to Ethan's house, he'll be on his way back."

"No, he won't. He's meeting the pastor at three. The church is halfway up the mountain. We'll be fine." She laughed. "Hell, Gage, you're the P. I. Where's your sense of adventure?"

"I left it in my other pants." He pulled onto the highway. "Hold that okra on your face. You don't want to look like you're storing nuts for the winter."

At exactly three o'clock, Gage maneuvered the Jeep into the tall grass beside the Spannagel's fence. He cut the motor and turned to Morgan. "So, what's the plan? You are going to tell me the plan, aren't you?"

"Break in, find the stuff, and don't get caught."

Gage sighed and opened the door. "Well, at least we have a plan."

"I'll take care of the guard. You find the key under the planter. Keep an eye on the road. Meet you in four. Mrs. Cowden may be half blind, but she can hear snow melt."

Morgan ran across the road and waded through the weeds until she came to the Cowden house. She slipped on the porch, rang the doorbell, and counted to twenty. Then she sprinted back across the road and jumped into the ditch. She ducked down, panting, feeling like she was ten-years-old again. She'd always loved ringing doorbells and running, but back then, the rush of not getting caught had been worth the risk. It would take several minutes for Mrs. Cowden to get out of her chair and lumber downstairs. When the old bat realized no one was at the door, she would either call the sheriff or start firing the hunting rifle she kept in the foyer.

Gage crouched in the high weeds beside the car. He leapt on to the porch, swiped the key from beneath the planter, and unlocked the Spannagel's front door. Morgan joined him in the living room.

"It's ten after three," Morgan said. "If Ethan dropped the paper off without talking to the pastor, we've got about ten—twelve minutes. I'll search upstairs for the pills. You look for the files."

Morgan opened Harlan's bedroom door and was surprised to find his room exactly as she'd seen it the day Harlan had died, with one exception: no pill bottles. She looked in his drawers and closet, lifted the lid of the old steamer trunk at the end of his bed. What had happened to them? Had they been confiscated by the police as evidence? Had Ethan thrown them away? The first thing she'd done after her grandfather died was rake all his medicine bottles into a bag and toss them in the trash.

She hesitated before opening the door to Ethan's room, then wrapped her shirttail around the brass doorknob and turned. She looked under the bed, felt under the mattress, opened and closed his drawers. A black suit in a clear plastic cleaner's bag hung in the closet beside a freshly laundered white shirt. Funeral clothes. She picked up the shoebox sitting on the closet floor and lifted the lid. The sweet, pungent odor of vanilla and jasmine rose up, permeating the air. She pulled the white tissue paper apart and tried to comprehend why she was staring at an open bottle of her favorite perfume instead of Ethan's shoes.

The soft, crunchy sound of tires rolling over gravel rumbled outside the bedroom window.

Her heart crashed into her throat.

She slammed the lid on the shoebox and shoved it in the closet.

"Morgan!" Gage yelled. "He's back! Time to haul ass!"

She ran into the hall. Halfway down the stairs, she remembered she'd left Ethan's bedroom door open. She spun on a dime, retraced her steps, and pulled the door shut. The sound echoed through the hall like a clap of thunder.

"Morgan!"

She started running. *OhGodOhGodOhGod.* She swung around the banister and stumbled down the stairs.

Outside, a car door slammed.

"Hurry! *Quick!*" Gage stood at the bottom of the steps. His eyes darted to the window. He held out his hand, and she clasped his arm. The strength of it pulled her toward him until she was airborne. His other arm circled her waist to steady her landing on the braided rug.

She hit the ground running.

"Back door," she gasped. "Through there."

"After you, my dear."

They sprinted around the dining room table to the kitchen, then dodged another table and trashcan before escaping out the back door. The key sounded in the front lock. Gage pulled the door closed, then pressed his fingers against the wavy glass windowpane to keep it from rattling. They ducked under the kitchen window and slid to a stop at the corner of the house.

"Slow breath," Gage said. "In your nose, out your mouth, count of four." He grinned at her. "Oh, and act natural."

The back door opened. "Sean?" Ethan said. "Are you out here?"

"Hey," Morgan said. The rasp in her voice gurgled like she'd been swallowing water. Her pulse pounded in her throat. She flashed Ethan a bright smile. The skin where she'd been slapped pulled taut against her cheekbone.

"I saw Sean's Jeep," Ethan said.

"Yeah, the transmission on the truck is acting up again. We were...uh..."

"Good seeing you again," Gage's low baritone boomed jovially. He held out his hand, and Ethan shook it. "Morgan's been a basket case, trying to figure out exactly who in this sleepy little burg would want to frame her brother for your father's murder."

Morgan shot him a warning glance.

"So, I suggested she come back to the scene of the crime. See if anything jogs her memory that might help Sean's defense. She didn't want to look around while you weren't here, but I told her that since the two of you are such close friends, and you have her best interests at heart, you wouldn't mind." He gave Morgan an indulgent, exasperated look, so exaggerated, it almost made her laugh. "But now our girl's having second thoughts."

"It was just so...gruesome," she said. "We should have waited for you."

"I was on my way to meet Pastor Byrd," Ethan said. "Then I realized I'd forgotten the list of scriptures I want him to read at Dad's funeral." He smiled tentatively at Morgan. "But if you think it will help Sean, I'll open the slaughterhouse for you."

"No, no." She glanced at the slaughterhouse anxiously. "I thought I'd be able to go back in there, but the memories are so...fresh. And now I...I just don't think I can."

Gage slid his arm around her shoulders. "Baby, you're trembling."

Ethan shot him a look of pure disdain. "Morgan, I think finding Dad's body has been more traumatic for you than you realize."

"Exactly what I told her," Gage said. "Maybe she'll believe it, coming from you."

"The autopsy is in," Ethan said. "I didn't think it would be back so soon. I think Sheriff Stallard must have hustled it through."

"Cause of death?" Gage asked.

"Hemorrhagic bleeding from an overdose of anticoagulants."

"Time of death?"

"Between one and three. Sheriff Stallard explained that once a person is dead, the heart stops pumping and blood stops flowing, so even though a massive amount of blood was lost when Dad was alive, his cause of death could still be determined." He looked at Morgan. "I shouldn't have said anything. You're white as a ghost."

"Are ghosts white?" Morgan shivered. "Sorry, Ethan. Sorry to cause so much trouble."

"No trouble," Ethan said. "Do you want to come inside? I could make you a drink."

"Thanks, but I think I should get back home. Sean's alone with the pickers."

"Pickers?" Ethan said. "You found pickers?"

"Only two," Gage said. "But they're hard workers." He edged his way up the driveway, still holding on to Morgan. "Isn't that great?"

"Great." Ethan's gaze never left Morgan's face. "Maybe now things will finally turn around for the orchard, and you can leave Riverbirch. You still want to leave, don't you?"

"Of course I want to leave. There's nothing for me here."

"Nothing, Morgan?" His pale eyes regarded her sadly. "Nothing at all?"

"Once Sean's name has been cleared and the harvest apples are in, only one thing could make me stay in Riverbirch."

"What's that?" Ethan asked hopefully.

"A bloody miracle."

Chapter 15

Gage backed the Jeep out of the weeds and headed down Milltown Road.

"Do you think he bought it?" Morgan asked. "Any of it?"

"No. Do you?"

"I thought I sounded pretty convincing. But you—" The dimple beside her mouth deepened. "'This sleepy little burg.' What was that about?"

"Well, it beat the hell out of, 'Oh, *Ethan!'*—*bat, bat, bat*—'I don't think I can go back in that scary old slaughterhouse again. It was *soooo* awful.'"

"Well, it *was* awful. What was I supposed to say? You're the one who told him I was having second thoughts."

"He was waiting for an explanation. Somebody had to say something."

"Too bad it was all for nothing."

"Oh, I wouldn't say that." Gage reached over and pulled a small trash bag from behind the front seat. He set it on her lap. "Merry Christmas."

She opened the bag and squealed. "Harlan's pill bottles! When did you—how did you—"

"While you were upstairs. They were in the mudroom at the bottom of a trashcan. I'm not sure how thorough the sheriff was, but I guess the she didn't consider them part of the crime scene."

"I wasn't upstairs five minutes. How did you locate them so fast?"

"I used to do this for a living. Without the benefit of a search warrant, I might add."

"How did you know to hide the pills in the car? Did you know Ethan would come back?"

"No, but I've learned not to take chances. In and out. As fast as possible."

"I might have to cross-stitch that on a pillow for you."

"Well, it's not going in the bedroom," he said, laughing.

"I just wish you'd been able to find the account folder."

"It's in the trunk."

She stared at him with her mouth open. "Unbelievable."

"They were in the china closet drawer. You know, the Hamster's not too bright."

"Why do you call him that?"

"Because he is one. If he was a turtle, I'd call him a turtle. He'd still be in love with you."

"He is not."

"Is too."

"Is *not*."

Gage lowered the window. "I get a very crazy-obsessive vibe from him. He probably has a picture shrine of you plastered on a wall somewhere. Or a Hannibal Lecter hole dug in the basement of his house."

"All I found was one picture. I don't think that qualifies as either crazy or obsessive."

"He probably snipped off a lock of your hair when

you weren't looking and sleeps with it tucked inside his pillowcase. That's where I hid my blankie at summer camp. Did you check his pillow?"

"Stop it," Morgan said, laughing. "You're the crazy one."

"No, I'm the hungry one."

She smiled at him, and his heart lurched. Then she looked at him with such unabashed affection, it made his legs go weak. They'd had a close call at the Hamster's house, but it had brought out the best in her. She'd kept her cool. Kept her head. They'd bantered back and forth like they'd been breaking into people's houses together for years. Why had he spent all those years working alone? He couldn't remember the last time he'd had so much fun.

The R-rated fantasies he'd spun in his head featuring Morgan had all been soft focus, wrapped in a kind of dreamy gauze, and about as romantic as a guy who'd never made it through a Lifetime movie could craft. They had nothing to do with the person sitting beside him, a woman with brains, and a wicked sense of humor, and a huge, caring, strong, brittle heart.

He liked this Morgan—the real Morgan. He liked her take on the world, the way she handled herself. The way she laughed at herself. He liked the way her smart, sassy mouth could take no prisoners one minute and tremble beneath his touch the next. He marveled at the way the light in her eyes could wrap around him, healing him, grounding him, making him believe the miracle of love was more than a myth someone had made up to torture lonely people. How could he risk giving that up? How could he walk away?

He couldn't. And he wouldn't.

Not without a fight.

The only chance he had—which, face it, was so slim, it barely existed—was to be honest with her. Completely, brutally, open-a-vein-and-bleed honest. Even that might not be enough. If he told her the truth, that the only reason he'd agreed to recover the flag was to help Jeremy, maybe, just maybe she would understand. And maybe she wouldn't.

"Are you up for barbecue?" she asked. "There's a place in Cherokee Bluff called Hog Heaven."

"I think that's a country-western bar."

"Well, you are in Tennessee."

"I'm always up for southern fried indigestion." He handed her his cell phone. "Mine seems to get a better signal. Call Sean and tell him we have the goods. Don't want him worrying."

After she checked in with Sean, Gage said, "You and your brother sound like good friends. I know you're twins, but some twins can't be in the same room without wanting to strangle each other."

"I've always felt protective of him. That it was up to me to keep the bad guys at bay."

"Like you're doing now?"

"Sean and I were born polar opposites. He was a sweet, gentle kid. I was Nellie Oleson. But don't let him fool you. That sweet, gentle kid has a will of iron. In his own quiet way, he usually gets what he wants. He can talk me into anything."

"Good childhood? Except for your parents dying?"

"Well, that did kind of put a damper on things. My grandpa was a widower when he took us in, and I think he married Opal so he wouldn't have to be a single parent. Of course, to his surprise, she ended up being anything but the motherly type. He raised us Old School. Sean got to drive the truck and taste the apple wine. I got to make apple butter and practice piano. Maybe that's why I detested the farm so much; Sean seemed to be having all the fun. Looking back, I realize he didn't have it so easy, but at the time, the freedom he'd been handed because he'd been born a boy, made me envious. And angry."

"But you still watched out for him."

"Someone had to." She lapsed into a long silence.

"What are you thinking about? I know the girl usually asks the guy that, but I'm willing to break tradition if you are."

"I was thinking about all the hours I spent practicing piano to win a music scholarship at UT. And how I only did it because it was my ticket out of Riverbirch."

"I thought you loved piano. What would you have rather been doing?"

"Almost anything."

"Whoa." Gage shook his head. "You've got a priceless treasure hidden in your house that could bring you enough money to give you what you've always wanted. And you don't have any idea what that is?"

"Exactly."

"Then we need to figure out what you want to be when you grow up."

Morgan laughed. "I'm pathetic, aren't I?"

He reached for her hand and brought it to his lips. "You're beautiful. And smart. And quite possibly the love of my life. But you are anything but pathetic. You want to know what pathetic is? Pathetic is not listening to your heart when every instinct inside you swears you should. Pathetic is spending your life wishing for what might have been, and not having the guts to do something about it. Does that sound like a crazy person talking?"

She squeezed his hand. "It sounds like a hungry person talking."

He glanced in the rearview mirror. The motorcycle was still behind them. He hadn't said anything because he didn't want to worry her, but he couldn't sit on it any longer. He tried to sound casual. "Do you know anyone who rides a motorcycle besides Denny?"

"The Wheeler twins ride them, and I think Deputy Nelson has one. Why?"

"One has been following us since we started over the mountain. I've given it every opportunity to pass, but if I slow down, it drops back. When we go around a switchback, it stays too close for me to see the rider's face."

She flipped the sun visor down and looked in the vanity mirror. "It's too dark to see anything but a pair of black shoulders hunched over the handlebars. It looks sinister. Like the faceless driver of a hearse that stops on the road in front of you and opens its door."

"I wish I had your imagination."

If Gage had been alone, he would have tried to lose the bike. But with Morgan in the car, he was forced to own up to his limitations as a mountain driver. He kept his eye on the rearview mirror and downshifted around the last series of hairpin turns. When he started over the bridge, he approached the stop sign, but instead of slowing down, he slammed his foot on the brake. The cyclist swerved to the right and skidded hard across the pavement, barely missing the Jeep's back bumper.

After the bike righted itself, the driver revved the motor a few times, then made a wide U-turn and headed back up the mountain.

"He's leaving," Gage said. "He just flipped us off. Well, that wasn't nice."

"Do you think it was Denny?" She squinted out the back window. "Why the hell don't they put a streetlight at this intersection?"

"If it was Denny, I think he was trying to spook you."

"One of the few things he excels at."

Gage glanced at her. "Do you still want to eat? I can take you home, if you want."

"No, we're safe. Denny's a coward. He only bullies women who are alone." She blew out a breath. "Look, I swore a long time ago, I wouldn't let Denny, or the fear of Denny, rule my life. And I'm not about to start now."

"Good girl." Gage pulled into Hog Heaven and cut the motor. "Popular place. Is this the local Saturday hot spot? I see kids and grandparents."

She laughed. "Of course, you do. Welcome to date night in Riverbirch, Tennessee."

****

Ten minutes later, they were seated at a rustic wooden table covered with a red-checkered cloth. The smoky sweet aroma of pork barbecue made Morgan's mouth water, and she realized she hadn't eaten since breakfast.

Rows of square tables and a long half-moon bar sat on a platform circling the dance floor. A split rail fence separated the diners from the dancers. Copper pigs, handmade quilts, and antique farm implements decorated the walls, giving it a cozy barn-like feel.

Country music boomed from the speakers. A line of dancers dipped and kicked in unison, whooping and clapping to the music.

"Is it always this lively?" Gage looked at the waitress's nametag. "Suter? Well, that's a name I've never heard before. But it...suits you." He shot her a blinding grin that sent blood rushing to the girl's cheeks.

Been there, Morgan thought.

"Why, this ain't nothin'," Suter said. "After the band sets up at nine, it'll be so crowded, you won't be able to fart sideways in this place." She smiled at him, a little breathless, and smoothed a few tendrils of hair off the nape of her neck. "You should hang around." She glanced at Morgan, his previously invisible date, and added, "Oh, and you, too."

After polishing off a plate of pork barbecue, coleslaw, cheese grits, and jalapeño cornbread, Gage leaned back in his chair and laughed. His deep, rich baritone rumbled across the table. Sean did that sometimes, laughed out loud for no reason at all, as if the sudden burst of joy inside him could not be contained.

"Dance with me," Gage said. "My Tush Push is a little rusty, but I think I can manage a slow dance without flattening your toes." He grinned and turned on his South Georgia drawl. "Whad'ya say, Miss Morgan? You're the best lookin' gal in this tiny burg. Have pity on me?"

"Well, you are my chauffeur."

He took her hand and led her through a pair of wooden posts to the dance floor.

She put her arms around his neck. His large hands

encircled her waist. She leaned into his shoulder and let the music swell around them, a familiar, heartbreaking ballad full of regret and longing, that never failed to prick tears behind her eyes.

She knew all about regret and longing. Regret gnawed at her soul when she pondered the fact that the loss of this man had set her on a solitary path, closing her heart to anyone. How had she let that happen? How could she have fallen in love with Gage, then turned around and married a man she didn't love, simply because her self-worth had hit the skids? If only she'd believed in herself then, believed the life she wanted to live would resurface someday after hobbling through the empty, painful fog of a broken heart.

"We are the sum total of our choices," she said.

"What?"

"It's from a Woody Allen movie. I just thought of it."

He kissed her lightly on the forehead. "Then choose me."

"I'm thinking about it."

What the hell was she doing?

The more time she spent with Gage, the easier it was to ignore the warning bells clanging inside her head. She'd relied on those bells; they had never steered her wrong. They had kept her heart from splitting into a million pieces. That's why she was having a hard time accepting the fact that in three short days, the longing she'd felt for him all those years ago had filtered into the here and now. Maybe it had never gone away. Maybe it had lain dormant like a bear in wintertime, hunkering down, sleeping through Christmas, barely anticipating the insatiable hunger it will feel on the first day of spring.

Why had he picked now to show up? Now, when the scars he'd left had almost healed and her life had gone on? She'd made peace with going through life as a solo act. She could go for days, even weeks without thinking of him. Alone was something she'd learned how to do. And she did it well. She still got a pang when she saw a couple walking hand in hand across the Deer Creek footbridge, or when the Wallace's dropped off their daughter for a piano lesson, and she could see them on the porch, bent over the new baby, eyes shining as they congratulated each other on their perfect life. Gage was a road she wasn't sure she wanted to travel again. She didn't want to walk over a mile-high suspension bridge in a windstorm again, either.

But, oh, God, he smelled good. She burrowed her face against his neck and breathed in his scent—male and sweet and addictive. She rubbed her cheek along the edge of his collarbone, back and forth, like a lost kitten who's found its way home. His thighs pressed against hers as they swayed to the music. His feather soft breath darted across her neck, sending a chain of shivers snaking down her back. Heat flared at the base of her spine. She closed her eyes. As long as she was in his arms, it was all so easy. She could blot out the rest of the world and pretend they were a normal couple, taking things one step at a time without waiting for the ground to open up and swallow her whole. He was charming. Convincing. Tempting. He was a trip to Disneyworld. All she had to do was suspend belief long enough to jump on the tram.

"Morgan?"

She pulled back and looked into his eyes. In the

soft amber light, his smoky brown gaze appeared more intense than she'd ever seen it. His dark eyes melted into hers, and she tightened her grip on his shoulders to keep her knees from buckling. He was so near, she could see the tiny blue flecks swimming near the dark brown-green irises. "Lacey's Pond in winter. That's what your eyes look like to me. It's so deep there, it hardly ever freezes over."

"Morgan, I need to tell you something."

"Spilling your guts on a dance floor is never a good idea." She laced her fingers behind his neck and drew him closer. "Kissing, on the other hand, is highly recommended."

"This is serious," he said. "I can't wait any longer."

"Neither can I." She leaned in to him until her lips were inches from his.

"Morgan, please. Let's go somewhere where we can talk. There's something about me you need to know."

She raked her lips across his, tasting them, teasing them. "Well, we can go somewhere." She pressed her mouth against his. "But I don't think..." Then kissed him again. "...we'll be doing much..." And again. "...talking."

****

It wasn't hard for Gage to rationalize waiting one more day to tell her. Especially when she was standing in the middle of a public dance floor kissing him like there was no tomorrow. In his wildest dreams—and there had been a few of those—he had never expected her to want him again. Or for him to feel the kind of happiness that wrapped around his heart and set him free at the same time. It was better than any dream he

Rebecca Lee Smith

could have manufactured. It exhilarated him. Terrified him. He vowed to hold on to the memory, because the one thing, in all certainty, that would split them apart forever was hanging over his head like an anvil waiting to drop. The only chance he had to keep Morgan in his life was to level with her.

And yet, he couldn't bring himself to do it.

Please, God, he prayed. *Let me fall asleep in her arms. Just let me have one more night with her, and I swear, I'll tell her in the morning.*

"You know, we're the Bible Belt," she murmured. "Are we breaking the law?"

"No, but we're damned close. Let's get out of here before somebody calls the sheriff."

He threw money on the table, grabbed Morgan's jacket, and led her outside through the swinging saloon doors. They clattered across the wooden porch and hurried past a rowdy, laughing group of people gathered around a concrete ashtray. They followed an overgrown path leading to a wooden gazebo at the side of the building, then ducked into the shadows behind a thick copse of river birch trees.

A sharp gust of mountain air blew against the base of his throat. It rustled the leaves as he pulled her under a limb and leaned her back against the trunk. He captured her mouth again, relieved that the heat they'd generated on the dance floor hadn't begun to cool.

Dusky moonlight filtered through the branches. Morgan's blue eyes glistened, half-closed with desire. Her lips curled into a smile against his. How many times had he fantasized about those lips, their velvety softness gliding over him, driving him to the brink and back again? A flood of gratitude swelled inside him, expanding his chest until he thought it would rip open. For one small moment in time, he was the luckiest bastard in the world. He was here. Awake. In the dream, with the woman he loved. The woman he had always loved.

She gasped and pulled away. "We could go to the car."

"Gear shift. No back seat." He nuzzled the tender spot behind her ear. "And I parked beneath a big. Tall. Sodium vapor lamp."

"Gotcha."

He ran his fingers along the smooth column of her throat and held her face in his hands, deepening the kiss, matching each flick and swipe of her tongue with a hunger he wasn't sure he could control. Her hips thrust against his, warm and pliant, and the tightening in his groin told him things were moving faster than he should let them. But before he could take a breath and tap the brakes, Morgan raked her hands across his back and held him tight, as if she were trying to dissolve into him. Her breasts pushed up and out, rubbing against him, nipples hard beneath her cotton blouse. Suddenly, tapping the brakes, or anything else, was the last thing on his mind. He slid his hand beneath the thin material and skimmed it along the scorching flesh above her jeans until he found the back of her bra. He held the connecting strap between his thumb and index finger, and with one expert snap, unhooked it.

A sharp intake of breath escaped her lips. It sent a shiver rushing through him, and he smiled into her shoulder. It had been a long time since he'd unhooked a woman's bra. Longer than he was willing to admit. Thank God, he still remembered how.

Morgan finished unbuttoning his shirt and began clawing at his belt. It was his turn to suck in air and groan. Loudly. If a possum was hiding within twenty feet, it would either start hissing at them or turn tail and run.

****

Morgan tugged on Gage's shirt, trying to extract it from his pants. She'd managed to unbutton the waistband of his jeans, revealing a soft thatch of dark hair curling over the plaid elastic on his shorts. But the zipper—the damned zipper—refused to budge. She tried to concentrate. Which wasn't easy with his mouth trailing molten kisses along the slope of her shoulder. His hands caressed the length of her bare back, then stroked the prickly spot where her bra clasp had fastened. She leaned into him and moaned, like an old Basset hound who's finally found someone to scratch under its collar. She cursed and gave the shirt one final tug. *Bingo.*

His hands were on the move again, systematically making their way to the front of her body. Her heart picked up speed. Her breath, when she could hold on to it, came in short, self-conscious pants. Heat burned a path across her abdomen, down her legs, turning them to Jell-O. She had about three more seconds until those magic fingers of his reached her breasts. Four until she threw herself on the ground and pulled him on top of her.

Gage chuckled and turned her around facing the tree. The pungent, earthy scent of moss permeated her nose. He lifted her hair and kissed the back of her neck, lingering in the hollow of her shoulder, then slid both hands around her torso, cupping her breasts. He grazed his thumbs across her nipples, back and forth, until she arched her back. Her hands crept upward along the damp bark until they overlapped. She lowered her head and cried out, aroused to the point of plunging into some dark abyss of heat and need. She longed to see him, touch him, feel the length of him. She needed to know he was as turned on as she was.

She twisted back around and reached for him, feeling his erection strain against his jeans. "No, Morgan," he said softly. "This one's for you."

He pulled her to him and backed her up to the tree, kissing her deeply. The rough bark scraped the exposed flesh at the base of her spine, but she hardly felt it. Every nerve ending pulsated to the rapid beat of her heart. Pale blue moonlight filtered through the leaves, threw uneven shadows across the fine, chiseled planes of his high cheekbones. He smiled at her, slashing the dimple on the left side of his face. Then he whispered her name. He might as well have lit a fuse. Desire exploded inside her, and she was tempted to close her eyes and let his touch sweep her into the stratosphere. But she couldn't.

Not tonight.

Tonight she needed real. And it didn't get more real than standing backed up against a tree with her legs spread and a man's hand inside her pants.

He gazed at her with so much longing, it hurt to breathe. Wasn't this what she'd always wanted from him? The reality she'd yearned for? Wasn't this what she had lost all those years ago and was terrified of letting back into her life? Into her heart?

And then he touched her, and pure sensation took over, and it didn't matter anymore.

He unzipped her jeans and swept his right hand along the soft contour of her stomach, beneath the silky vee of her panties, until two fingers slipped inside and found the mother of all epicenters. His stroke was relaxed and persistent, self-assured without trying too hard. Within seconds she was able to blot out the world and ride the slow, rhythmic wave to the top. When she came, she came hard, rocking into him with a shudder, gripping his shoulder, clutching his hand in mid-stroke to stop the sensory overload. She fell against him, gulping in air as if she'd swum up from the bottom of Lacey's Pond.

And then she began to laugh.

"Holy—" she said, panting noisily. "All right, Mr. Kirkland. I have two questions for you. Where did you learn to do that? And when can you do it again?"

He laughed and pushed her hair back from her face. Then he kissed her lightly on the lips. "This may be the wrong time to say this. My timing's always been a little off." He grinned and shook his head. "Okay, a lot off. But these last three days with you have meant the world to me."

"They've been...not so bad," she agreed. "Well, except for the dead body. And my brother getting arrested. And your uncle trying to steal our land. And the fire at Bad Moon."

"I don't want this to end. If I thought for one minute you could forgive the irresponsible kid who was too stupid and too scared to stand up for the only thing he ever wanted, I'd do anything to make it up to you. Your memory has haunted me for so long, I—" His voice caught. "The heart doesn't give a damn how much time has passed, or how badly it's bruised, or how hopeless things are. The heart wants what the heart wants."

"Didn't Woody Allen say that, too?"

"The man's a genius." He placed his hands on her shoulders. His dark gaze held hers. "I don't want to turn back the clock because then I wouldn't have Jeremy. So I have to believe that all roads lead where they're supposed to lead. Do you believe that? Do you believe me?"

"See, that's the thing. I believed you before."

"I know you did. And I know trust is something that has to be earned. All I'm asking is for another chance to earn that trust. And to let me love you."

She lifted her hand. "Don't say that. Don't use that word."

"All right, 'like' then." He wrapped his arms around her. "Please, let me like you, Morgan. Let me like you a whole, whole lot."

They readjusted their clothes and walked, arm in arm, through the wet grass.

"What did you want to tell me?" she asked. "You said it was important."

"I'll tell you tomorrow. Tonight, I just want to make the rest of the world go away. I want to hold on to this. To you."

She turned to him. The lilting strains of "Copperhead Road" and the soft, syncopated thumps of the line dancers drifted across the lawn. "Tell me what's wrong."

He swallowed a sigh. "I'm trying to hang on to this little piece of hope I suddenly have with you. I wish I were a better person. Someone who didn't make mistakes. Someone you could be proud of. Someone you could forgive. I have to believe that no matter what happens, everything will work out, and I'm not just some poor, unsuspecting pig, trotting merrily into the slaughterhouse when I don't have a chance in hell of coming out alive."

"Maybe it's your destiny. You can't screw around with destiny."

"Destiny," he said. "That's an odd thing to start believing in at my age. But I do. Three days ago, my son wouldn't look me in the eye. And now, because of you, he's smiling and calling me Dad again. Three days ago, I was a man still living under my uncle's thumb, so bogged down with regret and guilt, I didn't know if I'd ever dig my way out. Three days ago, you were a memory I've spent the last twelve years trying to forget. And now, you're...here."

"Tell me what you don't want to tell me. Just do it fast. Like ripping off a Band-Aid."

Morgan's cell phone rang. She fished it out of her purse and snapped it open. "It's Sean."

"Morgan, Morgan!" Sean cried. "You've got to come home! I'm goin' crazy here."

"Slow down. What's happened?"

"It's Jeremy," Sean said. "He's gone."

"What do you mean, Jeremy's gone?"

"He's not here. I've looked everywhere. He's not in the house. He's not in the barn. He's just...*gone*."

Chapter 16

Gage snatched the phone out of Morgan's hand and roared into it. *"Where is he?"*

"Put it on speaker," she said.

The panic in Sean's tinny voice cut through the night. "I don't know. I went to the shed to get the stirring paddles, and when I came back he was gone. Gage, I don't know."

Gage pressed the heel of his hand into his forehead. "Now, listen to me, goddammit! You find my boy. And you find him now!"

"Denny?" Sean said. "What are you doing here?"

"Denny!" Morgan yelled into the phone. "Are you there?" Gage thumbed the volume to high. *"Sean, put Denny on! Let me talk to him!"*

"Denny, where's Jeremy?" Sean said. "What have you done with him?"

The phone went dead.

"Oh, Jesus," Gage said. "He's got Jeremy."

He turned and started running toward the Jeep. He was already inside and fumbling for the key when Morgan climbed into the passenger seat.

"Where are the lights?" Gage cried. "Where's the damned clutch?" He scratched at the dashboard, smacking every button with his hand. *"Where the hell are the friggin' lights?"* He glanced at her. "I've got the key in the ignition, but I can't find the lights."

Morgan opened her door and got out.

"What are you doing? Aren't you coming? We have to hurry!"

"I'm driving."

"No, you're not." He switched the lights on and groped the gearshift, searching for the brake release. "Where is it? *Where is it?*"

She opened his door. "Scoot over." When he didn't budge, she said, "Gage!"

He stared at her, wide-eyed and terror-stricken.

"I'm used to the car. I'm used to the mountain. I can get us there faster."

His gaze locked with hers, and for a moment she thought she was going to have to pry his hands off the steering wheel. But then he nodded and let go. He hoisted himself over the gearshift. She fastened her seatbelt and slammed the Jeep in reverse, jolting them backwards. She tore out of the parking lot, ran the stop sign before the bridge, and started up the mountain. As she rounded the first series of switchbacks, he raised his hand and gripped the *Oh, Jesus* handle. Then he leaned his head against the crook of his arm and closed his eyes.

"How could I have left him?" he whispered. "He's so little. How could I have left him alone? The person following us on the motorcycle might have been Denny. I should have turned around and gone back to be sure. But I didn't. I made myself believe Jeremy would be all right because I was desperate to spend time with you. I'm always trying to trick myself into rationalizing everything." His deep voice cracked. "I'm a terrible father. I ought to be shot."

"Calm down," she said. "Honey, it's gonna be all right." The East Tennessee accent she'd spent years trying to lose returned with a vengeance. "Denny won't hurt Jeremy. He only wants the flag. Call the sheriff, and have her meet us there."

Gage pulled out his phone and punched in 911. "I can't get a signal. I can't get a freakin' signal! What kind of place is this that I can't get a freakin' signal?"

"You're in the mountains, hon. God's country, remember?" She glanced at him, then focused on slowing down and speeding up as they flew around an S curve. She rolled the window partway down and breathed in the loamy, earth-scented air, a smell that never failed to soothe her. The lights from the Jeep cut across the tree trunks, sliding from one Carolina pine to the next like high-speed laser beams. "It'll be okay. I promise. Denny's not gonna hurt Jeremy. All he wants is the flag. When we get to the house, I'll give it to him. I'll hand it over, and everything will be fine."

"Does Sean have a gun?"

"A gun? No. I don't think so." She pushed her hair out her eyes. "We won't need a gun."

"Okay." He took a deep breath and blew it out, slow and steady. "If anything happens to Jeremy, I'll never forgive myself. I'll never forgive anyone again."

She reached out and squeezed his hand. "Gage, it's okay. We'll find him."

As they neared the bottom of Blackstone Mountain, a stillness gathered around him, and she wondered if he was mentally preparing himself for what might lie ahead. She barreled down Milltown Road, then slowed before she rounded the curve to the orchard entrance.

"Cut the lights," he said. "Then ease the Jeep into the lower yard away from the utility lamp." When she came to a stop, he swung out of the front seat and said, "Stay here."

"Like hell."

"Then stay behind me. I can't worry about you right now."

The sweet aroma of apples, mingled with the sharp, smoky scent of a wood fire filled the air. White plumes of smoke drifted over the barn like ghosts waiting for midnight. The four floodlights on the side of the barn shone upwards, illuminating the large wooden apple quilt block over the door.

Morgan followed Gage. He skirted the side yard and crept along the shadowed fence line. When they reached the house, he put his hand out to stop her, then pointed to the massive rhododendron bush growing near the far side of the porch. A tiny slice of chrome glinted in the light. Through the thick, stobby branches, she could make out the outline of a black motorcycle.

"Is that his bike?" Gage asked.

"I'm not sure. Do you think he's inside the house?"

"I don't know." Gage started up the side porch steps. "But I'm going to find out."

"Wait a minute!" she whispered. "Don't you want to sneak in the back door? Wouldn't that be the smart thing to do?"

"I'm not doing the smart thing. I'm doing the fast thing. If he heard the car, he knows we're here. He's waiting for us, watching our every move. Back door, front door, it doesn't matter."

Gage wedged his broad shoulders between the screen and the door. He placed his hand on the brass knob. "And Morgan? Just so you know. If that son of a bitch has laid so much as a finger on my son, I will kill him."

He opened the door and walked inside.

Morgan edged into the foyer behind him. Her heart banged against her ribs.

The tiny lamp on the piano cast distorted shadows around the room. The drawers from her grandfather's roll top desk had been emptied, a chair overturned. A path of sheet music trailed across the flowered rug.

Gage stood for a moment, head down, listening, then quickly circled through the dining room to the kitchen. He crept through the laundry room, in and out of the office, down the back hall. He opened and closed doors without making a sound, moved silently across old hardwood floors that creaked if someone looked at them. For the first time, she was seeing the real Gage doing the thing he'd been trained to do, the thing he loved, the thing he did best. Watching him in stealth mode both fascinated and reassured her. It took the edge off her fear, kept the adrenaline from bouncing her off the ten-foot ceiling.

He came back and stopped at the staircase. He held his finger to his lips and pointed upstairs. Then he disappeared into the shadows with his hand poised above the light switch.

A scraping noise echoed on the second floor near her bedroom. A tremor shuddered down her spine. Her mouth went dry. Her pulse hammered in her ears, swishing and pounding like she'd fallen overboard and had to fight her way to the surface.

Soft footsteps thumped along the upstairs hall.

Morgan glanced at Gage, hoping the sight of him

might quell the panic rising in her throat. His gaze focused on the top of the stairs, every muscle in his body tight and ready to spring. She reached out and curled her fingers around the hall tree. Denny was a big man, a head taller than Gage, but she had no doubt that if Denny wouldn't listen to reason, Gage would beat the crap out of him anyway.

A man swung around the wooden banister. Morgan could tell at once it wasn't Denny. This man was wiry and agile, and was tripping down the stairs like he'd been called to breakfast.

The man crossed the center landing. When he pivoted toward them, she heard Gage suck air through his teeth. The man never looked up, and by the confident swagger in his step, it was clear he had no idea two people were waiting for him.

When the man reached the bottom step, Gage flipped on the overhead lamp, bathing the room in white light.

The man stopped in mid-step. He blinked at Gage, shook his head, then blew out a long, loud sigh and grinned. "Jesus, Gage. Whatcha trying to do? Give me a heart attack?"

"It had crossed my mind," Gage said.

"Where you been, dude? Tyson thought you'd disappeared." His gaze shot to Morgan and lingered, lazily traveling from her neck to her knees. "Well, damn, Gage. Now I see the reason you're still hanging around here. Can't say as I blame you."

"You two know each other?" Morgan asked.

"Uh, oh," the man said. "Gage has forgotten his manners." He shoved the clear plastic box he was carrying under one arm and held out a surgically gloved hand. "Cal Leonard, ma'am." When Morgan ignored it, he grinned again, "And she's got principles. Hell, Gage, no wonder you didn't finish this job. I'd have ditched it too if I was gettin' some of this."

Gage stared at Cal like a man who's come face to face with his worst nightmare, and can't grasp the fact it's real. The only thing that moved was the knot in his jaw, clenched so tight, the artery in his neck bulged.

"Gage?" Morgan said. "What's going on?"

"Cal, have you seen my son Jeremy? He's eleven, but he's just a little guy. I think I showed you a picture of him once when we were on stakeout. Have you seen a big, gray-haired hippie-looking dude? I think they're together, and—"

"Yeah, I saw 'em. Out by the barn. I checked to see who was here before I ducked into the house. The kid's okay. They're cooking something in a big vat."

"Thanks, man." Gage turned to go.

"Not so fast." Cal pulled the box out from under his arm. The faded gold stars of General Johnston's battle flag were visible through the thick plastic. Cal reached behind him and slid a handgun out of his belt. He pointed it at Morgan. "No one's going anywhere. Not until I make it outta here with this flag."

"Please, Cal," Gage begged hoarsely. "My boy's been missing for over an hour. I have to see if he's all right. Just let me go to him."

Cal's eyes narrowed. "I'm a better shot than you, Gage, remember? And I say you ain't goin' anywhere." He laughed and held up the box. "Women always think they can hide stuff where nobody will find it, but that just ain't the case. In old houses like this, there's always a loose floorboard or two. Usually in a bedroom underneath a rug and a rocker. You taught me well, Gage. It only took ten minutes to find the honey pot. You been here for days. Why couldn't you find it? Or maybe you didn't want to find it."

"That flag belongs to me," Morgan said.

"Not according to your ex-husband's father," Cal said. "And he's paying one hell of a finder's fee to get it back. Old Gage here could have made a killing off it if he'd kept his pants zipped up nice and tight. But keeping your pants zipped ain't your style, is it, old buddy? Too late now. The flag is mine." Cal laughed and shook his head. "She don't know about you, does she? She don't know why you came here."

Gage's leg came out of nowhere. It kicked the gun out of Cal's hand, and sent the box flying. Before Morgan had time to blink, he had pinned Cal against the wall and was towering over the smaller man like a school bully. Morgan picked up the gun.

"Let go of me!" Cal cried. "I'm only doing my job. *Your* job."

"Are you here by yourself?" Gage asked.

"Yeah," Cal said. "I always work alone. You know that."

Gage loosened his grip. "Then get the hell out of here. And tell Tyson I said if Denny's father wants his flag back, he'll have to get a warrant."

"What's gotten into you, man? Has this chick already got you whipped?"

Morgan pointed the gun at Cal. "You want me to whip you, too? Because I can do it. Now, get the hell out of my house." She kicked the box toward him. "And take the flag with you. I don't want it."

Cal glanced at Gage and hesitated.

"Go ahead," Morgan said. "Gage isn't going to give you any trouble. Are you Gage?"

"Morgan, please," Gage said. "Don't do this." He glanced at her. The guilt and humiliation in his eyes only made her angrier. "I know I should have told you. I *tried* to tell you. But please, don't give him the flag."

"Shut up," she said. "Take it, Cal. And may you never have a moment's peace with the money it brings."

Cal scooped the box from the floor and rushed out the door.

Gage took the gun from her hand. He flipped it open and checked the chamber. "Loaded. I guess Cal gets points for that. I have to find Jeremy." He ran out the door and bounded down the porch steps two at a time.

Morgan followed him. The wind whipped hair into her face, and she raked it out of her eyes. Fury rose in her throat like acid. "You *bastard*," she cried, running alongside him. "Is that why you came here? To steal the flag from me? You only pretended to help Sean so you could weasel your way into our house." She hurried to keep up. "Everything you told me was a lie. *Everything*. You're no better than your uncle. You're no better than Denny."

"You're wrong, but I don't have time to explain." He stopped at the corner of the barn. An eerie silence surrounded them.

"I don't hear anything," she whispered.

He glanced at her as if he were seeing her for the first time. "What are you doing here?"

"I'm helping you find Jeremy. But only because I like the kid. You can rot in hell."

"Fine," he said. "But this is how it's gonna go." He

held his baritone down to a low rumble. "I'm going in alone. If I get into trouble, you hightail it back to the house and call 911."

"You are not going in there alone."

"Yes, I am." He stood beside the barn door. "You stay here."

"Not a chance."

"I mean it, Morgan. Do not move."

"You keep saying that like I'm going to do it. I've had it with you."

He pointed the gun toward the black sky and clasped his wrist in his other hand with a practiced assurance that sent a chill through her. Whatever made her think she knew this man? Or would ever know him? He had lied to her. Betrayed her trust. And now he was standing outside her apple barn, ready to crash through the door and fire a bullet into her ex-husband.

"Open the door," he said calmly. "And stay behind me."

She squeezed the handle and pulled the barn door toward her as quietly as she could. When the opening was large enough, Gage stepped through.

Fluorescent lights burned brightly overhead, illuminating the dusty corners, reflecting off the apple butter equipment. Gage held the gun in both hands with his arms straight out. He turned quickly to the left and right, then upwards to the loft, his eyes darting all around. Satisfied they were alone, he pointed toward the back door. A fine film of perspiration glistened across his upper lip.

He pushed the narrow rear door leading to the yard behind the barn with his foot. A gust of wind caught the door like a sail, banging it hard against the outer wall.

White wood smoke billowed past Gage into the interior of the barn. The bittersweet aroma of scorched apples rushed through Morgan's sinuses. Outside, the enormous built-in kettle sat beneath a work lamp Sean had attached to the corner of the barn. Light sliced through the brown apple mash. Rolling bubbles exploded on the surface.

Gage stepped across the threshold. He held Cal's loaded gun in front of him like a saber. He stopped beside the kettle. "Oh, Christ," he said. He spun around. Shock and rage spilled across his face. "Jeremy!" he called, softly at first, his voice a frightened, mournful cry. Then louder as the terror in his heart struck him full force. "Jeremy! *Jeremy! Jeremy!*"

Morgan waved her way through the drifts of white smoke. "Gage, what—"

"Don't come over here!" he cried. "Get back in the barn."

But it was too late. Her gaze had already caught a movement in the copper kettle, a dark log-like cylinder gently bobbing up and down. She wiped her burning eyes and waited for the smoke to clear. Above the thick, simmering liquid, a hand attached to the buttoned cuff of a denim work shirt surfaced. It paused in midair, as if beckoning her closer, then sank into the bubbling brown mash.

Morgan swallowed a scream.

A death mask of Denny's face, red and bloated and hideous, rolled up out of the swirling liquid with its eyes wide open. Strings of waxy flesh where his eyelids should have been dripped across the bridge of his nose. A gaping gash cut across the right side of his forehead, splayed open to reveal a wedge of white skull. He bobbed for a moment like a top heavy pool toy then flipped over onto his face. His braided ponytail undulated in the boiling apples like a silver snake.

Morgan stood paralyzed. She stared at the arc of blue plaid covering Denny's back, unable to breathe. Unable to look away.

How many times had she wished Denny dead? A hundred? A thousand? But not like this. Not anything like this.

Gage grabbed her arm and jerked her away from the kettle. "Don't look at him. Look at me. *Morgan!*"

She forced herself to shift her gaze to Gage's face.

"Help me find Jeremy and Sean."

Sean. *Where was Sean?* A fresh rush of adrenaline shot through her veins, snapping her brain awake. "Sean!" she shouted, turning first one way then the other. *"Sean!"*

Maybe Jeremy and Sean were hiding somewhere together. But where? She looked around frantically then kicked at the stacks of wooden crates beside the kettle. She shoved them out of the way, lifted them up, looked beneath them. She knelt beside the wide work table her grandfather had nailed together with two-by-fours. Jeremy was small but resourceful. If Sean and Denny had fought, he might have crawled beneath the table to hide in the shadows.

"Jeremy?" she called.

No answer.

"Where are they?" Gage stood with his back to her, staring at the top of Pip's Hill. "Do you think they're in the woods?" Bathed in a wash of pale moonlight, the scrubby weeds growing on the hill looked exotic and beautiful as they moved in the breeze.

Morgan started for the shed.

"I already tried the shed door. It's locked."

A low moan thrummed beneath the work table.

"Jeremy!" Gage cried.

Morgan whirled around. She dropped to her knees and ducked her head under the wooden slats. "I looked under here, but I couldn't see anything." Gage squatted beside her. He peered into the blackness.

"Jeremy? Son, where are you?"

"It's me," Ethan said. He stretched out his arm. "I think I passed out." She could barely make out his lanky form lying curled in the corner. "I can't move my leg. Denny pushed me down, and I fell over a crate."

"Where's Jeremy?" Gage demanded. He reached into the far corner beneath the table, clasped Ethan's hand, and pulled him out.

"I don't know where the boy is," Ethan said. "After the fight broke out, he took off." He looked at Morgan. "I had a bad feeling about you tonight. That's why I'm here. I tried to call, but it kept going to voicemail. I came over to make sure you were all right. When I got here, Denny was threatening Sean." He grimaced. "*Owww*, that hurts. I think he broke my foot."

Gage lifted Ethan and set him on a crate, then paced the length of the yard. "*Jeremy*! Where are you, son? Everything's okay now. *Jeremy! Jeremy, answer me!*"

"Where's Sean?" Morgan grabbed Ethan's open collar. "Where is my brother?"

Ethan held his foot and groaned. He pointed to the supply shed. "In there. Denny worked him over pretty good then locked the door. I think he's unconscious."

Morgan's heart crashed against her ribs. She ran to

the shed and felt beneath the eaves until she located the extra key hanging from a nail. With shaking hands, she unlocked the door and flipped on the light. A single bulb hung from its cord like a noose. She looked around, panicked, until she spotted Sean lying on his back beside the lawnmower.

"Sean!" She ran to him and dropped to her knees. His right eye had swollen shut. Purple welts mixed with dirt and sweat covered his jaw. His lower lip laid split open and bleeding. Blood trickled down his neck. She put her hand on his chest. She knew better than to move him.

"Gage!" she shouted. "Over here! I need help."

Gage was suddenly beside her. "How is he?"

"Alive but unconscious."

"I can't get a signal on my cell. I'm going back to the house to call for help on the land line."

"Any sign of Jeremy?"

"Ethan said he ran up Pip's Hill."

"Into the woods?"

"Yes," he said.

"Then I know where he went."

"Where? Tell me." He put his hands on her shoulders. "Morgan, tell me!"

"It's a secret place I showed him, about half a mile in. It'll be faster if I go. You'll never find it at night." She reached behind the door. "Sean always keeps a flashlight back—here it is." She flipped the switch and shone the amber arc of light across Sean's still face. "He looks bad."

"Can't I come?" He grabbed her arm. "Jeremy's my son. If anything happens to him—"

"You've got to stay with Sean and Ethan. I know

exactly where Jeremy is. I'll bring him back. I promise. You have to trust me." She looked into his eyes. "Like I trusted you."

****

The spit in Gage's mouth turned to ash. His heartbeat thudded in his neck. The panic he'd managed to hold at bay in front of Cal pressed against his chest until it ached. His gaze tried to focus on everything at once, do what he'd been trained to do. But he couldn't move. He sat helpless while images and sounds slid from real time into slow motion: Sean bleeding on the floor, Ethan moaning outside, Morgan standing at the door, looking at him like he was the scum of the earth. He wanted to tell her he was sorry, that he was getting what he deserved for deceiving her. But all he could manage to say was, "I didn't know it would feel like this."

"What?"

"Being a real father. Not knowing where your child is. Whether he's safe or hurt or—"

"I'll find him," she said.

"Please, Morgan. That's my life—that's my heart out there."

Morgan nodded. "I'll find him." Then she was gone.

"It's okay," Sean mumbled. "She knows those woods like the back of her hand."

"Hey, you're awake," Gage said. "I think you're gonna be okay. I'm going for help."

"No, wait." Sean put his hand on Gage's arm. "I know who you are. I've known all along. You're the guy Morgan fell in love with at the Harvest Festival. The one who broke her heart."

"Why didn't you say anything?"

"Because I was selfish. Harlan had researched your company. He was sure you could save the orchard." He swallowed and squinted up at him. "You're not a bad guy, Gage. You just can't forgive yourself. She still loves you. I think she'll always love you." He moved his leg and groaned. "I can't walk. The son-of-a-bitch kicked me in the knee."

"Well, he won't be kicking anybody else." Gage got up. "I'll be back as soon as I can."

Gage turned. He'd almost forgotten about Ethan sitting on the crate, watching them. "How's your foot?"

"It hurts," Ethan said. "But don't worry about me. I'm tougher than I look."

"Good. Just hang on. I'm going for help."

Gage ran through the barn and down the path. He slammed through the gate at the bottom of the hill and raced up the steps. He pushed open the door then scanned the room for the phone sitting on the open roll top desk. He started for it, then stopped. The faint, high-pitched screech of the screen door sent a jolt rushing though his chest. He glanced over his shoulder.

A spray of white sparks exploded behind his eyes. He fell forward to his knees. The sound of metal striking metal hammered through his skull. The edge of his peripheral vision squirmed and crawled like an exposed ant colony beneath a rock.

Something pawed at his side pocket. He tried to lift his head.

The last thing he saw before the clanging in his brain took over, and the rolling waves of darkness obliterated his sight, was the shimmering outline of a person, standing over him, holding Cal's gun.

Chapter 17

Morgan grabbed her denim jacket off the hook by the barn door. She wished it was heavier. The brisk autumn wind cut through it like a knife. She wondered what Jeremy was wearing. The thought of him shivering in the cold, alone and afraid, quickened her steps.

She trudged up the hill, hardly feeling the thistles and scrub grass scrape her bare ankles. She kept her head down and put one foot in front of the other until she reached the top. The egg shaped moon darted in and out of a bank of feathery clouds, sweeping moonlight across the steep meadow. She had held off using the flashlight to save batteries, but once she reached the forest, she would have no choice but to switch it on.

She stopped to catch her breath. The muscles in her calves burned through to the bone. She leaned over, with her hands on her thighs, and gulped in air. Deer moved nearby, rustling through the thick underbrush, snorting softly to each other like ponies. Sean could imitate them perfectly. At dusk, when the does ventured into the orchard to snack on the windfall apples covering the ground, Sean would snort at them, and they would answer back.

Her gaze swept down the hill toward her grandparents' house. The wistful, comforting ties of home rushed through her, filling her with love. Suddenly, she was ten years old again, galloping down the hill at dusk with the season's first snowflakes swirling around her face, knowing that inside, her mother had lit the kitchen fire and was waiting for her with a bowl of hot potato soup and a pair of loving arms. Lights filtered through the filmy curtains, warm and inviting. No one would suspect anything bad had ever happened there. Of course, from the other side of the street, the house in Amityville probably looked normal, too.

Wisps of gray smoke floated up from the fire and drifted across the sky. From where Morgan stood, the fence blocked her view of the built-in kettle. But it was there. Bubbling away. As if it were sitting on the patio of some cannibal's house in deepest, darkest Africa, with the body of her ex-husband sloshing up and down. The image of Denny's dead, ravaged face loomed behind her eyes, and she shoved it away. She couldn't think of that now. She couldn't think of anything. Not Gage, or his betrayal, or her brother lying unconscious and bleeding on the tool shed floor. She was on a mission. Maybe the most important mission of her life. The terrible ache in her heart would have to wait until she found Gage's son and brought him home safely.

She zipped her jacket, switched on the flashlight, and set out through the thick woods. The harsh, labored sound of her own breath roared back at her with each faltering step. It had been a long time since she had walked through the woods at night. She'd forgotten how claustrophobic they could be with only a ten-foot path of light to follow. The dank, earthy smell of dead leaves and moss flooded her senses. It brought the memory of Gage touching her in the copse of birch trees crashing back into her head.

She'd known better than to trust him. Known better than to let him under her skin. How stupid she'd been. How pathetic and weak. He'd planned the whole thing: sending Sean the letter, showing up with his eleven-year-old son who just happened to be the same age as her dead child, prying open her heart and making her wish for the things she could never have. She hated him for deceiving her. But she hated herself more for letting him shine a light on her life and showing her how lonely and empty it was.

Her eyes filled with tears. She stumbled on the rocky path. "Damn him," she said, batting at her face with the back of her hand. "Damn Gage Kirkland to hell and back."

She ducked under a broken hickory branch and stopped. Where was she? She should have passed the line of chestnut trees by now, but everything looked different. She glanced around, trying to get her bearings. Then she swept the light across the vine covered trees in front of her and retraced her steps. *"Jeremy!"* she shouted. *"Where are you?"* Could she have veered off the path? It wasn't much of a path, just a wide, tamped down corridor local hunters used to bag the wild turkeys that screeched and scuttled through the woods. She hadn't been walking very long, but the dark kept closing in. Her surroundings looked grotesque and unfamiliar. Maybe she hadn't gone far enough.

A sharp scratching sound echoed behind her. She shone the light on the ground. The sound moved away, rustling through a mound of tangled underbrush like an animal on the run. The adrenaline overload generated one chilling thought after another. What if Jeremy had fallen into a cave? Or slipped and tumbled into a sinkhole? What if Finch and Mendoza were tracking her? What if they'd come to the farm to threaten Sean and ended up killing Denny? How much had Jeremy seen before he ran away? Too much? Enough to put him in danger? Were Finch and Mendoza after Jeremy to silence him?

She picked up the pace.

The flashlight beam bounced off the trees. The scrub cedars on either side of the path took on an eerie, one-dimensional façade. Their scraggly fronds bobbed in the wind like lace fans and smelled of Christmas. She pressed on, stopping every twenty feet to shine the light along the treetops until she spotted a long, swinging vine of kudzu attached to a high, rounded branch.

She knew where she was.

The line of chestnut trees appeared in front of her. She started running, slashing her way through the overgrowth, tramping through the long grass. She made the left turn, climbed around the rocks, picked her way through the twisted kudzu vines, and flung the car door open. "Jeremy, I'm—"

Empty.

Her heart sank. She shone the light inside the car. Up and down, back and forth, as if she thought he might somehow, magically spring out of thin air.

"Oh, God, Jeremy," she whispered. "I was so sure."

She pushed the door closed and leaned against it, staring into the dark.

Where would he have gone? Ethan said he'd headed up Pip's Hill, but he could have turned right instead of left and taken the long way down to the orchard. By now, he knew his way around the farm. He could be hiding in a tree, or in the ditch across the road, or in the dense mass of wild honeysuckle surrounding Lacey's Pond. He could be lost on the other side of Deer Creek, wandering around, still looking for the kudzu car. The kid was book smart and brilliant. But he was still eleven.

A bloodcurdling shriek cut through the night. Morgan slapped her chest and swallowed air. The knowledge that it was only an owl warning its mate that man was in the forest didn't stop her from jumping out of her skin. "Calm down," she whispered. "Just calm the hell down."

She swung the light across the bank of trees. Thick coils of kudzu blanketed the crowns, streamed down from the branches like long, graceful arms. Most Southerners considered kudzu a curse, the vine that grew a foot each day and couldn't be killed by a plutonium bomb. But she had always loved it. In a few weeks, it took a plain, ordinary tree and transformed it into something ornate and majestic. Many of the old-timers still believed evil spirits lived in a kudzu forest, ghosts who'd been kicked out of the house for bad behavior and had nowhere else to go. To Morgan, trees wrapped in kudzu were anything but evil. They were mysterious and comforting. They were home.

She took a deep breath and stepped over a tangle of vines. "Okay, kid. Let's find you."

The path was easier to navigate on the way back. She focused on her feet and tried to make time without stumbling. As she walked, she formed a plan. She would check the orchard and pond first, then double back to the woods. If she still hadn't found him, she'd go to the house and tell Gage she'd been wrong. By then, the ambulance would have taken Sean and Ethan to the hospital. They could call the sheriff and assemble a search party.

"Morgan?"

She stopped. Had someone called her name?

Fear snaked across her shoulders, pricked at the skin behind her neck. She pointed the flashlight at an oak tree, half expecting to see the light glint off Mendoza's gold tooth. "Who's there?" she cried.

"It's me," Jeremy said.

"Oh, God, kid. You scared the crap out of me." She began to laugh.

Jeremy stepped from behind the tree. His *Family Guy* T-shirt was torn across the shoulder. Dirt and sweat streaked his narrow face. "I found the kudzu car. I found it in the dark."

"Without a flashlight? You must be part bat."

"Well, the waning gibbous moon helped, and after a while I could see pretty good. It's called dark adaptation. The eye uses a chemical called rhodospin to recognize light by absorbing photons. When a molecule—"

"You knew we'd come looking for you. Why didn't you stay in the car?"

"I got scared. I was afraid Denny knew about the car, so I hiked back to the path and hid behind that tree. What took you so long?"

"I got lost," Morgan said. "By the time I found the car, you'd already left."

"I...I'm sorry." His voice cracked.

"Oh, honey, it's okay." She put her arms around

him. "You followed your gut. And that's always the right thing to do." She took his hand. "Come on, we need to start back."

"Denny showed up and wanted to know where the flag was, but Sean wouldn't tell him. Then Denny said he'd leave. He pretended to go, then he turned back and hit Sean in the face. He kept on hitting him, and Sean said, 'I'm not gonna fight you, Denny. You're whacked out on drugs. It wouldn't be fair.' Then Denny picked up the big stirring paddle and started to hit him with it. So, I told Denny you didn't have the flag. I said you'd sold it."

"But I haven't—"

"Well, you *could* have sold it. I found two buyers on a Civil War website who were very interested. It was all I could think of to make him stop hitting Sean."

"Well, it was an inspired idea." She took off her jacket. "Put this on. You're shivering."

"It is k-kinda cold out here."

"You are one brave kid."

"No, I'm not. I took karate. I should've stayed and helped Sean. Is he okay?"

"He'll be fine."

Jeremy looked up, his eyes suddenly wide with panic. "Where's my dad? Is Denny still there?"

"No, honey," she said, "Denny's gone. Your Dad and Ethan are waiting for us."

"Are you sure he won't come back and hurt my dad?"

"You don't have to worry about Denny. He'll never hurt anybody again."

Moonlight spilled across the grass as they made their way down Pip's Hill. Lights from the house glittered through the twisted branches of a lone dogwood tree. The bitter stench of an extinguished fire hung in the air. Halfway down, Jeremy started to run.

"Hold it!" Morgan rasped.

"Why? I want to see my dad."

"Just wait." She caught up with him and held his arm. "Things don't look right."

"You said my dad and Ethan would be waiting for us."

"I know, but the porch light isn't on. If your dad called an ambulance, he would have turned on the outside lights. Get behind that honeysuckle bush and wait for me." Jeremy hunkered down. "I'm going to check the shed and make sure they've taken Sean to the hospital." She put her hand on his shoulder. "Jeremy, I'm serious. Do not move."

Morgan edged her way around the fence, careful to stay in the shadows.

Something was wrong.

She'd bet her life on it.

Dread coiled up her spine, leaving a damp line of perspiration in its wake. She glanced up. The three-quarter moon she'd been so grateful for in the forest had vanished behind a rolling bank of clouds. She crouched beside the fence and peered through the wooden slats. The shed door stood ajar. A long shadow moved across the ground, then stopped. Its hands pawed the air, then fell.

Sean.

She opened the gate and ran to him. "Don't move!" She knelt down. "Where's Gage? Did he call the ambulance?"

Sean groaned and looked up. One gray-green eye

had swollen shut, the other was glazed over in pain. "I...I don't know. I keep waking up and passing out again. I talked to Gage. I remember talking to him." His words came out thick and slurred. "Where's Denny? He was here, and then he—"

"Denny's dead."

"Oh." He rolled onto his side. "You might want to move your foot. I think I'm gonna be sick."

"No, you're not. Do you have your cell phone with you?"

"It's in the truck. I think. God, I can't think. My head's thumping like a bass drum."

"Lie still. I'll get help."

"Morgan?" Jeremy's reedy little voice traveled to her on the wind.

Morgan scrambled to her feet. Jeremy stood by the open gate with his arm wrapped around the fencepost.

"Dammit, kid!" Morgan shouted. "I told you to stay put! I told you not to move! I told you to glue your butt to that honeysuckle bush, and—"

"Stop yelling at him," Sean said. "You would have done the same thing."

"I can see my dad through the window. He's sitting in a chair, staring straight ahead."

Morgan put her arm around him. She stooped down until she was on his level. "Listen to me. I need you to sneak down to Sean's truck, open it as quietly as you can, climb in, and find his cell phone. It may be on the seat. It may be on the console. Then I need you to call 911. Tell them we need help. Say you're at Morgan's orchard. They'll know where to come." She held onto his shoulders. "If you can't get a signal, go down to the road and turn left. Then run as fast as you can to the

Jenkins' farmhouse. Here's the flashlight."

"But my dad? Why is he just sitting there?"

"I'm going to find out. Do what I said, and don't go in the house."

"Okay, but—"

"No *buts*. Sean is counting on you." She squeezed his upper arms and stared into his anxious brown eyes. "*I'm* counting on you."

"Okay, Morgan."

"And Jeremy? Be careful."

He grinned and gave her a thumbs up, looking so much like his father, she wanted to cry. He headed down the hill toward the back of the house. If Finch or Mendoza were holding Gage hostage, at least the kid would be safely out of sight.

Morgan started for the house. Every nerve ending bristled against her clothes.

She left the path and zigzagged down the hill, moving from one clump of wild honeysuckle to another. At the bottom, she eased herself through the gate and ran past the old water pump to the south side of the house. She flattened herself against the clapboard and glanced at Jeremy. He had made it to Sean's truck and was standing on the running board, trying to open the door.

Light from the living room window spilled into the yard. Square shards of white and amber slashed across the grass. Morgan pushed her hair out of her eyes and placed one hand on the high windowsill. She rose up on her toes, keeping her face in the shadows, and peered into the room.

Gage sat in the stuffed armchair beside the fireplace. His hands rested on the arms, and he stared straight ahead, exactly as Jeremy had described him. Morgan craned her neck.

"Well, hey, Morgan," Ethan said. "Come on in. Gage and I have been talking about you."

Thank God, Morgan thought. It was only Ethan. His leg must not have been hurt badly after all. But why hadn't he or Gage called an ambulance for Sean? They probably couldn't get through. It had happened to her grandpa once when he'd fallen off the harvesting machine and drug himself up to the house. Living in the sticks was like living in a third world country.

She didn't understand why Ethan and Gage were sitting in the house while Sean was outside hurt and bleeding? Why weren't they trying to help him?

Panic rose in her chest then settled into her abdomen, leaden and cold. Adrenaline gushed into her veins, urging her to turn her eyes away and run.

And yet, she still refused to believe the worst.

She stepped up on the porch as if she were moving through a dream, as if a power source she couldn't fight was pulling her along, forcing her to fulfill her destiny. She glanced in the front window. Gage caught her eye and shook his head no.

She hesitated.

And tried to wrap her head around what was happening.

The screen door screeched open. The shadow of a man slid across the floor. Ethan stood in the doorway, still holding Gage hostage with Cal's gun.

"Like I said, Morgana. Your friend and I have been talking about you. Of course, I've been doing most of the talking." He smiled, still pointing the gun at Gage. "But I think all that's about to change."

Chapter 18

Gage's heart dropped.

The look on Morgan's face was enough to send him flying across the room to her. But he didn't dare move. Not yet. Not while the Hamster was pointing a loaded gun at his head. He gripped the chair until his fingers throbbed and tried to channel the fight energy coursing through his limbs. *Focus! Focus, dammit!* His need to protect her was threatening to eclipse the reasoning center of his brain. But getting himself blown away wouldn't do anybody any good. Least of all him.

Why hadn't she run when she had the chance? Why hadn't she saved herself? Had she found Jeremy? Had she come back to tell him his son was still missing?

If only he could turn back the clock. One hour. Two. How could he have put Jeremy and Morgan in so much danger? He'd always been good at reading people, a skill that had kept him breathing on more than one occasion. But he hadn't seen this one coming. Ethan Spannagel had made him uneasy from the get go. Why hadn't he realized the man was a complete nutcase?

"Ethan, I don't understand," Morgan said. She sat on the piano bench, folded her hands in her lap, and glanced up at him as if they'd just sat down to tea.

"Honey, what's going on?"

She still trusted the bastard. Gage could see it on her face.

Gage's eyes darted between the two of them, waiting for the opportunity to make a move, not sure what the hell it was going to be. Ethan stepped back to relax the arm aiming the gun, and in that split second, Morgan's gaze shot to the door, to the window, to Gage, then back to Ethan's face. *She doesn't trust him at all. She's as petrified as I am.* Why should he be surprised she was a master at hiding her feelings? Hadn't she done the same thing three days ago when she'd pulled into the driveway and found him standing on her porch like the Ghost of Christmas Past? She'd barely blinked an eye then, too.

He looked at her, and his heart swelled with admiration. Her hands trembled in her lap, and she clasped them tightly, all the while looking at Ethan just as calm and cool as you please.

Ethan steadied the gun. "Your boyfriend doesn't know what's going on either."

Morgan snorted. "He's not my boyfriend. If he were the last man on earth, he would not be my boyfriend. If he were the last living, breathing man walking upright in the universe, he would not be—"

"I think he gets the picture," Gage said. "And for the record, she's not my girlfriend either. My girlfriend is short and cheerful and...blond."

"I don't believe either of you," Ethan said.

"By the way," Gage said, "where's Jeremy? Still roaming the countryside? I can never get that boy to come home, even when it's raining." He tried to control the fear his voice. The only way he could get the upper hand was to follow Morgan's lead and keep his emotions in check.

Morgan's eyes cut to him, then back to Ethan. "He was scared. I guess he went up Pip's Hill and doubled back to the orchard. Don't worry, he'll find his way home. He got that hiking merit badge in Scouts last year, remember?"

Okay, Gage thought. *Jeremy is not a Boy Scout; she's talking in code. Did she find him? Is that what she meant?* He stared at her, willing her to understand he needed more information. *Please, Morgan. I know you hate me. But let me know my boy's okay.*

"Jeremy's a great kid," she said, still watching Ethan. "He's small for his age, but he's smart. And wherever he is, I'm sure he's fine." She looked at Gage and held his gaze for a long moment. "He's just fine."

Relief washed over Gage. This time he could not mistake what she meant. Jeremy was fine. She had told him his son was fine.

"Why do you care so much about this man's kid?" Ethan snarled. "You said you didn't want kids."

"I said I couldn't have kids. I never said I didn't want them."

"Bullshit!" Ethan shook his head vigorously. "You'll say anything with him in the room."

"That's not true," Morgan said.

"Yes, it is." Ethan's hair fell across his wide forehead in long, unwashed strings. His pale white-blue eyes stared at Morgan like a drugged out gallery owner Gage had had under surveillance once. He didn't think drugs were Ethan's problem. Ethan's problem was he was bat shit crazy. And obsessed with the woman Gage loved.

Gage turned his head. Pain ignited behind his eyes. He held his arms rigid and gripped the armrests, determined to stay conscious and concentrate. Passing out was not an option.

If he could get Ethan to move to the left, so if Ethan fired the gun, the bullet would go past Gage's head instead of through it, he might have a chance to subdue him. He didn't think Ethan would shoot Morgan. Not as much as he cared for her. But Gage couldn't risk taking that chance. Not when someone's mind was as far gone as this dude's.

Every plan Gage came up with had too many risks. At best, the situation was uncertain and volatile. At worst, he and Morgan could be blown across the room into next week.

Gage lifted his head off the back of the chair. He tried to ignore the wet oozing behind his left ear and the sledgehammer pounding the back of his eyes every time he blinked. His stomach roiled with cheese grits and ribs. He swallowed the bile at the back of his throat. Vomiting was not an option, either. If he moved fast enough, he might be able to position himself between Ethan and Morgan. As long as he could get there before the gun went off.

There was always a catch.

Ethan stared at her. "You want him. And if you say you don't, you're lying."

"I don't lie," Morgan said.

Ethan circled the room and stood behind Gage. The cold muzzle of the gun touched the back of Gage's neck. "Well, you're lying now. You're pretending you're not together so I won't kill him. But you *are* together. I saw you tonight at Hog Heaven. You couldn't keep your hands off him."

"You were there?" Her blue eyes widened in disbelief. "You followed us?"

"I've seen the way he looks at you," Ethan sneered. "The way you act around his kid. You wish his kid was your kid, because you can't have any of your own." He took a shaky step toward her. "So, stop lying."

Morgan swallowed a gasp. Her back stiffened. Her fingers skimmed across the needlepoint seat cushion, then clutched the edge of the piano bench until her knuckles turned white. Sorrow settled in her eyes. Gage had never seen her look so sad, and he wanted to gather her in his arms and make it disappear. He worried that by spilling the beans she couldn't have children, Ethan had hit a nerve so profound, she might fall apart. But instead, she lifted her chin and looked Ethan straight in the eye. When she spoke, the sudden appearance of her soft East Tennessee accent betrayed the blow she had been dealt. "Ethan, honey, you've been under a lot of stress since your father passed. But if somethin' else is botherin' you, then you need to let it all out and tell me what's wrong. We're buddies, remember?"

"I don't want to be your buddy. Don't you understand? I want to be your—" Ethan's face crumpled. "You used to love *me*, Morgan. Why don't you love me anymore?"

"I do love you. You're one of the dearest, sweetest people I know."

"Really?" Ethan said.

"Well, how dear," Gage said. "And how sweet. But I'm not sure how far that sentiment is gonna fly, once he shoots me in the face."

****

Morgan held on to the piano bench as if it were her salvation.

Her eyes followed Ethan like a cornered cat. His gaze wandered to the mirror above the dining room sideboard. He scrutinized himself, then frowned, as if he recognized the man holding the gun but couldn't quite put a name to the face. She'd stopped trying to talk to him. He didn't want to talk to her. He wanted to get back at her.

Like Gage had predicted, it had all come back to bite her on the ass.

In the past, Morgan had relied on Ethan's friendship. He'd always come through for her, never judged her mistakes, never let her down. He'd been a good friend, even though she'd taken him for granted. He'd hinted at his feelings, but she'd ignored them. Because as long as she ignored them, she didn't have to face the fact that if she rejected him, he would not want her in his life. She'd been too selfish to let him go. Another mistake she was sorry for. It had been cruel to let him believe they might end up together someday when she knew in her heart that would never happen.

And now, she could only pray that he loved her enough not to kill them all.

She glanced at Gage.

His steely gaze scanned the room. The knot in his jaw moved back and forth. She could almost see the wheels turning behind his eyes, trying to anticipate Ethan's next move. His hands held onto the edge of the chair, the muscles tense and ready to catapult him across the room. He looked strong and formidable, but behind his head, an amoeba shaped bloodstain had spread across the blue slipcover, and when he turned his head to look at her, his face couldn't hide the pain.

She steered her gaze away from Gage and focused on Ethan.

"Ethan, please," she begged. "You and Sean have always been friends. He's lost a lot of blood. Please let me call an ambulance and get him some help. He's my brother."

Ethan laughed. "And you would do anything for your brother, right?" He shook his head. "Jesus, Morgan, you hate this farm. You *loathe* it. But when your brother asked you to stay, you stayed. No questions asked. See, I knew if Sean thought the farm was going under, he'd talk you into staying. Because you're the strong one, and that's what you do. When has your brother, or any of your family, been able to do anything without your help?"

Morgan stared at him. "What do you mean Sean thought the farm was going under?"

"Good question," Gage said. "And I think I've got the answer. Ethan is the one who cooked the books, only in reverse. He made it look like the orchard was in financial trouble because he had a pretty good idea that Sean would convince you to stay and help get it back on its feet." He looked at Ethan. "Am I on the right track?"

"Shut the fuck up," Ethan said.

"How could you do this?" Morgan said. "Sean's been working sixteen hour days trying to save the orchard. He and your father did everything they could think of, called in every favor my grandfather had. And it was all a sham?"

"I wouldn't have let it go on forever," Ethan said. "I wanted to buy some time until I could convince you this is where you belong. Here. With me. We were starting to get close again. You felt it, too. I know you did. Until this...this *jerk* showed up with his kid. I tried to scare him away by shooting out his windshield, but the godammed jerk wouldn't leave."

Morgan crossed her arms. "Yes, I think the word *jerk* is a very apt description."

"I tried to tell you tonight why I came here," Gage said. "At the restaurant. But then we started dancing, and as the man waving the gun said, you couldn't keep your hands off me."

"Oh, please," she said. "It was the other way round, and you know it. Don't blame me because you didn't have the balls to tell me you had a hidden agenda. *God*, I should have known better than to trust you. But you have this infuriating habit of showing up at the exact moment I need someone. I should have gone on pretending I didn't remember you. And then, you made me believe you cared about me. 'Oh, I'll help you, Morgan. I'll get your brother a lawyer. Never mind that I came here to steal the flag that could pay for that lawyer.'"

Gage leaned back. "This may not be the best time to point out that if you cared as much about your brother as you say you do, the sale of that flag could have sustained the orchard."

She glared at him. "That's why you came back that night. Not to ask a favor for your son. Not to see me. But to steal the flag. You'd heard Sean was in jail. You thought I'd be at the sheriff station with him. You expected the house to be empty."

"I came back for Jeremy's sake. And because I wanted to see you." Gage pressed his hand against his head. "I needed to know you were real."

"I should have kicked you to the curb the day you got here. But I wanted so desperately to believe you."

"You *can* believe me. The moment I saw you again, I knew I could never take anything from you whether you stole it or not. Didn't I tell you to take the flag to the bank where it would be safe? Didn't I let Jeremy find you a buyer for it? Didn't I—"

"Didn't you what? Show up after twelve years and expect me to fall in love with you again? In all those years, did you ever look for me?"

"No, but—"

"You're a private investigator, for Christ's sake. And you never even looked for me."

Ethan slammed his fist against the upright piano. *"Shut up!"* he cried. Vibrating piano keys chimed beneath the mahogany lid. "Hasn't anybody noticed I'm holding a gun on you?" He looked at Gage. "So, you're the one."

"The one?" Gage asked.

"The one who got her pregnant then dumped her. The one who broke her heart and screwed her head up for the rest of us."

Gage stared at Morgan. "You were pregnant?

Morgan nodded slowly.

"I didn't know," he said hoarsely. "Why didn't you tell me?"

"What was I supposed to do? Show up on your doorstep holding a baby, in the snow, like the upstairs maid in a Victorian novel? You didn't want me, remember?"

"But I did want you," Gage said. "You're all I've *ever* wanted. At twenty-two, I wasn't strong enough to fight my father and Bert. I was too naïve to realize I could have been a good father to Jeremy without marrying his mother. I wanted to leave Suzanne as soon as Jeremy was born, but I couldn't walk away. Jeremy needed me. And I couldn't ask you to wait."

"You should have let me make that decision," she said.

Gage took a deep, ragged breath. "I have to ask you—the child. What happened to the—"

"Denny threw her against a chair," Ethan said flatly. "I was the first person she called."

"I had an ectopic pregnancy," Morgan said. "My abdomen hit the back of the chair so hard, my fallopian tube ruptured. I would have lost the baby anyway."

"But can you still—"

"Conceive? Yes, but since I only have one ovary and one fallopian tube, it will be twice as hard."

Gage's eyes glistened. "Not such a bad thing, having to try twice as hard. It could be fun."

"I should have killed Denny then," Ethan said. "I should have." His focus was beginning to wander. "I should have gone to Atlanta, found Denny, and killed the bastard. But tonight, I finally did it. I smashed his head in, then pushed him into the kettle. It felt so damned good." His eyes settled on her face. "I...I did it for you, Morgan. Everything I do is for you." He sniffed and wiped his face with the back of his hand. "Why don't you love me?"

"Ethan, I'm sorry," she said.

Ethan laughed. "She's sorry. She's *sorry*. All of this was for nothing—the orchard, Dad's death, Sean, Peach."

"What about Peach?" Morgan asked.

"He started the fire at Bad Moon," Gage said. "To get rid of Peach, right?"

Ethan lowered the gun. "That slut was going to move in here and help Sean with the farm so you could leave again, Morgan. I couldn't let that happen. I had to make sure you stayed here. With me."

Morgan shook her head. "And the fact that Peach swears she has a copy of Harlan's will and you could lose a chunk of the estate if he named her as a beneficiary didn't enter into it?"

"How did you know about that?" Ethan asked.

"I listened to the voicemails Peach left on your father's cell phone," Morgan said. "Peach thought he was going to leave her set for life. But she sounded unsure about it. I wonder if Sean warned Harlan about her. Your Dad and Sean were pretty close."

"Stop it!" Ethan spun around. For one terrifying moment, Morgan thought he was going slam the gun into Gage's head.

"Shut up about my father and Sean! My father thought I was weak because I didn't want to work in the slaughterhouse. He made fun of me, ridiculed me, told the men working the chutes I was a sissy because I couldn't stomach the blood. But he treated Sean like a man. Sean didn't have to do anything to gain his respect. Sean was Robert Maguire's grandson, and he could do no wrong. My father said Sean was more of a son to him than I had ever been. So, you know what? Let Sean bleed to death. I don't care. Sean Maguire makes me want to puke."

"Is that why you framed him for your father's murder?" Gage asked.

"Well, *yes,*" Ethan said. "I'd seen that fancy knife

of Sean's in Dad's toolbox, and it pissed the shit out of me. He and Dad were always using each other's tools, swapping them back and forth, laughing and joking. When I came home and found them standing in front of the slaughterhouse with Sean hunched over, patting his arm like he was so worried about him, it ran all over me. I watched them through the window, and all I could think of was that knife. And how it would look in my father's back."

Morgan opened her mouth, then closed it again.

"He'd told me that morning his nose wouldn't stop bleeding, so I knew he was going downhill. He said the palms of his hands kept bruising when he tried to open the pasture gate. It was only a matter of time before he started hemorrhaging. After weeks of giving him fish oil and Vitamin E, and pouring warfarin-laced maple syrup on his cream of wheat, I did not want to miss the big payoff. But then Sean left, and Finch showed up with that Mexican."

"What did Finch want?" Gage asked.

"To threaten me, I guess. He was on to me. He knew about the books, about the pickers. He knew I was the one who paid them double not to work for you. The more Finch took care of things so Bert wouldn't have to get his hands dirty, the more he learned what was really going on. After your grandfather died, Bert thought he could get your land for a song. But he hadn't counted on Finch double-crossing him. When Finch realized how much some of the U.S. wineries were willing to pay to access the perfect soil for Chambourcin grapes, he decided to cut Bert out of the deal.

"Harlan—my dad—was a sharp man. A complete

asshole in the father department, but sharp. He knew about Bert's plan to grow Chambourcin grapes, so he held back the money Bert was paying him to let the orchard slide into bankruptcy and put it in a savings account for Maguire Orchard to grow their own grapes. That's when he discovered I'd changed the orchard accounts and threatened to tell Sean. And he would have, too. He would have done anything for Sean. I'm sure he was planning to tell Finch about me to teach me a lesson, but Finch had already figured things out."

Gage leaned to the left, his eyes hot and feverish. The crimson stain on his neck had darkened and spread across his shoulder. A rivulet of fresh blood ran from the back of his neck into his shirt collar. Morgan knew that no matter how deep the wound, or how much pain he had to endure, the second Gage got the chance, he would charge across the room and try to wrestle the gun away from Ethan. Even if it killed him.

Morgan couldn't let him risk his life for her. This was her fight with Ethan, not his. And somewhere outside, a brave little boy was counting on his father to stay alive long enough to watch him grow up.

"Put the gun down," Morgan said. "We can work this out. Your father's funeral is tomorrow. No one has to know anything. We'll get through this, Eth. I'll get you some help."

"I don't need any help," Ethan said. "I need you."

Morgan pushed herself off the bench. The hair on her arms rose, pricking the skin beneath her cotton shirt. A wave of cold slid across the back of her neck, then slipped down her spine. She turned and faced Ethan.

"Morgan, don't," Gage said softly.

"Ethan." He raised his pale dead eyes to hers. "Everything will be okay, honey. I promise. Just give me the gun."

"I can't," Ethan whimpered.

"Why not?"

He pointed it at Gage's face. "Because I don't want to. Because I want you to watch this jerk die. You're in love with him. You've always been in love with him. And when he's gone, I want you to feel empty and alone and hopeless. Just like me."

Chapter 19

The sudden clatter of feet outside sent Morgan's heart racing to her throat.

Gage's eyes darted to the window.

Ethan shoved her out of the way and stood over Gage, mashing the barrel of the gun into his neck. "Don't even think about it," he growled.

The front door swung open. Wind rushed into the room, scattering dead leaves across the floor, rattling the glass.

"*Dad!*" Jeremy cried. "*Hey!* You let go of my dad!"

"*Jeremy, run!*" Gage screamed. "Let him go, Ethan, please. He's a little boy. Let him go."

"Can't do that," Ethan said. "Come on in, little boy. You're about to experience something that will keep you in therapy for years."

"*No!*" Morgan said. "I won't let you scare him like this." She wasn't sure whether it was strength or insanity that thrust her across the room, but she travelled quickly, and with purpose, ignoring Ethan's warning and the shocked, terrified look on Gage's face. Her heartbeat thundered in her ears, like a drum propelling her into battle, until she reached Gage's son in the doorway and pulled him behind her, then encircled his thin arm with her fingers to hold him in place.

"Get out of the way, Morgan," Ethan said evenly. "I'm not afraid to shoot you. You're nothing to me now."

"Then shoot me," Morgan said. "But I'm not moving."

"Did you hurt my Dad?" Jeremy wriggled beneath her grasp. "Because if you hurt my dad, I'll...I'll—"

"It's okay, son," Gage said. His voice cracked with emotion. "*Shhhh*. I'm fine. Everything's gonna be okay."

"Not a good idea to lie to your son," Ethan said. "My father lied to me my whole life, and you see how I turned out."

Jeremy tapped Morgan's shoulder from behind.

"Forget about the poor bastard in the kettle," Gage said. "You're holding a woman and a child hostage. Where can this go?"

"I don't know," Ethan said. The gun trembled in his hand. "I don't care."

"Just calm down." Gage's gentle baritone brushed over each word, soothing and low.

Behind her, Jeremy shifted to the side, then slid the cool metal neck of the baseball bat into her hand. Her fingers shook as she slowly drew the bat around to the front. Her heart knocked against her ribs.

She knew what she had to do, but the thought of slamming a bat into Ethan's head made her sick to her stomach. She'd been ready, even eager, to break Lawrence Finch's toes. But Finch wasn't Ethan. Ethan had loved her, understood her, been her friend. But that was all in the past. Now, her old friend, wild-eyed and vicious, was standing over the man she loved, holding a gun to his head. Ethan Spannagel was one more thing she'd been delusional about. He had hurt her family. He had tricked her into staying in Riverbirch. And now, he was going to kill her.

She grasped the bat tightly. If her aim was good, one decent swing could knock the gun out of his hand. But her aim had always been rotten. No, her best bet was to hit him in the head.

Adrenaline streamed through her arms like an electrical current. She eyed her target, the swirling cowlick growing above Ethan's collar, and pulled the bat back. A sudden flash caught her eye.

She glanced at the wall behind Gage. A white glint darted across her line of vision, like a spark ricocheting off glass. Her gaze shot to the oval convex mirror hanging above the sideboard. She looked at her own distorted reflection, then dropped her gaze to meet Ethan's eyes, staring at her intently behind his shiny silver frames.

Fear shuddered through her.

Ethan twisted around. He ripped the bat out of her hands and sent it hurtling through the front window. The high-pitched crash shattered the air. Morgan bent over to shield Jeremy from the splintered glass. It flew at them, covering the windowsill, sticking to the rug and floor like ice crystals. Gage was on his feet, bounding toward them in a blur.

Ethan yanked Jeremy out of Morgan's arms. He held him, squirming, out in front of him, then swung around and pointed the gun at Morgan. He blinked his eyes like a mole surfacing into sunlight.

"Ethan, *no!*" Morgan cried. "Let him go!"

He glanced at Gage. "You take one step closer, and

I'll shoot them both."

Gage stopped. He held his hands out, palms up.

"That's better," Ethan said.

Gage reached out and pulled Morgan behind him. "Stay," he whispered.

She stared at the back of his neck in horror. A ragged gash carved the flesh behind his right ear. Blood dripped from a wet, matted circle of hair. He swayed slightly then steadied himself. Every muscle in his body had tensed, but his breath came in quick, shallow pants, so faint, she could barely hear it. A surge of heat pulsed from his hand to hers. "You all right, son?" he asked quietly.

"Yeah, Dad," Jeremy said.

Ethan jerked Jeremy back, then shook his own head as if he were trying to shake the cobwebs out of his brain. "I wish my dad was here," he said in a quiet voice. "If Harlan was here, he'd know what to do. He'd know how to fix this."

"I know what he'd say," Jeremy said.

"Shut up," Ethan said.

"He'd tell you to back your way out the door, then run as fast as you can to your car. You've lived in these mountains all your life, right? I bet you know a lot of shortcuts. More than the sheriff, probably. If you hurry, you can get a head start before she gets here."

"The sheriff?" Ethan's eyes narrowed. "How does the sheriff know—"

"I called 911," Jeremy said. "I used Sean's cell phone, like Morgan told me to." Jeremy glanced from Morgan to his father. "She should be here real soon. So, if you're going—"

"Jeremy's right, Ethan," Morgan said. "You should

get out of here. But I wouldn't take too long to think about it. Because if you're planning on staying out of prison for murder, attempted murder, assault, breaking and entering, arson, and kidnapping, then you need to go...*now*."

Ethan moved toward the door with Jeremy in tow.

"I'll let the boy go when I get to the car," Ethan said. "If either of you move, I'm taking him with me." He slowly backed his way across the floor. Broken glass crunched beneath his feet. When he reached the door, he pushed the screen door open with his left shoulder and stepped backwards across the threshold.

A bloody arm came out of the dark. It grabbed Ethan around the neck and jerked him onto the porch. Ethan cried out. The gun fired. A bullet whizzed over Gage's head, shattering a wall sconce above the piano.

Gage looped his arm around Jeremy's torso and jerked him away from Ethan. He shoved him at Morgan then lunged for the gun in Ethan's hand.

"Could you speed things up?" Sean asked, still holding Ethan's head in the crook of his arm. "I've got about two more seconds before I pass out again."

"Sure thing," Gage said. He grabbed Ethan's arm and banged it against the oak pedestal table. The gun launched into the air, knocking an earthenware bowl of apples onto the floor, then slid across the rug like a shuffleboard puck. Gage seized Ethan's shoulders and slammed his face on the floor. "Not so tough without a gun in your pocket. Or were you just glad to see me?" He looked at Morgan. "I could use some help here."

Morgan located a roll of duct tape in the pantry. She tore off strips and handed them to Gage while he bound Ethan's hands and feet.

"You bitch!" Ethan hollered, wriggling on his stomach.

"Did you just call me a bitch?" she asked. "Is that the best you can do?"

Ethan reeled off a string of curses.

"I think I've heard enough," Gage said. He righted the bowl of apples and selected a large Rome Beauty. He blew on it then buffed it on the front of his shirt. "I'm sure the Maguires can spare one of these." He stuck it in Ethan's open mouth, stifling a howl. "Now that the orchard is doing so well."

Sean held on to the hall tree. "So, it's over?"

"Yeah," Gage said. "And thanks, man. Nothing like having the cavalry show up in the nick of time."

"Just so you know," Sean said. "Your son is the one who saved you. He helped me back to the house, thought up the plan, and went in as a decoy. That kid's almost as brave as he is smart. We would have gotten here sooner, but I kept passing out. And now, I think I'm gonna stumble out the door, lie down on the porch, and wait for the real cavalry to arrive."

Morgan rocked back on her heels. She looked up as Gage's dark gaze met hers. "You're hurt," she said. "You need to sit down before you fall down."

"I'm fine."

She had forgotten to steel herself against the flip-flop her heart always did when he looked at her. She pulled her gaze away and scrambled to her feet, then picked up the cordless phone and dialed 911.

Jeremy came out of the dining room. He stood shyly in front of his father. "Dad? You've got blood on your neck. Are you okay?"

Gage smiled. "I am now." He put his hand on

Jeremy's shoulder. "Thanks for saving us, sport. How did you think of such a brilliant plan?"

"I read a magazine article at my therapist's office called, 'How to Get a Raccoon Out of Your House.'" He grinned up at Gage. "I figured it would work on hamsters, too."

Gage laughed, then pulled the boy into a bear hug and held him tight.

Morgan reeled off the information to the operator, including the gasp inducing fact that her ex-husband was simmering face down in a kettle of apple butter. When she was sure all available help was on the way, she stood watching Jeremy and Gage. The sharp realization that she would never be part of their lives tightened in her chest. She hated Gage for dangling the possibility of happiness in front of her then snatching it back with a lie she didn't know how to forgive.

Hot tears pricked her eyes. Seeing Jeremy and Gage together, forging a bond that would shelter them from the rest of the world, filled her with longing. The pain of loss cut into her, slashing its way through her heart until it hurt to breathe. In another, kinder universe, Jeremy might have been destined to be her little boy. But he wasn't. And never would be.

"Morgan, forgive me," Gage said. "I had my reasons for recovering the flag. Good ones. But after seeing you again, I never could have gone through with it."

"Right," she said.

"I'll get the flag back. I swear. If I have to fight my way through hell and half of Georgia, I'll get it back for you."

She laughed and shook her head. "How stupid do

you think I am, Gage? Stupid enough to hide something as rare as General A. S. Johnston's personal battle flag under a floorboard in my bedroom? The flag your friend Cal took was a fake. I bought it at a gift shop in Gettysburg. Twenty-six bucks, plus tax."

"Where's the real one?" Gage asked.

"At the bank. In a safety deposit box. Exactly where you thought I should put it. I can think of one other place I'd like to put it, but for now, I think I'll leave it at the bank."

She walked out the door and knelt beside Sean. "Help is on the way, little brother. You're gonna be just fine."

Sean groaned. He clasped the hand she offered. "This feels like the time I fell out of the tree playing Superman and broke my collarbone."

"Yes, it does. A little."

"You sat beside me and waited for the ambulance, remember? While Opal paced up and down, crying and hollering like it had happened to her."

"Emergencies aren't really her strong suit."

"It's not gonna work out between you and Gage, is it? I was hoping it would."

"No."

Morgan looked at the sky. Stars twinkled like beacons full of false promises, coaxing the world to send them wishes no matter how futile they might be. The three-quarter moon was still there, shining down on all of them, watching their mistakes, keeping their secrets.

She'd never been very good at forgiving and forgetting, but it was time she learned how. She was older now. And stronger. And smarter. Time to put the past behind her once and for all. Time to take Sean's advice and swing out over the lake, let go of the rope, and pray she remembered how to tread water.

"Morgan?" Gage said softly.

Light spilled through the screen, casting a checkered pattern on the painted floor. The wind had died down. The bitter stench of the doused campfire hung in the air. Morgan shuddered, thinking of Denny. Would she ever smell a wood fire again without remembering this night?

"Morgan," Gage said. "*Please.* Look at me."

Her heart ached. She pressed her hand against her chest to make it stop. Why couldn't she let go of the hurt and give him a chance? Turn around and fall into his eyes? Open her heart to him and let the past slide away like a handful of water dribbling through her fingers? Why couldn't she forgive him?

Forgive him for what? For deceiving her? For putting his child first all those years ago? For putting his child first now? Or was she still unable to forgive him for not having the courage to stand up to his father and uncle? For letting her go when she loved him so dearly? For leaving her with a baby that could only live in her dreams, and the memory of one perfect day? It had taken her years to get over him. Years to make sense of her life and learn to live without the things she thought she needed to make her happy. What would she do with all that happiness anyway? Wrap it in cotton wool and hide it under her bedroom floorboard, terrified that a thief might come in the night and steal it away?

She extricated her hand from Sean's and went back inside. She picked up the guitar Jeremy had left beside the piano. "Here," she said. "I want you to have this."

Jeremy's eye lit up. "For real?"

"For real. Forever."

He let go of Gage and clasped the guitar to his chest. "Wow. Thanks, Morgan."

"I'm not going to be able to give you lessons, but I know a lot of great bluegrass artists in the area who would love to take you under their wing. I'll...I'll contact a few and text you."

"If you can get a friggin' signal," Jeremy said, laughing.

"On second thought, I'll use a real phone." She smiled and held out her arms. "Come here, you. Gimme a hug." Jeremy threw his free arm around her waist. She hugged him tight, patting his back, rubbing the sharp outline of his small shoulder blades. It always amazed her how fragile he felt, and how having him in her life, even for a few short days, had begun to fill the empty hollow of her heart. She kissed the top of his head, then ruffled his hair. "Have a great life, kid. And do me a favor—give your old man a break once in a while."

She could feel Gage's eyes burning into her as she walked back to the porch. She resisted the urge to turn around and drown in them. It was the self-preservation thing. His eyes had always been her undoing. If she looked into them, knowing it was the last time, she wasn't sure she would be able to walk away. The crack in her heart would split wide open.

She wrapped one arm around the porch post, grateful the tears she'd been fighting had decided to wait until Gage and Jeremy were safely gone. Her gaze swept down the flagstone walk, across the road to the Jenkins' cow pasture, over the dark, hulking shadow of

Blackstone Mountain, to the black twinkling sky above.

"Morgan, look at me," Gage said.

She didn't move.

"Don't throw us away, Morgan. *Please.* What we have together is magic. Who gets to feel like this in their lifetime? Who?"

"My dad wants you to look at him," Jeremy said.

"Morgan, *please,*" Gage begged hoarsely. "Please, look at me."

Morgan slowly shook her head no.

In the distance, so faint she could scarcely believe it was real, the mournful wail of a siren echoed through the deep, rolling hills of Riverbirch.

Chapter 20

Light poured through the narrow stained glass windows, throwing golden arched rectangles across the church floor. The oak pews had been polished until they gleamed. Flowers from the only shop in Riverbirch filled the urns on either side of the communion table. Ribboned sprays wishing Harlan a safe journey to heaven stood balanced on wire stands at the front of the sanctuary. Between them, a black box full of ashes sat dwarfed on a large pedestal where the casket should have been.

Morgan was glad Harlan had been cremated. The thought of him lying in a box ten feet away while she played his favorite songs, would have been difficult to get through without wanting to lay her head on the keyboard and weep.

After she and Sean had returned from the hospital, she'd lain awake mourning the loss of Gage and Jeremy. Before daylight, and sick of feeling sorry for herself, she went downstairs and combed through her collection of sheet music, searching for songs she thought Harlan might like to hear. She closed her eyes and remembered the tunes she'd heard him whistling the last two years as he tromped from the office to the barn and back again. She settled on "Amazing Grace" and "Shenandoah" for the prayers and a selection of

Harlan's all-time favorites to underscore the beginning and end of the service. If she played them slowly and reverently, she doubted the religious conservatives in the crowd would recognize "Folsom Prison Blues" and "Hunka Hunka Burning Love."

The small church was filling up fast. Morgan smoothed her blue flowered skirt and began to play, segueing seamlessly from one song to the next. Sheriff Stallard scooted beside her on the piano bench.

"How are you doing?" the sheriff whispered. "How's Sean?"

"I'm fine," Morgan said. "Sean's sitting in the back between the Wheeler twins. His kneecap is in a cast, but he wouldn't stay home. Seems he's a lot tougher than I've been giving him credit for." Morgan licked her thumb and turned a page. "Have you charged Ethan yet?"

"Oh, yes. I let Deputy Nelson do the honors."

"But what about the evidence? Will there be enough to—"

"Put him away for the rest of his life? Oh, sweetie, you can count on it. We went back to the slaughterhouse and recovered a bloody print off the underside of the steel railing. When we told Ethan it was a perfect match to him, we got a full confession."

"Seriously?"

"Yes. And he admitted stabbing his father's corpse with Sean's knife. So, that lets Sean off the hook."

"Thank God."

Sheriff Stallard patted Morgan's shoulder as she got up. "I know we're at a funeral, but cheer up, dear heart. When you get to be my age, you'll realize that things usually work out the way they're supposed to."

"Tell that to Harlan."

Morgan glanced out at the congregation. Her heart lurched.

Gage and Jeremy stood in the arched doorway at the back of the church, talking to Opal. When they started down the aisle, Gage eased Jeremy's baseball cap off his head and motioned for the boy to slide in beside him on the last pew.

Morgan took a deep breath and shoved the pain to the back of her heart. She would deal with it later. Right now, she needed to concentrate on the music and make Harlan proud.

Today was going to be harder to get through than she thought.

****

Gage couldn't remember the last time he'd seen the inside of a church.

Suzanne's funeral had been held in a chapel at the funeral home, a decision Suzanne's father had made since he considered her death a suicide. Gage hadn't agreed. He believed Suzanne's death had been facilitated by an illness she never quite had the strength to manage on her own. He could only hope that someday Jeremy would come to the same conclusion.

"Morgan's playing the piano," Jeremy whispered. "Are you gonna talk to her?"

"I don't think so," Gage said. "She won't even look at me."

"Girls never look at you when they're pissed off. You have to do something nice for them, give them flowers and stuff, first."

"Duly noted," Gage said.

Gage settled himself in the pew then turned his

attention to the front of the church. Seated safely on the back row, he could drop all pretense of mourning a man he'd never met and openly stare at Morgan all he wanted. She was sitting at an old piano, engrossed in her sheet music, playing some hymn-like song that sounded a lot like "Take This Job and Shove It." Her skirt, made out of some kind of flowy fabric, fanned out across the piano bench. The white scoop-necked shirt beneath her fitted denim jacket was low enough to hint at her full, creamy breasts. She'd pulled her dark hair back from her face, and he watched, fascinated, as the silver hoops in her ears bounced against her neck each time she turned a page. Her skin seemed to be lit from within. She looked beautiful, and ethereal, and sexy as hell. In the warm morning light, she damned near took his breath away.

After the invocation and prayers, Pastor Byrd showed an amazing amount of restraint by not preaching one of those hell and damnation sermons he was known for to the standing-room only crowd. Instead, he focused on Harlan's memory as a man who was well loved and respected by the Riverbirch community. No mention of Ethan, or the fact he'd been arrested for his father's murder. But everyone sitting in the Higher Ground Baptist Church sanctuary knew the tragic circumstances surrounding Harlan Spannagel's death.

The minister invited the congregation to join him after the service in granting Harlan's last wish; accompanying him to scatter Harlan's ashes among the river birch trees beside the cold, rushing water of Deer Creek. He asked anyone who wanted to say a few words about Harlan to come to the pulpit and speak. A few members of the congregation shared some lighthearted memories amid tears and laughter. As they walked back to their seats, each one patted Sean on the shoulder as if he were Harlan's son.

"Before we conclude," Pastor Byrd said. "Does anyone else have something to say?"

Gage cleared his throat and got to his feet. His heart pounded hard in his chest.

As he walked down the aisle, all eyes were upon him, including Morgan's. He avoided direct eye contact, knowing he'd never get through the next three minutes if he let himself look at her. He grasped the sides of the pulpit and gazed out across a sea of expectant faces. He tried to keep his voice steady. "My name is Gage Kirkland, and I...I have something to say. It's a little off topic, I guess, but I think it's important." Opal smiled at him, blindly nodding encouragement. "I didn't know Harlan Spannagel, but I understand he was a great friend and mentor to Sean Maguire. Harlan spent the last two years of his life managing Maguire Orchard. When Robert Maguire got sick, Harlan jumped in and helped him carry the load, because that's the kind of man he was. He took pride in his work, and in the friendships he forged in this community.

"Harlan wasn't perfect. He made mistakes. But everyone makes mistakes." He glanced at Morgan. "Big ones, small ones, it doesn't matter. What matters is how you learn from them, and if you're willing to spend your life making them up to the people you've hurt, the people you love, the people who mean everything to you." He stopped. "But I digress." He shook his head and grinned. "I've always wanted to say that. Anyway, we're here to celebrate the life of Harlan Spannagel, and I think I know what would make Harlan happy."

"Besides a pint of moonshine?" someone yelled from the back.

The congregation tittered and laughed.

"Harlan was a character," Gage said, laughing. "Look, I realize I'm an outsider. But I would feel privileged to be a part of this community because I know how much you care for each other. In Riverbirch and Cherokee Bluff, everyone may know your business, but everyone has your back."

"You got that right," one of the Wheeler twins said.

"I'm sure you've all heard that Maguire Orchard, which Harlan took such pride in sustaining, has fallen on hard times. Many of you are farmers, and you know what it's like to weather a storm. Well, folks, this storm's a doozy. Harlan is gone, Sean has a broken kneecap, the Maguire's harvesting machines had to be sold to pay Mr. Maguire's medical bills, and the apple pickers the orchard depends on are unavailable. The apples are ripe and ready to pick, and if we can't get them off the trees, they'll be lost forever. If that happens, Maguire Orchard and Apple Butter Barn may not survive the winter. What I'm asking—what I'm begging you to do—is to show your community spirit and love, and give the good people at Maguire Orchard a helping hand."

Gage's voice gathered strength. "If everyone pulls together, we can get this done today. And even though my son Jeremy and I will be moving away, today I can show him why a small town is the best place on earth to live. My uncle will provide a catered picnic for everyone who comes to help. If you haven't eaten the food at Hog Heaven, I think you'll like it." He smiled.

"I ate there last night, and it ended up being one of the most memorable dinners I've ever had. So, what do you say, folks? Let's take Harlan to his final resting place at Deer Creek, hold him in our hearts, then do something nice for the people he loved most."

Gage turned to Morgan. He smiled shyly, then gave a little shrug. He held her gaze and looked deep into her eyes. Her big, beautiful, surprised-as-hell eyes. And for one miraculous moment he thought she might forgive him. Their eyes melded into each other, going deeper and deeper, soul to soul, until she broke the spell and looked away.

His heart sank.

So that was it, then.

He turned and walked down the aisle. At the last pew, he held out his hand for Jeremy to take, and without a backward glance, the two of them pushed open the double church doors and walked into the bright September sun.

****

"Aren't you even going to talk to him?" Sean reached across the cast on his knee. He scooped up a stray soccer ball and tossed it back to the group of squealing children running through the orchard.

"You're the fourth person who's asked me that question," Morgan said.

"Well, if you're going to speak now or forever hold your peace, then you'd better hurry. Most of the apples have been picked, and I don't think he's staying for dinner."

"I don't care what he does."

"You don't mean that." Sean looked at her and sighed.

303

"If I talked to him, what would I say?"

"Well, *thank you* for starters." He gestured to the women emptying bags of apples, the men hauling bushel baskets to the truck. "Look what he's done for us. For *you*. He's made all this happen. He's worked like a dog today. I don't think he's stopped for a second. Or taken his eyes off you."

"All right. I'll admit, he's worked hard. And he's singlehandedly saved the first harvest. But is that supposed to make up for the fact he came here to steal the flag? That he lied to me about it? That he used me?"

"Oh, come on, Morgan. Stop whining about that damned flag. You knew what Denny was like when you married him. Are you surprised to find out he stole a Civil War flag from his father and bribed you with it to keep his ass out of jail?" When she didn't answer, he said, "No, I didn't think so."

"But Gage came here to recover the flag under false pretenses. If he and I hadn't reconnected, he would have taken it back to Atlanta and accepted the finder's fee."

"The money was for his child. For Jeremy. Gage was desperate to get him the help he needed to deal with his mother's death. You would have done the same thing for me. For anyone you loved."

"Maybe," she said grudgingly.

"Gage is a good guy." Sean laughed softly. "He's a little hotheaded at times, and about as stubborn as you are. And he's got some strange ideas about turning this orchard into a moneymaking machine."

"Like what?"

"He wants to open it to the public—picnics in summer, hayrides and hot cider in the fall, pick-your-own-apple parties, funnel cakes, Saturday night line dancing in the barn. In addition to Chambourcin grapes, he thinks we should grow a pumpkin patch."

"What is this? 'If you build it, they will come?'"

"Oh, he's full of ideas. Life with him wouldn't be boring. And you know how you hate boring." He laughed again. "Come to think of it, I told him the same thing about you. His passion for catching bad guys and thugs concerns me a bit, and you might have to work on curbing his appetite for adrenaline." He grinned. "But I think you're up to the task."

Morgan crossed her arms over her chest. Her eyes flicked around the orchard, searching for Gage. She'd spent the last three hours knowing exactly where he was at any given moment, and now she couldn't locate him. Finally, she spotted him, and her heart wobbled in her chest.

Gage stood on the edge of the flatbed truck, gazing out at the orchard. His hands rested lightly on his waist, one hip slung to the side. Streaks of burnished sunlight, shining low in the sky, shimmered around his tanned arms like a halo. He bent to hoist a bushel of apples, then set it on the truck beside the others. He wiped his hands on the back of his jeans, quickly glanced her way, then resumed his stance and continued to gaze at the horizon.

What was he thinking about? Staring so intensely at a bunch of bare limbed trees? His new life? There was no question he was leaving. By the time she'd returned from Harlan's sendoff at Deer Creek, he and Jeremy had already packed their things and loaded them into the Mustang. She and Gage had sidestepped each other all afternoon, avoiding eye contact, making sure they had no reason to speak, staying as far away from each other as possible. Even Jeremy had kept his distance, realizing, she guessed, that his life was going to carry on somewhere else.

The night before, she had mentally said her goodbyes to Gage, then spent a long, sleepless night trying to distance herself from him. But the next morning, he had crashed Harlan's funeral and said all those wonderful things. She had listened to his low, sexy southern drawl melt each vowel, and she couldn't stop needing him, or wondering why she was destined to repeat the worst part of her life over and over again.

As the day wore on, it grew worse.

The sweet power of his smile wrapped around her heart. Raw emotion burbled in her chest. Every time she filled another burlap bag, and caught him glancing her way, electricity surged through her. She could feel his heartbeat, his breath, the warmth of his skin against hers. The magnetic pull of him, stronger and more poignant than she thought she could bear, wouldn't let up. It spiraled around her, spinning and churning until she wanted to scream at it to stop. To give her a few moments peace. Until the tender, empty place inside her heart closed up again.

"Morgan," Sean said gently. "Gage has spent his life trying to do the right thing. For his wife. For his son. And now, for you. He's never stopped loving you. I don't think he ever will."

The evening breeze blew against her cheek, cold and damp. She wiped her tear-streaked face with the back of her hand. "Am I crying? Why am I crying?"

"Because you love him. And he's leaving."

"Is he?" she said in a small voice.

"I don't care if you think your happiness is hiding out in Nashville or New York or Timbuktu. If you can't open your eyes and see that it's standing over there on that truck, then you are the densest woman in the world, and you don't deserve him." He pulled himself to his feet and used his cane to hop toward her. He put his arm around her. "Listen, twin of mine. Your heart may have been stomped on a few times, but I know how strong it is, and how big it is. And I don't want you to live with the kind of regret that will eat away at your soul."

She wasn't sure when she pulled away from Sean and started running through the orchard. One second she was standing beside her brother, wiping tears off her face, and the next, she was flying through trees, dodging ladders and apple baskets, parting groups of astonished people like the Red Sea. She stopped at the back of the flatbed truck and stood, gulping in air, holding the sides of her flowered skirt bunched in her hands.

Gage slid a bushel basket to the back of the truck. When he turned around, he gave a little start at the sight of her, then quickly lowered his head and reached for another load.

"Can you help me up?" she said.

"I thought you weren't speaking to me."

She held out her hand. "Can I not speak to you up there?"

He turned back to her and, in one fluid motion, clasped her forearm and swung her onto the truck bed.

"Are you really leaving?" she asked.

He stopped, still holding on to her arm, and looked in her eyes. The last rays of sunlight cut across his angular face. "Why, yes, I am. I thought I might move to Nashville. Jeremy can find a guitar teacher there, and I can help revitalize and reinforce small businesses in these exciting but uncertain times."

"I thought you liked small towns."

"I thought you hated them."

A crowd was beginning to gather.

He looped his arm around her waist and pulled her to him. "I've heard Nashville is the biggest small town in America. That sounds like a compromise to me."

"What about children? You know I probably can't get pregnant."

"That won't stop us from trying. In the meantime, we'll adopt."

"What about Jeremy's therapy?"

"Bert's paying for it. And I'm letting him. Besides, with you in our lives, I think Jeremy is gonna be just fine."

"Am I in your life? I don't want to be just a shadow on the ground."

"Baby, you are my life."

"Let's wait till the harvest is over," she said. "This is only the first wave of apples. And look at these kind folks surrounding the truck, staring at us like we're the midnight show. We wouldn't want to deprive them of hayrides and hot cider."

"We could wait until the first snow. I'd love to spend winter in the mountains with you. Drinking apple brandy by the fire."

"Seeing where this might go. Learning to like you calling me baby."

Gage leaned over and nuzzled her neck. "Sleigh rides through the meadow. Ice skating on Lacey's

Pond."

"Christmas," Morgan murmured.

"New Year's Eve."

He held her face in his hands and covered her mouth with his. Thundering applause, loud hoots and whistles erupted around them.

"Forever," Gage whispered.

"Forever is a long damn time," she said, laughing.

"That's okay." He kissed her again. "It still won't be long enough for me."

A word about the author...

Rebecca lives with her husband in the beautiful, misty mountains of East Tennessee, where the people are charming, soulful, and just a little bit crazy. She's been everything from a tax collector to a stay-at-home mom to a house painter to a professional actress and director.

When she's not churning out sensual romantic mysteries with snappy dialogue and happy endings, she likes to travel, go to the Outer Banks for her ocean fix, watch old movies, hang out at the local pub, and make her day complete by correctly answering the Final Jeopardy! question.

Visit her at www.rebeccaleesmith.com.

Thank you for purchasing
this publication of The Wild Rose Press, Inc.
For other wonderful stories of romance,
please visit our on-line bookstore at
www.thewildrosepress.com.

For questions or more information
contact us at
info@thewildrosepress.com.

The Wild Rose Press, Inc.
www.thewildrosepress.com

To visit with authors of
The Wild Rose Press, Inc.
join our yahoo loop at
http://groups.yahoo.com/group/thewildrosepress/

www.ingramcontent.com/pod-product-compliance
Lightning Source LLC
Chambersburg PA
CBHW070547260626
47161CB00002B/535